BOULEVARD

JIM GRIMSLEY

Boulevard

A NOVEL

ALGONQUIN BOOKS
OF CHAPEL HILL
2002

Published by
ALGONQUIN BOOKS OF CHAPEL HILL
Post Office Box 2225
Chapel Hill, North Carolina 27515-2225

a division of
Workman Publishing
708 Broadway
New York, New York 10003

Library of Congress Cataloging-in-Publication Data
Grimsley, Jim, 1955–
    Boulevard : a novel / by Jim Grimsley.
        p. cm.
    ISBN 1-56512-251-8
    1. New Orleans (La.)—Fiction.   2. Gay youth—Fiction.
I. Title.
PS3557.R4949 B68 2002
813'.54—dc21   2001055238

10 9 8 7 6 5 4 3 2 1
First Edition

For Madeleine St. Romain

For if they do these things in a green tree,

what shall be done in the dry?

Luke 23:31

Contents

BOULEVARD

The
Pornographer

Newell took his duffel down from the baggage rack, slung the strap over his shoulder, and climbed off the bus onto the pavement. A breathless feeling, that first step into the open air. Stowing the bag in a coin-operated locker, he pocketed the key and unfolded the map of the city he had bought by special order from Ed White's filling station in Pastel. The closest street sign read Tulane Avenue, and he found it on the map, the fact giving him a rush of happiness, to know the name of the street, to understand where it ran in relation to all the rest. He took one step away from the bus station, then another. He was walking along Tulane Avenue in the city of New Orleans.

That morning the city was new to him, and he could hardly imagine himself standing among such huge buildings as these, on streets with names like Carondelet, Gravier, Poydras, Magazine, St. Charles, words that ran through his head like notes of music. He guided himself through a tangle of streets and slivers of buildings, after only a couple of wrong turns, to Canal Street, where he took in the width of the thoroughfare—so many lanes for cars going each way, and more lanes down the middle, where city buses were running. He walked past shops, closed at this early hour, places to buy clothes, drugstores, fast food restaurants. Here was New Orleans early in the morning, hardly awake yet, but already it was like nothing he had ever seen.

The street he wanted lay on the other side of Canal, and he had said the name in his head a hundred times in the last few days, Bourbon Street, a place he had heard about from Flora and Jesse, who had come here twice for the Mardi Gras. If his dream came true today he would live on Bourbon Street, somewhere on it; and if that failed he would find some other place in the French Quarter, because he wanted that more than anything, not simply to live in the city but to live in the center of it. So he turned onto Bourbon Street from Canal, on the side of the street occupied by the wall of a store called Maison Blanche, beyond which, even at that hour, a fair number of people were walking around, some of them with the look that maybe they had been here since the night before.

He would get accustomed to this smell of vomit and

piss, he thought, as he headed down the tilted sidewalks. Tired workers in uniforms were taking up street barricades, and traffic moved sluggishly along the cross streets. The buildings were low, decorated with ironwork, wooden doors sagging, stucco flaking and falling off; restaurants, Takee-Outee stands selling egg rolls, bars, more bars, places to buy nightgowns and underwear in multiple colors, more bars, with patios and balconies, bars where you could watch women strip off their clothes, and farther down, places where you could watch men and women. A marquee showed black-and-white glossy pictures of the strippers, Tammy and Nanette and Roberto, names he remembered for a moment, then forgot.

He walked a long way before he found a newspaper box, fumbled with the quarter before slipping it in the slot. The newspaper was called the *Times-Picayune,* and his copy was printed on green paper, a fact that so distressed him he rolled up the paper and hurried away from the vending box without reading the headlines. But at the next box he saw all those papers were green too, so he supposed it was all right.

On his map, in the center of the French Quarter on the river side, he had marked a place called Jackson Square, and now he headed toward it down St. Peter Street. He had only a vague notion of what a square might be but emerged from the street in front of a big gray church. Mist hung over the stone plaza in front of him, the stones covered with pigeons looking for something to eat, and he walked into the crowd of feathers and cooing, headed toward one of the iron benches in front of the church. He sat on the bench and looked around. The square was a big open space, but the buildings looked like nothing he had ever seen before, the church rising up gray and austere, stone buildings flanking it, proper and harmonious, with historical plaques about the builders and the history. Behind him, facing the church, lay a green park enclosed in an iron fence. The park gates stood open at the moment, but there was a sign giving the hours of business. He sat in the mist with the green newspaper in his lap and flocks of pigeons at his feet, the air so wet he could feel the moisture on his skin, the gray of the mist muting everything. A sound cut through the morning, a long lowing, and he understood it was a ship's horn he was hearing because he had heard a ship's horn on television before, but the real sound raised the hackles on his neck, the horn blew on and on. He could tell the sound was coming from behind him. That would be the river, he thought, and he started to walk toward it, because he knew what river it was.

He would learn the names: Jackson Square, St. Louis Cathedral, the Cabildo, the Pontalba buildings, the Moonwalk, Jax Brewery, the French Market, Café du Monde, all these mysteries would be explained to him in time, but this was his first walk to the river, and once he stood on the levee, one could understand that the sight might move him, because it was the Mississippi, and this bend of the river had created the city behind him. He could feel the power of it, the river flowing past him, gray and sooty, wind lifting over the water, a white ship passing upriver with a tug for an escort, a seagull riding the breeze near the wharf. He stood there for a long time, looking at all of it, taking it in. After a spell of that, he sat on one of the benches along the Moonwalk, opened the paper, and started to read.

Skipping over the article about President Ford and the First Lady at Camp David, skipping over the article about Richard Nixon planting flowers in the garden at San Clemente, Newell searched for the classified ads about rooms for rent in the French Quarter. There were listings for Metairie and Elysian Fields and Gretna, but these were all for houses or apartments, and besides, he had no idea where any of those places might be. The rented room list was actually quite short, and he studied it closely, spreading out his map as best he could in the breeze off the river. Not a single room on Bourbon Street. But some of the addresses were close, according to his map, which had a special section on the French Quarter. He found rooms on St. Ann, Governor Nicholls, and Ramparts, and more across Ramparts and Esplanade, outside the French Quarter but close by. Was he ready? He folded the map and was heading for the first place, on St. Ann, until he remembered it was early, hardly anybody would be ready to rent a room at such an hour. So he tucked the map into his pocket and folded the newspaper section by section.

He sat with the river flowing past him, studying the tiny houses on the distant shore, reminding himself that this was the Mississippi River, that he was sitting in New Orleans, and this seemed to him a great accomplishment. Never mind the worry that now he had to find a room to rent, a place to stay. That he had to find a job and go to work. Never mind any of that, at this moment he could do nothing more than watch the river.

But he was hungry after the trip and decided he ought to eat something, so after a while he left the Moonwalk and retreated across the levee to the Café du Monde, where a lot of people were sitting and eating off little plates and drinking coffee. Since there were so many people and so many round white metal tables outside, he sat in a chair, and pretty quickly a girl about his own age rushed up to him to ask what he wanted. It turned out all the Café du Monde sold was coffee and doughnuts, except that the doughnuts were called something else, a word the waitress said three times, *bay-nyays*, with Newell simply looking at her, at which point she said, "They're doughnuts with powdered sugar on them. And café au lait." She hurried off to take somebody else's order, and finally he saw the word she was talking about, *beignets,* on a sign in one of the windows, and he took a deep breath. What he had really wanted was some fried eggs, but he would gladly eat the doughnuts instead. The city was already showing itself to be a complicated place. A restaurant that served nothing but doughnuts, full of people, laughing and chattering.

The doughnuts were hot and sweet, but he kept blowing the powdered sugar up his nose, at first. He got one order and another, and paid for each out of the bills in his pocket. He knew you were supposed to tip a waitress like this, but he could only guess how much, so he laid a quarter on the table and added a nickel as an afterthought. The coffee, which was what café au lait turned out to be, had a rich cream in it and ran smooth as silk down his throat. He hardly ever drank coffee, but he thought he might like this kind, after a while. His stomach felt better with something in it.

For an hour or so he walked, at first in a place called the French Market, where a lot of produce vendors had already opened for business, and later along Esplanade, a wide avenue darkened with trees, with a green median running down the center, which anyone who lived in New Orleans would have known to call a neutral ground. Newell crossed onto it and walked down it, among the trees and plantings, with traffic on both sides of him.

Newell arrived at the address on St. Ann by a roundabout route, and stood patiently at the door waiting for someone to answer. The woman who came to the door was well dressed and carried a tiny dog in the crook of her arm, and when she quoted the price of the rooms, the dog silently licked her wrist. Newell thanked her for her trouble and went away, because she was asking way too much money for a room, and he didn't mind letting her know that. He walked to the place on Governor Nicholls, for which the price of the rent was listed in the paper, three hundred dollars a month, and the room turned out to be in the back of a service station across Ramparts from the Quarter. The room had only one tiny window, high up in the wall. The bathroom consisted of a toilet and sink and no shower or bathtub. A sweet, balding man in a sleeveless T-shirt was showing the room, and Newell looked for a polite moment or two, and then said he had some other places to see but might be back.

He walked from place to place, to all the listings in the newspaper, and found nothing under three hundred dollars a month, which was more than he could pay with no more money than he had. Jesse had told him to stay at the YMCA, which he could rent by the night, till he found a job, but Newell had balked at that suggestion. But he might need to stay there tonight, he thought, and by then he was hungry again, so he found a place to buy a sandwich, a roast beef po' boy that dripped gravy and mayonnaise onto the wax paper in which it was wrapped. He wanted to ask for a phone book, but the people in the sandwich shop were too busy, so he finished his sandwich and wandered for a while.

He visited a few of the shops in the lower Quarter, pretending to browse like a real customer, a store full of used books, including some books by Robert Heinlein and Poul Anderson for a quarter apiece, a store full of old postcards and glassware, stores full of Mardi Gras masks and costumes, places such as he had never imagined, though he kept a poker face and acted as if he had seen it all before. He ambled along Barracks, nearing Decatur Street, when he walked into a shop near the corner, which turned out to be a junk shop, tables and shelves of junk everywhere you looked, and the ceilings must have been twenty feet at least, wall-papered with dark paper that had stained even darker with age. A sign had been lettered onto the front window by a careful hand, and the sign, in contrast to the building, was bright and well kept. "Hendeman's Rare and Used," the sign read, but what? Everything, apparently, including old ashtrays, a wooden baby carriage near collapse, several wooden buckets, jars of beads, masks hung on the walls and piled on the shelves. Across the room behind a counter a woman was watching him. She had broad shoulders and hips and a narrow waist, and was dressed in a light, flowered dress with a buff-colored sweater wrapped around her. A large cat prowled the counter near her elbow, fluffing against her hand, till finally she shoved it away in irritation.

She was as handsome as a man, he thought, when he was close enough to see her face. Square-faced, high cheekbones, a strong jaw, full flaring lips, heavy eyebrows, her hair done up in a loose bun. "Are you looking for something?" she asked in a pleasant, husky voice.

"Do you have a phone book?"

She lifted a white-covered directory to the counter and set it in front of him. "Do you want the phone?"

"No ma'am. I just need to look up the address of the YMCA."

"Well, that's on Lee Circle," she said, "I can tell you that."

"Lee Circle?"

"Yes. You take the streetcar uptown, and you get off at Lee Circle."

"How do I know it's Lee Circle?"

"Because it's a circle," she said, "and you know who Lee is, don't you? Robert E. Lee."

"Oh." He was distracted, opening his map to see if he could find the place.

She found his map to be amusing, he could see by her smile. She had some papers she was looking at, and she went back to doing that, correcting something with a pencil. After a while she asked, "You're looking for a place to stay?"

"Yes ma'am. I been looking all day. All the ads in the paper."

She smiled at him, started to say something, changed her mind. Then changed her mind again. "Most people in the Quarter don't put an ad in the paper if they have a room to rent."

"Why not?"

"Because they don't have to. And anyway, they would be afraid of tourists. Or out-of-town people. Most people from the Quarter would put out the word to their friends they had a room, and wait."

"Well, there's ads in this paper for rooms," Newell fanned the paper up and down, "but there's not a single place that's fit to live in."

She shrugged. "The YMCA is nice. You won't mind it."

"I know."

After another moment, she walked into her office, a door behind some filing cabinets, and he figured she was tired of talking. He looked up "YMCA" anyway and wrote the number on a scrap of paper. He closed the phone book and laid it down, and as he turned away her voice stopped him. "Do you have a job?" She had put on a pair of glasses and had a ledger in her hand. She set the ledger on the counter and opened it to a page and started to make entries in it.

"No ma'am. Not yet."

"Most people aren't going to rent you a room if you don't have a job."

"I can get a job. It looks like there's a lot of restaurants and places around here. I can do something. I worked in a grocery store in Pastel. And I graduated from high school."

She wanted to smile, he could tell, and he supposed he had said something foolish. "Well, I'm sure you'll be fine," she said.

He headed for the door without thanking her, thinking she was making fun of him, but again her voice stopped him. She was looking at him with her hand on the cat's back, smoothing its fur.

"I have a room, upstairs."

He stopped and turned. There were no stairs anywhere in the room.

"Would you like to see it?"

He nodded.

She sighed and closed the ledger. Unlocking a drawer, she pulled out a ring of keys and put them in her pocket. She led him outside to the street, then unlocked a narrow door next to the store. This door, which looked like a tall piece of fencing, opened to a narrow passageway that led to the interior of the block. He followed her to a courtyard full of green, the sound of water running somewhere; he could see a fountain through a pair of archways, to the right of which rose stairs, and she led him up those to a narrow doorway. She gestured to another door down the gallery from the one she was unlocking, "There's an apartment there, somebody's living in it. This next one is the room that's empty."

The room was tall and narrow, with a single casement window at the front, and a set of narrow French doors leading to the balcony that ran along the front of the building. A ceiling fan hung from the ceiling, and when she flicked a switch on the wall it began to turn slowly. At the back of the room, behind a white door, stood a bathroom with a bathtub, a sink, and a toilet. High up in one wall of the bathroom was a window, admitting dingy light. The two rooms seemed dark to him, but the main room was clean and big enough, with a bed in it, and a wooden wardrobe, a chair, a small table, and a small refrigerator with a lamp on top of it.

"The last fellow who lived here skipped out on the rent," she said. "He had owed me for two months. And he had a job."

"It's a nice room," Newell said.

"My husband used it for an office, when he was an astrologer."

Newell had no idea what to say. He wandered in the room and felt the money in his pocket and wished. When he turned around, she was watching him.

"If you can pay me two months rent in cash right now, I'll let you move in," she said.

"How much is that?"

"Two hundred fifty dollars a month. That's five hundred dollars."

This was nearly all he had. But he pulled the money out of his pocket at once and counted five hundred dollars into her hand.

"You pay me the rent in cash on the first of the month, beginning with July," she said. "I keep this second month's rent in case you skip out. You can have these last few days of May for nothing."

He had less than a hundred dollars left. In a month he would have to give her two hundred fifty dollars more. If he didn't, she would keep his extra two-fifty and kick him out in the street. Looking at her, he had no doubt she would do exactly that. The thought left his mouth dry. But he nodded and said, "That's fine."

"Come downstairs and show me some I.D."

In the shop, where ceiling fans were creaking overhead stirring the cobwebs on all the bric-à-brac, he showed her his Alabama driver's license and his library card for the Polk County Public Library. He also showed her a picture of Flora in front of the trailer on the outskirts of Pastel. "She's my grandma."

"So if I find you dead in that room up there one morning, she's who I should call?"

The question unsettled him some, but he nodded. She wrote down Flora's address and phone number and gave him a receipt for his five hundred dollars. That was when he learned her name was Louise Kimbro. He had expected her to be a Hendeman, because of the store window. She gave him keys and showed him which was which. "Jiggle the handle on that toilet," she said, "or it'll run all day. And don't leave the lights on when you go out. And be careful you lock that balcony door."

He took the keys and hurried away, thinking he could reach the bus station before too late, to fetch his bag. Tomorrow he would look for a job. He had already forgotten about Louise by the time he reached the door, and she stood watching him. Something about him reminded her of Arthur. She liked Newell's looks, his dark hair and watery green eyes. She liked his thin, pale body standing in the doorway, looking out at Barracks Street as though it were a moonscape. She liked something about him that she could never have described, something languid and lean. Back in the junk shop she listened for his footsteps on the stairs beyond the wall and slipped the rent money into an envelope and stuffed it into a filing cabinet in one of the rooms behind the junk store.

Later, when Owen brought the delivery truck to load her Thursday deliveries, she realized what it was she had recognized. Newell had Arthur's voice, the same gentle, drawn-out vowels, the same note of music in the speech. But the revelation was fleeting, since, along with the truck, Owen had brought his daughter, Millie, a ripe, pretty thing, and Louise never could keep her eyes off that girl.

Newell rushed to the bus station as fast as he could, through the boiling afternoon heat, partly out of excitement at the prospect of unpacking in his new room, and partly out of a sense of panic that he had spent all the money he had saved, so quickly, just like that. He should have rented a room by the night at the Y till he found a job, that would have been more prudent, wouldn't it? Because now he had only thirty days to find a job and earn enough money to pay the rent on time. Now he had less than a hundred dollars to his name.

As long as he was walking with the distractions of the French Quarter, of Canal Street, around him, he could stop thinking about how poor he was, he could stop being afraid he would end up homeless on the street. He fished the key out of his pocket and opened the locker in the bus station, where several buses were idling at the gates, loading passengers for destinations everywhere a person could imagine. He had enough money left, he could take the bus home again, now, while it was safe.

When he set the duffel on the bare mattress of his new bed, he realized with a thud that he would have to buy sheets. He had brought none. Looking around the room, he realized he would have to buy a lot of things, including nearly everything that he took for granted in a bathroom. His money was bleeding away from him, dollar by dollar. Why hadn't he thought of this when he was packing, when he could have swiped a bar of soap from Flora, and some towels, even a set of sheets?

He had brought his clothes and his cassette tape player

with the five tapes he had managed to buy during high school. He had brought his high school diploma and his birth certificate, which Flora said he was sure to need when he got a job. The clothes fit neatly into the wardrobe, which had drawers at the bottom, with plenty of room to spare. The cassette player he put on the table beside the bed. This was the whole of his unpacking. When it was done, he sat in the chair for a while, looking at the room, feeling short of breath.

He counted his money. A little over ninety-five dollars. He had to have soap and toothpaste, shampoo, deodorant. He had found a blanket in the bottom of the wardrobe, and it smelled pretty clean, so he figured he could make do with that for a while, since he had no idea how much sheets would cost, or pillows, or anything like that. He was lucky there was furniture in the room at all, he supposed, feeling a bit foolish to have brought so little money, to have been so naïve as to think the move would be so easy.

The proportions of the room, the simple bed and table, chair and dresser, pleased him, however, and he could look around and know that this was where he lived now, with an address, with a lock and keys. All he had to do was find a way to pay for it.

Spreading out the newspaper, he studied the want ads. He felt better when he saw listings for restaurant jobs and hotel room service jobs, cashiers and clerks, work he figured he could do pretty easily, if only he could convince somebody to give him a chance. He marked some of the places he wanted to apply tomorrow, after consulting the map to make sure he could find them, and since he was living near downtown he was within walking distance of nearly all the jobs he read about.

He folded up the newspaper and counted his money again, then went downstairs. He stopped in the junk shop to ask Louise where the best place was to buy what he needed, and she told him how to find the A&P on Royal Street. He found it easily and wandered among the cramped shelves. The store was crowded, people were stepping around each other constantly, and Newell found himself caught up in the game after only a few moments. So many men, in particular, here. Young men in flannel shirts and tight jeans. In tight T-shirts with the sleeves cut away. Young men with beards, sideburns, moustaches, chest hair bristling out of their shirts. Men of all colors and sizes, sliding among the canned goods and displays of produce. Buying liquor, which shocked him. In Alabama you could not buy liquor at a grocery store like this. He had come to a new world, for sure.

He spent more money than he meant to, nearly thirty dollars. With his bag in his arms, he walked down Royal Street, gas lamps lit at the doors of buildings, high balconies hovering above, the sidewalk uneven. The street was a wall of buildings, fences, and gates, and he had the feeling that all this was to hide what went on inside these buildings, these courtyards. Over the tops of fences he could see the backs of houses, many with smaller buildings running perpendicular to the back. These must be what were called slave quarters—he'd seen a slave quarter apartment described that way in the classifieds. Rooms where slaves had lived. Devorah, his friend from high school, might have lived in one of those rooms, in those days.

Every stranger's face he passed seemed mysterious in some way. By the time he reached his room again, his heart was pounding from the newness of it all, the beautiful shapes of the buildings, the uncomfortable feeling when he looked at the slave rooms, contrasted with the graceful twists of wrought iron, the Spanish moss draped over a brick wall, the glimpse of an interior garden, a fountain singing behind a closed wooden gate. A city full of everything, bad and good. He had done the right thing by coming here, he was sure of it, no matter how risky. Even if he failed, even if he ran out of money and had to go home, he was right to try.

He had bought all the soaps and shampoos he needed, a washcloth, a can opener, plastic spoons, some cans of soup. He could eat the soup cold, he figured, three cans a day, and that would have to keep him alive until he found a job. Tonight he began with a can of cold chicken noodle, opening the can and drinking the broth, spooning the noodles into his mouth. The noodles had a satisfying texture, he ate greedily, and he knew as soon as he had eaten that the three cans of soup a day would never feel like enough. But he had less than seventy dollars now, and he had to stretch the money as far as he could.

He studied the ads in the newspaper for a while, and

stepped onto his balcony. Barracks Street was so close to Decatur it was considered by many people to be a dangerous part of the Quarter, and Newell may have felt something of that character as he stood on the balcony. Close enough to the waterfront he could smell it, dank and dusky. He stood at the iron railing for a long time, one foot in the lower rung, leaning out, watching. The empty shop on the corner attracted some young men to stand under the awning, and cars stopped there, and one or another of the young men slid into the cars and rode away. This happened intermittently as he stood there, till the corner emptied. The figures moved with mysterious knowledge—he could only study them and wonder. More young boys came, and the same thing happened. After a while the corner emptied, and nobody came, and he went inside.

His watch said after eleven. He had meant to call Flora, but by now she would be asleep, with sheets of toilet paper wrapped around her hairdo. So he took off his clothes, cleared the newspaper off the bed, and standing on the balcony, shook out the blanket, in the night in his underwear, certain somehow that no one was watching, that it hardly mattered whether anyone saw, then returned to the room and locked the balcony door. He lay on the bare mattress with his folded jeans for a pillow, the scratchy blanket on his skin, windows open, breeze moving through the room. He was glad for the ceiling fan. But he would have to buy curtains for the windows. He would have to buy a hot plate and some pots and pans.

He slept, exhausted by the day and the bus ride, the overnight journey; all night he dreamed he was on the bus again, riding along the highway with the Gulf of Mexico sliding by the window, in and out of sight. Crossing wide spans of water, the bus gliding as if on a cushion of air. All night he dreamed he was still traveling to the city, still arriving. But he was already lying in a room of his own, already in his own bed. When he woke up and realized where he was, he felt afraid and glad all over again.

A can of cold chicken rice soup for breakfast, and water from the tap. He would have to buy a glass—he should have thought of that the night before. But he would surely pass the A&P again today. Or find one in the junk store downstairs. He dressed in his best Sunday pants, a dark brown polyester that never showed the slightest wrinkle, dark blue socks, shiny black shoes, and a white shirt with long sleeves. At the mirror in the bathroom he stopped to reflect that he was pretty good looking, with his hair combed the right way. He flossed his teeth and brushed them till they shone. He wished he had some cologne to make himself smell good, but at home he had always used Jesse's big bottle of Brut. He strapped on his watch.

First he called Flora, collect, from a pay phone inside a grocery store. She accepted the charges with resignation and said, "Good lord, Newell, I was about worried to death, I just knew somebody had drug you off somewheres."

"I'm sorry, I just was reading the want ads last night and I forgot to call. I had to find a phone. They're not on the street where you can see them."

"New Orleans is a different kind of a place." Flora spoke as though she ought to know.

"I like it. I'm out looking for a job this morning. Wish me luck."

"I wished you'd come on home is what I wish."

"It'll be all right, I got plenty of money left. I got me a nice room. It's not on Bourbon Street, where I wanted it, but it's close. It's on Barracks."

"Oh," she said.

Silence for a moment. "Well, I don't want to run up your bill."

"You better not," she agreed.

"I'll call you again when I get a job. When I get a phone."

They said the other things they were accustomed to say, that he was her little squirt and she loved him, and he wished she would stop calling him a squirt, but that was all it was, she said, that was all that made him in the first place.

He applied to a lot of restaurants in the French Quarter, including Brennan's, the Court of Two Sisters, the Magic Pan, the Coffee Pot, Café Sazerac, and he applied at bars like Pat O'Brien's, the Oyster Bar, and even Preservation Hall, which was apparently famous for something he didn't even know about, jazz. Some of the places he could tell right away he would never be hired, like the Café Sazerac, where all the waiters were a lot older than Newell; others, like Pat O'Brien's, hardly seemed like the kind of place he had come to New Orleans to find. But he had already decided he would take anything that was offered. He applied at the downtown hotels to work in room service, even applied at a place that was still under construction and couldn't hire anybody before the first months of 1977, almost a year away. He applied at a couple of banks to be a cashier, though he could tell he was not the right kind of person to get that kind of job—he was dressed the wrong way, he had the wrong air about him. More restaurants along Canal and Carondelet and up St. Charles, where the streetcars ran, places that catered to the downtown lunch crowd. In every place it was a plus that he had an address but a minus that he had no telephone. He would call them himself, he said, or come by again.

But he found he sparked more interest in the restaurants in the lower Quarter, a place called Circle K on Dauphine and Dumaine, and two places on the other side of Esplanade, the White Biscuit and Betty's Kitchen. These restaurants were staffed by men his own age with managers not much older, and the customers were mostly men as well. In these restaurants, the fact that he as yet had no telephone hardly seemed as much of a hurdle.

This was Friday, his second day in New Orleans, but by the end of it he had walked the streets from Poydras to Frenchmen, and he had introduced himself to the managers of nearly a dozen restaurants. So he went home in the heat of the afternoon, lay across the bare mattress and rested.

He fell asleep without intending to, and woke near dark, a breeze stirring through the open door to the balcony. He walked to the door, smoothing down his hair and straightening his shirt—the smell of the river again, heavier in the afternoon heat, but no boys on the corner today.

Now he could see that he was not the only one living on the street; a number of the second- and third-floor balconies showed signs of habitation, including porch furniture and potted plants, hanging baskets made of twisted twine. He studied the balconies up and down his block for a while, the day darkening, the sky bloody red.

He ate a can of soup and walked to the riverfront, straight up Decatur among what seemed to be abandoned warehouses, till he came to some stores that were open but very dark, machine shops, maybe, or garages, and then to retail places, a Christmas store, tourist shops that featured something called pralines and boxes of beignet mix. He came to Jackson Square and wandered among the tourists with their cameras and souvenirs. At the end of the square the gray cathedral loomed over the plaza, where portrait painters were still working, switching on electric lamps, determined to paint as long as the tourists were willing to sit and pay. Newell idled in this setting, reading the historical plaques on the buildings, learning about the Cabildo, the Spanish colonial administration, the Pontalba buildings, soaking up breezes that carried the dank smell of the river. Beneath all the other sounds came the lowing of ships' horns, cargo carriers moving upriver to the container docks. Memorabilia shops for the tourists and supply shops for the artists crowded the square around the church. Newell stood in the shadow of the tall tower, watching pigeons chasing one another on the stones of the square, squabbling over bits of hot dog and bread. On the plaza stood a hot dog vendor behind a stand shaped like a big hot dog on wheels, and the man behind the hot dog stood as tall as Newell but at least as wide as the wiener truck, a huge round man with his chin sunken deep into a waddle of fat, and bunches of fat hanging over his belt and along the sides of his trousers. He had a forlorn, weary expression, standing with his meat fork in hand, ready to spear a wiener for anyone who might feel the need.

At the door of the church sat men and women who were begging for money from the people going in and out of the church. He walked among them and looked at them closely, their gray clothes, their filthy skins, their voices cracked as they asked him for money. He ignored them except for looking at them, but he could hardly tear his eyes away from their misery, since he was nervous that he might end up this way himself, homeless, as he assumed these people were, living in the dirt of the street.

Others watched him, though he was scarcely aware that anyone noticed him at all: others watched him standing at the edge of the crowd of tourists on the square, in his awkward clothes, his hair combed back from his face, so fresh from the country. He was new in town, and there were always people to notice that, to watch him avidly as he stood beside the gate to the park. A look of yearning about him, palpable to anyone who cared to notice.

Instead of heading home at once he walked up Bourbon Street and back, and the vitality of the French Quarter at night overawed him; he could feel the whole constellation of its life around him, the layers of streets and cars and people, the ghosts of skyscrapers hovering in the shadowy sky. The long street engulfed him like a dream. He passed along the strip bars, the music bars, the country bars, the jazz bars, the piano bars, the ragtime bars; he stopped at a full-size picture of Chris Owens at her own show bar and wondered what it would be like to be a beautiful big-breasted woman like her, to have raven hair that tumbled and rippled down your back, to be so popular that you could have your own nightclub. He ambled along the street, which was closed to cars except at the corners, where traffic crossed on the cross streets. He marveled at the balconies of the hotels, the apartments draped with Boston ferns, clematis, confederate jasmine, ivory, warm lights spilling down through the ironwork. He stopped to smell the egg rolls at the Takee-Outee, wished he dared spend the one dollar seventy-five cents required, because the smell made his mouth water, but he walked away from the rows of shish kebabs and the egg rolls and the skewers of fried shrimp, the grease glistening under the lights. He stood in the doorway of an arcade where teenage boys were playing pinball or some of the new video games, with quarter after quarter to slide in the machines, and the boys all different shades of brown hunched over their games, their buttocks clenching and unclenching with each play.

He stood on the curb outside and looked first one way, then the other, up and down Bourbon Street, a riot of bobbing heads and color, voices rising and horns blowing, scratches of music, now and then some single voice rising distinctly above the rest, like the hawker in the doorway at the strip club where the female impersonators were strutting up and down the stage behind him, visible through the doorway as they passed along the runway, bright and colorful: a man who was pretending to be a woman and making money for it, a clear sign that the world was larger than anything Newell could ever have learned about in Pastel.

At a certain point on Bourbon Street the streets were no longer barricaded and the tourists no longer wandered, but there were still a lot of people walking on the street, nearly all of them men. He passed a corner where two bars faced each other, and the doors of the bars were all open, so that he could see inside as he was walking. The bars were also full of men, lounging on stools facing outward, or leaning against the bars, posing, very few of them talking to anybody, listening to the music that pounded from beyond the doors. Newell walked past the doors and through the crowd on the street, and he could tell people were watching him critically; he knew he had on the wrong kind of clothes, that he looked like somebody who wasn't sure where he was. Trying to keep his eyes to the ground, but unable to avoid staring at the men on the streets and in the bars, he made his way down one block, then two, and after a while he came to the sign for Barracks, and turned there and found his way home.

He stood in the middle of his room with the thought in his head that he had been for a walk down Bourbon Street and had come back from it, that Bourbon Street and the French Quarter were still out there if he wanted to go back, and the feeling of anticipation filled him completely, so that he was for the moment unworried about money, about finding a job, about all that. For a moment he was simply delighted to be here, at home in his one, narrow room with the breeze blowing through the open balcony door.

But when he lay down under the blanket he found himself thinking only of the latter part of the walk, when he had passed through the invisible barrier on Bourbon Street into the country of men, where men had been all around him, watching him, and he had watched them in return, with no need to say anything about it. He tried to remember a particular face to think about, to dream about, before he fell asleep. But the faces were a sea; he kept going under when he thought back to those moments, thinking from one face to another.

On Saturday rain fell morning to night, a low drizzle along the streets. He had only two cans of soup left, so sometime today he would have to go to the A&P again and spend more money. But he lazed in the room most of the morning, stood out on the balcony for a long time. Even in the rain a few people with umbrellas were walking, and some of them went into the junk shop downstairs. Later, when he was drinking water again out of the bathroom sink faucet, he thought maybe he could go downstairs and see if there was a plastic cup in all that mess in his landlady's store.

Enough people were browsing that he felt comfortable to look as long as he liked, and people were steadily in and out of the store. Some of them were buying the junk in the store and some of them were bringing junk for Louise Kimbro to buy. She had a section of old furniture, a section of used small appliances, a section for lamps, a huge stack of window transoms of many sizes, shelves of glassware in this shape or that. In the glass section he found a milk white glass with raised diamond-shaped beads on it marked for seven dollars, and he thought that was not the kind of glass he had in mind. But she also had tables and tables of the purest junk, dirty baby dolls, broken baby strollers, rusted Gene Autry lunchboxes, old checkers sets, pots and pans of every shape, size, and state of repair, and, finally, a table full of nothing but plastic dishes. He found a cup in a pile marked for twenty-five cents, and he took the cup to the counter to wait his turn.

Louise had help this Saturday morning—Owen's daughter, Millie, who was learning to work the cash register while Louise recorded in the ledger each item that was sold. The line moved a bit slowly because Louise took her time with the ledger, and because Millie was pretty and stopped to flirt with nearly everyone. When it was Newell's turn he set down the cup and pulled out a quarter and a nickel for the tax. Louise hardly recognized him at first, so intent was she on writing the words, "Light blue plastic Loyola University cup." When she looked up at him she did recognize him, though, and she said, "You're shopping for that apartment, I see."

He noted that the room had now become an apartment. "Yes ma'am. I need a drinking glass."

"Did you find a job yet?"

"No ma'am, but I looked all day yesterday."

"You'll get something." She nodded, moving to the next customer and adjusting her glasses. Millie took his money and thought he was cute—Louise could read Millie like a book. Louise flashed with jealousy and wondered whether she ought to tell the stupid girl she was wasting her time, but by then Newell had headed for the door again, and Louise found herself watching him too. Something in the way he moved drew the eye.

"Keep your mind on what you're doing, Millie," she said, and returned to the ledger, writing carefully.

Newell washed the cup with the same soap he used for bathing, figuring that would clean it well enough, and save him the cost of dishwashing detergent. He rinsed it a dozen times, tasted water from it, and put it on the top of the toilet. He ate a can of soup. He read the one book he had brought from Pastel, a science fiction novel called *The Time Traders* by Andre Norton. He sat with the book in the light of the lamp, rain falling beyond the balcony outside, a steady cloud of water as far as he could see. He stepped outside once, studied the street, the rooftops, the clouds, figured it could rain forever, and he had to buy more cans of soup. But he read for a while and waited, and sure enough the rain lightened, became a mist again, and he headed out at once.

Rain fell over everything, street and sidewalk, roof and gable, falling into all the courtyards invisible to him, beyond the walls of the houses that came right up to the edge of the sidewalk, down all the carriageways and passageways he glimpsed as he walked. He hurried from gallery to roof overhang along the streets, managing to stay fairly dry. In only a few blocks he came to a sign that said "Verti Mart" over an open door.

He went in and wiped the beaded rain off his forehead. The store was tiny, the shelves shoved tight together, and he had to wander, bending a bit to see the lower shelves, before he found the soup. The price was higher than the A&P, so he only bought three cans.

When he stood with the cans he noticed several other men in the store, all about the same age as Newell or a few years older. They were watching him, waiting to see if he would watch them back, not as a group but each alone, so that on the walk to the cash register it was as if he were being plucked by magnets, these big-eyed men with their neat haircuts, their trim moustaches. He bought the soup and the friendly looking, trim cashier smiled and said, "A little wet out there, honey. Better watch you don't melt."

"Oh, I won't." He felt awkward, wishing suddenly he could think of something else to say. He rolled the top of the bag into a wad and headed for the door, once again crossing past the other men who were shopping or looking at magazines, but who were watching him at the same time, and watching each other, and watching the door to see whoever else might come in.

He found he had been holding his breath and at the door let out a long sigh into the rain. He hurried under the same roofs, the same galleries, and when the rain began to come down harder he found himself on Barracks close to home.

In his room he picked up the book but thought about the store for a long time, holding the book open to the page where he had stopped reading. Gazing into the rainy day, he could not recall a single face, except the sweet cashier who had taken his money so politely. He read the book for a while before dropping it to daydream about the men, through the afternoon and into the evening.

Sometime later the rain stopped, and his restlessness called him out to the streets. He walked down Barracks and up Chartres this time, and pretty soon learned that more men roamed this street as well, congregating in particular in front of a bar called Travis's a few blocks from where he lived. Men had spilled out the door onto the sidewalk and even into the street. Walking past, picking his way through the crowd, he was almost holding his breath again, wondering whether anybody noticed him. Music from inside the bar, lights, somebody dancing on a barrel, a whiff of a joint. The crowd thinned, and soon he had passed and wanted to go back. Wanted to go into the bar. Where everything would cost money. So instead he walked to Jackson Square again, and crossed the levee to the Moonwalk. The river was low and he climbed down to it, as close as he could get, sitting near the moving surface. He sat there for a long time staring into the dark water, watching lights from the bridge in the distance reflected in the river, cars moving across the bridge in a steady stream, clouds rolling overhead. He was hardly thinking of anything, but now and then he would feel as though he were walking through that crowd of men again, simply taking stock of the feeling, the men around him, having come together to that bar for a reason, to look at one another, to drink from plastic cups, to listen to loud, loud music. He sat by the river in a posture as if he were listening to something under the water, or trying to call something out of the river, waiting there for something to climb ashore. Waiting beside the river because no one could charge him any money for doing that.

He walked home again but took a different route, down Bourbon Street, out of his way if he were in a hurry, but he had nothing in particular to do. He walked up Bourbon a couple of blocks, not so many people here as last night, because of the rain; the T-shirt shops and arcades and strip clubs all appeared a bit bedraggled and forlorn. A hawker called out half-heartedly, "Hey fellow, these girls in here are for real," but Newell ignored him.

He had seen an adult bookstore in these blocks,

glimpsed it in his walking over the last two days, and he found it again, on St. Ann near the edge of the Quarter, in the bottom floor of a narrow three-story building, galleries over the street and on all three floors, curlicues of iron. He walked past slowly and looked inside. A blond kid about Newell's age slouched over the cash register. Beside him were racks of magazines with men on the cover, naked, he could see that much from a distance, before he passed the open door. Looked like nobody was in the store, though it was Saturday night.

Maybe if there had been some other people, he might have gone in himself. But he would never walk in that door by himself with that cashier staring. So he turned around, walked past the store again, took another peek at the magazine covers, then headed down Bourbon Street for home. By the time he had walked a few blocks, the rain began again, and he traced his route home wherever he could find a shelter, under the abat vents of cottages, the projecting roofs, the galleries and balconies, not yet knowing any of these terms but understanding, as he walked and saw, that these buildings were not like anything in Pastel. These buildings were a language unto themselves.

Monday when he woke, the streets were quiet, the rain still falling, and the junk store closed. He realized as he was soaking in the tub that this was Memorial Day, the last Monday in May. Not much use to look for jobs on a holiday. He had eaten his final can of soup and had nothing to eat, so even in the rain he would have to walk to the A&P. He would have to go that far, at least, because he considered it unwise to pay the soup price at the Verti Mart. So if he was walking that far, he could pass the adult bookstore again, maybe look inside.

He read till late in the morning, till he was very hungry, almost sick with it. On the walk, he found that, by choosing a careful path, he could find shelter most of the way, even without an umbrella, provided the rain fell moderately. He bought the soup without incident, and a candy bar to ease his stomach, and headed to St. Ann, noting the location of the bookstore near the edge of the Quarter. The store occupied the front of the building, three windows and a door across the front, the windows battened with shutters, hinges like fleurs-de-lis, the casement doors all of glass with wooden shutters to protect them, the door standing next to a carriageway that led into the heart of the block. Galleries of subdued wrought iron surrounded the house on the two sides that he could see. A handsome building, well kept, the stucco painted a pleasant buff color, the shutters a deep green, the iron-work gleaming black. He dodged the rain, stood under the gallery, took a breath and stepped inside.

The store was bigger than it looked, running deep into the house. Round, incandescent lights hung down from the ceiling, and up there ceiling fans were turning too, shadows weaving back and forth. Rows of magazines lined shelves against the street wall and parallel, leading to a counter where the blond guy was lounging. Around the corner from the cashier booth on both sides curtained doors led to rooms Newell couldn't see, and a sign over each door said, "25¢ Movies." A list of the movies was taped to the doors—he scanned the list but could hardly read the writing.

A big-bellied man stood to the side of the cash register and watched the store laconically. A few men were drifting among the shelves, eyes glued to the magazine covers, and a couple of men were looking at the names of the movies. The old man puffed his cigarette and smiled at Newell in a lopsided way, showing yellow teeth. "Happy Memorial Day," he said. "I'm a veteran. Do you believe it?"

"Mac," one of the men called, "we can't read what's on this list, sweetheart."

"I ain't your fucking sweetheart," Mac growled, lumbering toward them with his pants hiked to his lowest rib, his buttocks pressed perfectly flat at the back. He pulled out his glasses and slid them on his nose. "Louis, you skinny son-of-a-bitch, what the fuck kind of Chinese writing is this?"

Newell wandered to the magazines at the side while Louis, the blond guy at the cash register, shrugged and rubbed behind his ear with a finger. Newell slid his eyes down the rows of magazines. He looked at the price tags, seven, eight, ten dollars. Men of all sizes and shapes, all descriptions, naked or nearly naked, hunched over one another in various contortions, he found himself glancing at each cover and away, then back, then to another cover, while the old man Mac harangued his clerk and the two men who had started the quarrel disappeared through the curtains.

Dangerous to be here, Newell thought, because he had some money in his pocket. He lifted one of the magazines from the rack. It was wrapped in a plastic sleeve, the top taped shut. All he could see was the cover and the back. But the man on the front reminded Newell of O'Neal McCarter in Pastel, a burly, broad-shouldered country boy who had graduated from high school before Newell; here he was on the cover of this magazine, his body hard, white-skinned, black hair on the chest, a stomach like polished metal. He wore leather pants with the button open, the zipper partly unzipped, and was looking into the camera, deep brown eyes. The price was twelve dollars, the magazine not very thick, though the paper was heavy and stiff. He set it back on the shelf.

"Good evening," Mac called to Newell on his way out. "You come on back, now. It ain't always so slow."

All night in his room he longed for the magazine, thought about the image of the man, wished for twelve dollars to fall down out of the sky. The man's eyes had fixed on Newell from the magazine cover and would not let go, even now when he was far away, as if he had known he could cause all these thoughts to run through Newell's head.

Rain, the washing of rain, all night in his dreams, flooding the streets, splashing onto the gallery floor, rain all night and nothing but the sound of it around him, as if he were adrift in a sea. He woke and slept, woke and slept, through the night, and wakened early with his eyes on the crisscross pattern of the muntin on one of the transoms. The fan was turning, air drifting over him, he lay still and waited for daylight. Stained plaster overhead. He stretched, hungry, his stomach in an aching, burning knot. He went to the bathroom, drank some water. He sat on the toilet with his head in his hands. Now he was thinking about the money, about the fact that he had so little left, and it had to last such a long time, he had to find a job; he had been here for days and nothing had happened except that he waited in this room while outside rain came pouring down.

He ate his last can of soup and his stomach eased some. Looking at the newspaper from five days ago, the addresses he had marked. He would visit them all again, he would only stop when he had checked on every single one. So he set out and walked in the drizzle from place to place, beginning with the Court of Two Sisters, following the whole way round in a circle out through Royal Street, to Magazine, along Poydras and back down St. Charles by foot, managers shaking their heads at him, telling him that it would be hard to hire him until he had a phone number, sorry but there's nothing here right now, that's the way it is. Back into the French Quarter, to hotel restaurants and employment offices, asking in each place the same question as earnestly as he could manage.

Finally in Circle K the manager sat him down and gave him a glass of water. "We may need a dishwasher," he said. "Come by in a couple of days."

"Really?" Aware that he should seem less eager, if he could manage.

"Come by in a couple of days. We'll see."

Even such a bit of hope made him buoyant, and he crossed into the Fauborg Marigny to check at the White Biscuit and Betty's Kitchen. In both places, again, the managers behaved in a much more friendly way toward him, and in fact they both seemed to like Newell very much, though neither of them had any jobs to offer at the moment. The manager at Betty's Kitchen waved his hand at Newell and said, from his tattered office chair, "You can't get these queens to settle down in one job for long, sweetheart. We'll have something before long. You just keep coming by."

Newell understood the reference, the word "queens," he laughed politely at the tone. Walking home, trying to think about the Circle K, the possibility that he could earn money washing dishes, he thought of himself as a queen and could make nothing of it, nothing at all.

Shopping carried him as far as the A&P again, threading his way into those narrow shelves, carrying nine cans of soup, a box of crackers, a roll of paper towels, a roll of toilet paper, a box of plastic garbage bags, to the counter, where a sharp-shouldered, moustached cashier in a sleeveless T-shirt winked at him and ran his purchases back and forth over the new scanner that appeared to work only intermittently; when it failed the cashier tapped some number keys in a bored way and a price flashed up. Nearly nine dollars for hardly anything, the bag was so light when Newell lifted it.

Back in the room, when he opened one of the garbage bags and put the empty soup cans in it, a cockroach crawled out of one of the cans and across the back of his hand. He flung the thing off him and the can into the bag and smashed the cockroach with his foot. He washed his hand with a lot of lather and hot water.

He counted his money. Fifty dollars and some change.

An edge of summer heat touched the city that night, a feeling that the air remained too warm for comfort late into the night, not hot but not comfortable, and he found himself too warm under the blanket and too cool without it. Late, he drifted to sleep, woke, and drifted again, a rocking motion in and out of sleep, dreamless as far as he could remember, except for a moment when he was sure he was standing at his door to this apartment, afraid to walk to the courtyard because Shaquita Jarman, someone he had been afraid of in high school, was waiting down there to call him a cracker-head chicken-leg no-ass motherfucker again. He woke up for good near dawn, sighed, and got out of bed. The sky flushed pink, the buildings drew on colors slowly, he stood on the balcony, wondering what to do, maybe buy another paper and read the ads again.

He found some quarters on his desk, pulled on clothes in a rush, and went down the stairs and through the long, dark passageway to the street. He walked to the Verti Mart because he had seen papers on sale there, and sure enough it was open, and he bought a paper from another nice cashier. The same green newsprint as before. He must have looked at it funny, because the cashier looked at it too, and shrugged. "Newspaper been green for a while, honey. Lord knows."

"It must be recycled or something."

"Get out. Aren't you the cleverest thing?"

He took the paper to Jackson Square and read it with the pigeons rushing from side to side in scurrying clusters, fighting for a few crumbs. There were a few new ads for manager jobs and administrative assistant jobs, medical technologists and radiation therapists, positions to which he could hardly aspire. Some of the hotels listed here were the places that had already turned Newell down, or more or less turned him down in that polite but indefinite way, *we really don't know what we can do for you right now*.

So he read the paper itself, and he found himself surprised to learn that it was Wednesday; he had lost his sense of where he was in the week. The local news made no sense, about places like Plaquemines Parish, Shreveport, names completely unfamiliar to him, and even the national news, the latest about Jimmy Carter, for instance, or where Betty Ford was speaking this week, came to him as though diluted; perhaps because the paper was green, nothing he read in it seemed quite real.

He spent the day aimlessly, wandering along Canal Street, going into shops, wishing he had money to buy all sorts of things that he saw. Wandering down Ramparts, along Esplanade beyond the French Quarter, down Frenchmen into the Fauborg, noting everywhere the same kinds of curious houses built right up to the line of the street, or with fences along the street, and balconies and galleries, wooden curlicues, people sitting on steps, propping one leg, talking, chewing on the end of a match or puffing a cigarette. He took note of everything, all the while keeping his eye on the names of streets to make sure he knew how to find his way back to Barracks.

The next day he walked to the Circle K as soon as it opened, only to learn it was the manager's day off, and he would have to wait. He headed to the White Biscuit but lost his nerve at the point of going inside, heading home for a can of soup to ease his empty stomach, to count his money again.

Closing the shutters to darken the room, he lay on the bed in the dusky light and let the fan stir air across him. He tried to think of nothing at all. He could read the paper again, he could look again. He could look for jobs farther away. It was not time to panic yet, he still had some soup left, he had some money left, it would last for a few more days. He arrived at this point in his thinking only to find the fear returning, the knot in his stomach that told him he was failing, he would have to go home to Alabama, he would never make it here with so little money, he had miscalculated and would have to try again.

I still have the money for a ticket home, he thought, I can leave tomorrow if I want to; and once he thought this, he realized he would be all right, he could stay for a couple more days, at least, he could ask his landlady to give him part of his rent back if he left in a week, maybe. He already knew how much the bus ticket home would cost, about twenty-eight dollars, same as the price for the one-way ticket he had bought to come here.

So he could safely spend twenty or so dollars before he had to go home, and he could draw that out for a few days, at least. He could spare a few quarters to do a load of laundry at the corner.

After a while the ache in his stomach eased away, and he slept through the afternoon in the dim light. When he woke he felt calmer and figured he had panicked, but that maybe nothing was wrong, maybe he should simply get up from the bed and go out again, visit all those restaurants and hotels and offices again, pester them till someone gave him what he needed. Surely he would be able to do that? But his confidence faltered after he was awake for a while, when he thought of his little fold of money, when he thought of eating another can of soup for supper, and nothing the rest of the night but water.

The next day, even though he was supposed to go to the Circle K again, he was afraid to get up; he stayed in bed till afternoon, then dressed and walked as far as the Verti Mart to buy laundry detergent, soup, toothpaste, hurrying home again, with rain beginning to pelt the streets. He stayed in bed the rest of the day, read more of the science fiction novel, and dozed. Listless, hardly able to contemplate anything.

In the morning he made himself bathe and dress, down to forty-two dollars and forty cents. He walked to the restaurant, his stomach in knots. It was Saturday, and the manager, Curtis, was in the middle of a rush, so that he could pause to talk to Newell only for a moment. Newell figured that meant bad news, and Curtis kept dashing around from table to table anyway, so that Newell had to stand and wait. Curtis rushed by with a tray full of plates and glasses and said, "The dishwasher didn't quit, but wait a minute," he turned the corner. Newell's heart was sinking, there was no job, and here was suddenly Curtis again in his face. "But the bus boy left. Do you want to be a bus boy?"

He could hardly believe what he was hearing. "Sure."

"Well, I can't stop to talk to you right now. Come back this afternoon about three o'clock. Can you start Tuesday?"

"Sure. That's fine."

"Good. Come back and talk to me this afternoon."

Curtis rushed away, and Newell went on standing there, dumbfounded. After a while he realized he ought to leave, so he drifted to the door, walked outside, realized he could relax now, the anxious feeling could dissolve. He would come back this afternoon, he would talk to Curtis, he would go to work as a bus boy. He figured that was the job Curtis had been doing while he was talking to Newell, clearing the tables and carrying the dishes to the dishwasher and setting the tables again. For doing this he would earn money, and it was only the third of June—he had plenty of time to make the rent. He felt himself relaxing. He could stay.

When he returned at three o'clock, the tables were mostly empty, a few pairs of men or women sipping coffee. Curtis was sitting at a desk crammed against the corner near a blocked door. He had Newell sit down and fill out some papers and explained the tax forms. He told Newell the job paid four dollars fifty cents an hour plus tips. The waiters he worked with would each tip him at the end of their shifts. How much would depend on how busy the restaurant was, but if Newell felt like he was being cheated, he could say so. Had he ever worked in a restaurant before? Well, that didn't matter. What mattered in the Circle K was that Newell had to keep the tables clean, keep the water glasses filled, and look cute while he was doing it, so people would keep coming back to the restaurant to see him. Curtis said that with a perfectly straight face, and when Newell giggled, Curtis merely smiled, though in a rather tired way. "You don't think I'm kidding, do you? I wouldn't hire you if you weren't cute, sweetheart. Not to work out front."

He would work breakfast and lunch shifts Tuesday through Sunday, with Monday off. He was due at work by 6:30 A.M. every day except Sunday, when the restaurant opened later, and he would get off work by two in the afternoon every day. Absorbing every detail as if his life depended on it, Newell studied the rooms, the neatly placed wooden tables, the framed prints on the wall, drawings of men with no shirts and tight pants, big crotches, big eyes with long lashes, in pairs or groups, eyeing one another greedily.

"When is payday?" Newell asked.

"End of shift on Tuesday. For the week before. But you'll get your tips every day."

Walking home he could hardly believe it, that it was done, that he had a job, that he started in three days, that he would have to get up very early every morning, even earlier than for the IGA; he would have to buy a cheap alarm clock—he couldn't rely on his watch. But he could buy an alarm clock out of the forty some dollars he had left, a sum that appeared more substantial now that it only had to last a few days. He could buy something to eat besides soup, and starting on Tuesday, he could eat two meals a day for free at the restaurant.

He could buy the magazine if he wanted it, he realized, he could buy *Brute Hombre* with the picture of Rod Hardigan on the cover. Twelve dollars to own it, and he could afford it if he found an alarm clock that was cheap enough. So he went to his room right away and got his money, leaving twenty and taking the rest, heading to the junk store downstairs, figuring it was smart to check with Miss Kimbro first. She struck him as a woman who understood a bargain.

The junk store had a lot of traffic, this being a Saturday afternoon, but he explored the store till he found a row of clocks, still in their store boxes, marked for two dollars apiece. The clocks had alarms and lighted dials, and he figured he could plug one in by the refrigerator and set it on top, and if the dial was really lighted he could read the time from across the room. Two dollars was in his price range.

It was sitting on a book, an old one with a cloth cover, *The Flavor of the French Quarter*. The book was fifty cents. Inside were pictures of the buildings he was seeing every day. He picked up the book, too.

Miss Kimbro was working by herself this afternoon. With her reading glasses low on her nose, she wrote in her ledger, "General Electric alarm clock in original box and old book."

"So, you're doing all right up there?" she asked.

"I sure am. I found a job today."

"You don't say." She was frowning, but he could tell she was pleased. "Well, then, I guess you're all right now, aren't you?"

"Yes ma'am. I'm going to be a bus boy at a restaurant."

"We all have to start somewhere," she said, though he was not quite sure what she meant. "You can bring that clock back if it doesn't work, and try another one. Keep it in the box."

"When I get the money, can I get a phone up there?"

"Of course you can. Now run along, I'm by myself today."

He took the clock and the book upstairs, set the book on his bed, plugged in the clock. The second hand swept round and the face lit a soft amber color. He set the alarm for the next hour and waited to see if it would work. At 3 P.M. the alarm sounded, a nice loud buzz, and he figured it would be enough to wake him.

He looked at the book for a while. Read a page that defined what a "walled city" was, what an "abat vent" was, each with illustrations. The book was stuffed with pictures and facts. There might even be something in it about this very building he was standing in. Newell felt pleased that he could spare fifty cents on his education; it made him feel as if he might come to understand this place. But he was too restless, now, to read.

Outside, low, the sound of a ship's horn, the ship passing upriver, he guessed, toward the container docks. From other directions the sound of traffic, from across the wall a television in the neighbor's apartment. The low hum of the ceiling fan, a sound he hardly heard anymore. A drip in the bathroom sink. Here he was, he could stay here now, he could earn a living and keep his room, he could stay.

By the time he reached St. Ann, he was already picturing the rows of magazines, the glossy cover, the pimply blond at the cash register. He crossed the street, dodging one of the metal horse heads, opened the door and stepped inside. He walked down the long row of shelves past the cash register, and yes, this time it was the blond kid on the cash register. He looked about Newell's age, and Newell wondered how someone so forlorn-looking had ever landed a swell job like this one. But by then he had found the copy of *Brute Hombre*, the hairy-chested man on the cover, the harsh block letters of the title slashing him through the forehead. Shoulders like a span of bridge. Newell gripped the magazine, wrapped in plastic and sealed with tape, as though it were some sacred object. On the back another picture of this man, Rod Hardigan, this time wearing only a pair of leather chaps and some kind of skimpy underwear, his thighs bulging, his body managing to look as if it were bursting out of itself, Newell found himself staring and wondered how long he had been standing there holding the magazine.

At the moment only a couple of other people were shopping in the store. Newell took a deep breath and walked to the cash register where Louis—the name came to him now—Louis, with a spray of acne across his nose and cheeks, and long hair that could have used a washing, a hook nose, and nearly absent lips, where Louis took the magazine from him and stared at it as if trying to remember what he was supposed to do. Louis gave Newell a slack smile as the cash register shook and spit out a price, including sales tax. Newell accepted his change and the brown bag. Louis tried to count the money into Newell's hand but kept getting lost, started over twice, finally shoved the money at Newell and said, "Here."

From the back of the store walked the old man, Mac, whose hair appeared darker today, and Newell guessed he had probably put a rinse in it, like Flora did to her hair. "Howdy," Mac said, "pleasant day, ain't it?"

The job had left Newell feeling friendly and even a little confident, so he spoke up. "Yes sir. But it looks like rain tonight."

"You think so?"

"Yes sir. Later on."

"Well, then, you better run your little tail on home,"

Mac said, pulling a pack of Camel cigarettes out of his pocket. "Before you get wet. What did you buy?"

Newell handed him the magazine in the paper bag without thinking. Some quality of Mac disarmed him, caused him to believe the request was good-intentioned. Mac looked at the cover and rubbed his jaw, scratchy with beard-shadow. "You got good taste. That one is high quality."

"It sure cost enough."

"You're buying quality, son. You pay the price for color printing and good paper stock."

Newell took the bag again. Mac turned to Louis, blew smoke in Louis's face. "Hey, you pimple-face son of a bitch, did you bag up them new magazines yet?"

"I ain't had time."

"Well, you better get time. We're going to have some customers in here after a while."

Newell dipped his head to say good-bye, and Mac did the same, and Newell carried the magazine out of the store with a better feeling about himself, a less furtive way of thinking about the fact that he had bought a book with pictures of naked men in it. Quality, it was. He hurried down St. Ann to Decatur Street and walked straight down to Barracks. For the first time since he had come here he hardly noticed the city at all. He had rolled up the magazine in its bag and carried it in his hand like a brown baton. Forward with a brisk stride he walked, and arrived at the door to the long, dark passageway, walked through it into the loggia and up the stairs to his room.

He sat in the chair by the door to the gallery and held the bag in his lap. He slipped out the plastic bag, unfastened the tape, and pulled the slick magazine out of its wrapper.

Finding himself watching the eyes of the man in the photograph, between brown and hazel, with a translucence that created the illusion of depth, as if the man were actually seeing, as if someone were inside the photograph. The man with his heavy beard and shaggy chest, the tip of his tongue visible, touching the fullness of his lower lip, the slight look of pout, the languid slouch of the pelvis.

Inside the cover, on the very first page, under a title that said, "Rod the Rock," the same man stood facing the camera, naked this time, with his private parts showing, so that they could hardly be called private at all any more. Newell had seen only a few penises, mostly relatives and boys in gym, none as large as this, and he stared at it, arched forward from Rod the Rock's thick thighs, Rod staring out at Newell as if inviting him to touch it, to find a way to reach into the paper and touch it.

This was different from what Newell had done in Pastel, different from fumbling with his zipper in the bathroom, sitting on the toilet having some fantasy about Little Joe Cartwright from Bonanza, and hoping Flora stayed close enough to the TV that she couldn't hear the racket he was making. Afterward, straightening the jeans on his narrow hips, he'd head off to supper where Flora waited at the table with her mild blue eyes, uncurious expression, and open can of Pabst.

Here what excited him was a fixed object, a picture, floating in space. When he read the words again, "Rod the Rock," when he looked at the shape of the man's body, the mass of it, calling up some feeling, Newell felt himself as if he were dissolving into the picture, as if the world of that image were more vivid than the room on Barracks Street where the ceiling fan turned slowly. For a long time Newell hardly thought about where he was at all; he sat without stirring from the chair, only turning the pages, daring nothing more than to run his fingers over each page before he turned to the next, the gesture like a caress, as though he were actually laying his hands on this man's skin.

He had been breathing carefully, as though walking on a wire where the faintest breath could send him off balance; he understood instinctively, even as early as that, the need to gauge his pleasure carefully, to conserve it in order to draw it out. He closed the magazine and stood. From outside, car horns, the hooting laughter of someone on the street, music from one of the opposite balconies; he recognized the song and it made him smile, "I Need a Man" by Grace Jones.

He stared down at the magazine, frightened some by the feelings it aroused in him. He had played with one of his cousins once, in Pastel, a boy his own size named Joel, the same age as Newell, with the same family looks, but that had been only once, and Joel so resembled Newell that the act was almost like masturbation. All the rest had been only speculation, longing. He could hardly believe what he saw on these pages; images that had been in his head all this time. It was as if he had foreseen this as his future, because he had foreseen this man, or at least someone who would pose like him, wearing nothing, or so little as to be nothing, page after page. Newell opened the magazine to the pictures on the sawhorse, the pictures in the locker room, Rod dressed in leather. The images rushed through him and he took the magazine to the bathroom with him and lay it on the back of the toilet. As powerful as the feeling of arousal was the strangeness of the moment. Newell felt as if he knew the picture-man completely, had always known him, and furthermore wanted to lie down with him and be covered by him and run hands along him and gaze into his face. From picture to picture, from page to page, the pose changed, but the expression was always the same, always fixed on the camera, always impassive, grave, self-assured to the point of arrogance; and what was disturbing was that Newell wanted him to have exactly that look. Since Rod the Rock could have anything he wanted, it was fitting he should express no desire at all, except, maybe, a wish to reveal himself again and again.

When Newell came out of the bathroom and put the magazine away, in the bottom of the wardrobe out of sight, rain was washing the edge of the gallery, sweeping down at a slant out of the sky. He had heard nothing in the bathroom except the sound of his own breathing, but now he heard low, rumbling thunder, the air heavy with moisture even inside the room. He threw open the windows, protected from the rain by the roof of the gallery. What a sound, what a hissing, everywhere. Along the gutters in the street below the water was running a foot deep.

He turned on the lamp in the twilight and sat by the open doors watching the rain for a long time, then reading his books, first leafing through the picture book about the French Quarter, afterward picking up his paperback novel about two men traveling together back in time and the world they find there. He could relax and pay attention to the book for the first time since arriving in New Orleans, maybe because he had a job, or because he had begun the transformation he had foreseen when he was leaving Pastel. He understood his present world, the narrow room, the high windows, the torrent of rain, well enough now that he could surrender to the book, for a few hours anyway, till time to go to bed.

He called Flora the next day, Sunday, to tell her he had found a job. He caught her at home with a headache, puffing her cigarette audibly, sipping coffee, and trying to clear her throat. "Sweet Thing, I am so glad you called me."

"Yes ma'am. Well, it's good news, don't you think?"

"Well, I hope you don't have to work in food service for very long," she intimated. "Jesse has been in food service his whole life and look where that's got him."

"Yes ma'am." He understood from this that Jesse was sitting at the kitchen table too, scratching his nose or the inside of his ear, looking completely vacant, as he usually looked in the morning.

"You being careful in that French Quarter?" She pronounced it "korter."

"Yes ma'am. But I don't think it's dangerous."

"You'd be surprised."

"Really. I been walking around since I got here, even at night, and I never feel like anybody is following me, or anything."

"Well," she took a drag on the cigarette, "you walk around with that kind of careless attitude and somebody will drag you off in an alley one of these days, you watch. And nobody will know what happened to you."

"Yes ma'am."

"I know what I'm talking about. There's things that happen in New Orleans that you'd rather not even imagine." Her words took on a curious authority over the long-distance line. Jesse must have coughed, with the cigarette smoke swirling around him in that trailer kitchen, because Flora snapped, "Go in the living room if you can't stand my smoke, you tattooed son of a bitch."

"Are you going to church today, Grandma?"

"No. I didn't get my dress out the cleaners this week." They had made this joke before; they both laughed and felt better, and he imagined Jesse sulking in front of the TV with his toes buried in the shag carpet. "It's a lot of Catholics in New Orleans," Flora noted.

"I know. There's a great big church they go to. In a square right here in the French Quarter."

"I know exactly the one you're talking about," she

said, and after a moment added, "My phone bill would be sky high with the two of us gabbing about nothing."

"I'll get me a phone pretty soon," Newell promised, "then I won't have to call collect." He waited a moment, then asked, "You heard from Mama?"

The mention of his mother put Flora on her guard, no different than any other time. "No. I don't ever know when she's going to call."

"All right. Well, you tell her I said hey. If you talk to her."

They said good-bye, and there he stood across from the Verti Mart on Sunday morning. Wondering why he had asked about Mama, after such a long time. Wondering what had put her on his mind.

He stopped at the French Market and bought a few apples and a carton of salt, and hurried up the stairs carrying the bag. He sat in his room and bit into the apples and sprinkled salt on the crisp white flesh, savoring the apples and salt. He lost himself in a reverie, eating all the apples he had bought and sitting there, until suddenly there was a knock at the door.

There stood Miss Kimbro, framed by the courtyard behind her, carrying something with a cord. She stepped inside and looked around and shoved the thing at him and said, "This comes with the room. You can cook with it."

"I can?"

"Plug it in," she said, and looked around again, as if he might have changed something, as if she were searching for some change he might have made in the room. "It's a toaster oven."

"That's really nice of you," he said, and she shrugged, and he plugged the oven into a receptacle near the bathroom and set it on top of the wicker clothes hamper.

"Don't leave it on that hamper, it'll catch fire."

He moved the toaster oven to the little table.

"Do you like the room?"

"Yes ma'am."

"You think you'll stay here?"

"Oh, yes ma'am."

He could hardly tell whether she heard him or not. She stepped to the bathroom and looked all around it. She looked down at the toaster oven, turned a knob at the front of it. At once the inside lit a luminous orange. "It works," she said.

"Thank you."

By now she was opening the door and stepping outside. She stood with the door partly closed, one eye watching him. "Anyway, I just wanted to bring up the toaster oven, I have to get back to the shop."

"Thank you, ma'am."

"Oh yes," she said, and vanished.

In fact, she waited on the steps leading down to the slate floor of the loggia. She had no idea whether or not he was listening, she simply stood there, in a bit of breeze, with the sun bright and the warm breeze stirring. She had been distracted by the expression on Newell's face, as if the thought of a toaster oven terrified him, or as if the room terrified him, or the city did. She stepped carefully down the plank stairs. She should have a carpenter look at these steps. A good, young, strong carpenter to work in the hot sun, repairing these steps. She thought Newell would like that. At the bottom she looked up again, at the closed door. She could almost hear the silence inside. Stepping into the junk shop, she stood before the whirring blades of the oscillating fan, and a breeze swept across her first one way, then another.

The whole afternoon and evening were busy, in fact, and she hardly got a breath of air before ten, when she locked the front door; she stood on the street for a long time, wandered to the corner. Upstairs, beyond the open shutters, the boy's lamp was burning. He was sitting in the doorway reading. He had but the one lamp, maybe she ought to get him another. Still, she had given him a toaster oven. But it was clear from his reaction that he was not accustomed to being given anything at all.

On Tuesday morning he woke up when the clock said 5:30 A.M. He had hardly ever woken up so early before, and he stumbled to the bath tub and ran hot water. He lay in the tub waking and sleeping, waking and sleeping, till finally he washed and rinsed himself as best he could. He dressed in jeans and a T-shirt, like the other guys he had seen in the restaurant.

He headed for the Circle K with plenty of time. Some people were already seated in the dining room, and a thin waiter in a tight T-shirt slouched over them writing down their order. Curtis was at his desk, looking half asleep, yawning as Newell walked in.

"Oh, hi, it's you," Curtis said, and yawned again. He showed Newell the kitchen, introduced him to Felix, the breakfast cook, and Alan, the morning waiter. Umberto, the prep guy, was out back, washing out the garbage can with a hose, visible through an open screen door.

The job was simple. Newell picked up dishes and brought people water. When the tables were empty he cleaned them off. He was the only bus boy for the breakfast shift; someone named Tyrone came in to cover the late part of breakfast and lunch. Newell set to work. At first there was little to do, then suddenly the tables filled. Curtis only returned to help when there were too many dirty tables for Newell to handle.

Often Newell found Curtis watching, though pretty soon Newell was too busy to notice what anybody was doing. Alan tapped Newell on the shoulder and said, "Those people have been asking for water for fifteen minutes. You need to move your behind." Or came up to Newell and snapped, "If you can't clean these tables any faster than this I'm not going to tip you. I could do it myself this quick." Or, while passing to the kitchen, said, "Come back here and help me take out these plates to that party of eight. That woman at that table has an attitude about me." A woman was in fact scowling at them both from the table, and Newell set her plate in front of her, and she asked for something unfamiliar to him, and he took the message back to Alan and Alan said, "Well, here, take it to her." It was Tabasco, a bottle of hot sauce that the customer sprayed over her eggs. Half the morning Newell spent running around doing what Alan said to do and the rest listening while Alan offered another harangue about how slowly Newell cleaned the tables.

Help came and things settled down, and sooner than he could have guessed the rush was done. Curtis clapped Newell on the back in the kitchen door. "You lived through it."

"It was all right," Newell said.

"Except you're so slow and clumsy," Alan added, from the side.

"Shut up, Alan," Curtis said.

"I will not shut up. He's slow and he's clumsy with the plates."

"He didn't break anything."

Alan whirled away with his order pad. Curtis watched him go and said, "You did okay. But you need to wear a tighter T-shirt."

"A what?"

Curtis laughed nervously. "Your jeans are all right but your T-shirt's not tight enough. You need to wear a tight one. We have to keep the queens happy."

In the lull between breakfast and lunch Newell ate his own eggs and bacon, served without a word by Felix, who watched Newell eat the first couple of bites, then grunted and lumbered back to the kitchen. Alan ate his breakfast, too, but he sat at a different table, away from Newell, refusing to look at him or speak to him. But by then there were other waiters, Frank and Stuart, Curtis's boyfriend, and they were friendlier than Alan, and cuter.

Lunch shift shocked Newell with its intensity, so many dishes on the table, so many empty water glasses, everything to be done at once, and people crammed into the restaurant leaving only the narrowest space through which Newell could slide. He moved as fast as he could and hoped for the best. His whole mind focused itself on the need to note the level of water in a glass across a room, despite cigarette smoke swirling in the air and bodies moving this way and that across his field of vision; he concentrated on the balance required to haul a heavy tray of dishes over the heads of the customers, who were often staring at him as he moved, trying to make eye contact. He was assigned to Alan's and Stuart's sections and kept them clean as best he could, kept the customers flowing through, kept the water glasses full, and picked up the used napkins from the floor, but even so, Alan found plenty to criticize—that Newell was setting the tables the wrong way, that he took forever to fill a simple pitcher of water. That he was bumping into the customers as he walked, that he was so slow he couldn't help to carry out the food.

At the end of the shift Stuart tipped him eight dollars and some change and Alan refused to tip him at all, at first, until Curtis and Stuart took him aside and talked to him for a while, after which he gave Newell four dollars even and said, "You're lucky I give you that much, as slow as you are. I think you're in the wrong line of work, honey."

"Don't pay any attention to her," Stuart said, indicating Alan as the "her" in question. "Her stars are all in the wrong place this month."

"Fuck off, Stuart."

Stuart smiled and glided away. Newell imitated the glide though not the smile, and said, "I'll see you tomorrow, Alan."

So his first day was over, and all he had to think about till then was finding a tight T-shirt to wear. He tried on the ones he had brought from Pastel, six of them, including the one that had Bruce Springsteen's picture on the front; that one was tight, and one other green one from high school was also a bit tight.

He put the twelve dollars and some change from his tips with the rest of his money, which grew to nearly fifty dollars again. The fact pleased him, and he thought, I can start saving for the rent right now.

But at work the next day, with Newell in the Springsteen T-shirt, relations with Alan were even worse, and now Stuart was cold to him, too. Every dish Newell touched was the wrong dish, every time he carried out the water glass he went to the wrong side of the restaurant first, or when Alan asked for a simple glass of orange juice Newell needed ten minutes to find it. Up to a point it had made sense, but by the lunch shift Newell was wondering what bothered Alan so much.

"He really liked Travis, the last guy," Frank told him, when they were eating breakfast together, Frank lowering his voice to float just over his eggs and potatoes. "But

Curtis fired Travis for coming in late all the time and not showing up one day, and Alan has been pouting ever since. Because Curtis lets Stuart come in late as much as he wants."

"That doesn't have anything to do with me."

"Honey, to a princess like Alan, common sense like that does not matter one little bit."

"Well, I hope he gets used to me soon."

"It's because you're cuter than he is," Frank added, as if he had not already offered another explanation, standing with his cup of coffee. The restaurant had gotten quiet, around ten-thirty, just before lunch would start. "And younger."

Alan, sitting alone at the window, legs crossed like a girl, smoked a slow, drawling cigarette, his elbows sharp and dark against the window. Hair combed straight back, long sharp nose, thin lips, narrow eyes, soft chin. His parts had a look of hanging together only loosely, an uncertain whole. He's not cute, Newell realized, and, at the same moment, but I am.

Curtis had that day off, but was at work the next, when Newell wore the tight green T-shirt from high school, and the tight faded jeans with a slight flare at the bottom. Curtis said the T-shirt was better, was more like what he had in mind, and all morning he found reasons to talk to Newell, helping him with tables during the breakfast rush. Newell had to concentrate on his work and hardly thought about Curtis or what he might be up to, but as the morning wore on, Stuart began to harangue

Newell pretty much as Alan continued to do, get the water faster, there's too much ice in the pitcher, this orange juice is soured, didn't you check it?

For breakfast Felix prepared Newell a nice omelet, a change from the usual eggs. Frank handed Newell the plate, noting, "Well, I guess Felix is in love with you too."

"What do you mean?"

"He never fixes omelets—you have to beg him."

For Frank, Felix had made the usual breakfast, scrambled eggs and bacon, potatoes on the side.

"Who else is in love with me?"

Frank laughed. "Are you kidding?"

"No."

"Well, darling, Curtis is following you around like a puppy. It's got Stuart all upset. Haven't you even noticed? You cold bitch."

From there on through lunch he did notice that Curtis was more or less following him around the restaurant and Stuart was watching the whole thing, slamming dishes around and getting in a fight with Umberto, the prep cook, about the salad. Alan was meanwhile sitting calmly by the window, puffing the usual cigarette, off his feet for a moment, as he called it, but glaring at Newell whenever he passed.

You cold bitch. He liked the ring of the words, though he had simply been oblivious and not really cold. But he liked that he had appeared cold to Frank.

The work was what absorbed him, the novelty of it, which he knew would wear away; but for the moment it was what he needed. Alan and Stuart tipped him, if poorly, and his stock of cash grew, if slowly. Payday was coming. Saturdays and Sundays the restaurant was busy from the time it opened till the time Newell got off, and the customers were all in a jolly mood. The dining rooms became so crowded that every trip he made through the mazes of chairs and tables became a performance, and he became easy at making eye contact with the customers, for the most fleeting of moments, but enough to fulfill the apparent requirement; he twisted and shimmied through the chairs with his pitcher, his tray, his cloths for cleaning, and he forgot whether Curtis was watching him or not, he forgot whether anybody liked him, he did what he was supposed to do and remembered that he was getting paid money for it, and with the money he could pay his rent, and with that accomplished he could stay here, in the city.

At the end of the shifts on the weekend, even Stuart and Alan had to give him pretty big tips, they had made so much money off the tables themselves, and Curtis supervised the payout, not only for Newell but for Tyrone. Nearly forty dollars for each day, twenty from each waiter, more money than Newell had counted on. He could buy some decent sheets and a stack of clean, new towels.

On Tuesday he overslept by a few minutes and arrived at work a few minutes late, only to find the place in an uproar. Alan had caught Umberto looking in Curtis's desk drawers without permission, presumably for the cash bag from last night, as if it would still be there. Everybody was shrieking at everybody, and the dozen or so customers sat struck with mild astonishment. Newell went to the office, stuck his card into the punch slot of the time clock. Alan said, "Well, Umberto, if you're so innocent, what were you doing in there?"

"I was looking for a book of matches."

"We have matches right at the register."

"I wasn't at the register."

"Well, ten steps would have taken you right there. You were not looking for any matches."

"Everybody knows Curtis takes the deposit to the bank at night."

"Sometimes he doesn't."

Umberto waved his hand at Alan and headed back to the kitchen, and Alan followed him there to argue more. Alan came out in a few minutes and spotted Newell with an empty tray, heading to the tables where the customers were paying their bills and fleeing. "And don't think I didn't notice you were late."

"I forgot to turn on the alarm," Newell said.

"Convenient to be so forgetful. When the rest of us have to do double work."

"It was only ten minutes, Alan," he said, but this time he looked Alan in the eye. Alan wavered and looked away. Newell cleared the empty tables, his stomach already in a knot, and the week was only an hour old.

When Curtis came in and Alan rushed to tell him the story, Curtis called Umberto to the office in front of Alan and handed Umberto a book of matches. "Here," Curtis said.

"That's it?"

"Alan, what do you think you're doing?"

"He was going through your desk. You don't let people go through your desk."

"There's nothing in my desk," Curtis said, "I don't keep anything in it. I don't even lock it."

"You don't let people go through your desk." Alan waved one hand in the air and stalked away. "What kind of boss are you?"

At the end of the shift, Curtis handed Newell a pay envelope and gave him a receipt to sign. Inside was a check for one hundred and fourteen dollars and thirteen cents. "I can cash it for you if you sign it over to me," Curtis said, and Newell waited, and Curtis looked at him, and then turned the check over and said, "Sign it across here. Sign your name."

Later he went to Mac's, as he had come to think of the adult bookstore, and hung out there for a while. This time he changed three dollars for quarters with the woman at the cash register, a platinum blond he had never seen before. "Where's Mac?" he asked.

"This is his night to prowl with the alley cats." She gave him a grin, her lips caked with pink lipstick. "He'll be back tomorrow. You a friend of his?"

"No. I just speak to him when I come in."

Newell walked behind the curtain for the first time. The booths were a maze of partitions, heading off two ways, though not quite in straight paths. He wandered in the dark spaces, trying to read the postings for each movie in the blue-tinged light. He could not bring himself to enter any of the movies except the one called, "Roger," which was apparently a man by himself, and that seemed like a good way to start, to Newell, but he found there were already three people in the booth when he opened the door. In that tiny space there was hardly room for another, nice as they were to invite him.

When he headed to the store again, he took a wrong turn and found himself at a door to the courtyard. He had known the old house had a courtyard but was seeing it for the first time, ivy climbing one wall, a picnic table at the center. A man stood in the courtyard, big-shouldered, heavy-jawed. He looked like Rod the Rock, and Newell found himself staring. The man wore a dark jacket, a shirt open at the collar; he glanced at Newell, smiled, nodded his head. So handsome. Newell's heart was pounding. Someone called out, "Jack." A woman's voice, and the man moved toward the sound. It pleased Newell to have heard the man's name. Jack. Nodding to Newell again, Jack disappeared, and Newell waited there a moment, in case the guy should reappear.

Newell wandered among the magazines for a while, but since Mac was off tonight, he figured he would go away and come back again later in the week. Walking home, he was grateful for the quiet, the row of old street-lamps, the crooked pavements, the wall of buildings massed at the street. Once he left the bookstore, that doorway blended into the wall, as did all the other door-ways, hiding all the other rooms like that one, where anything might happen.

On Bourbon Street he stopped and bought a tight,

white T-shirt with the words "Vieux Carre" printed across it, and the outline of an ornate gallery, intricate ironwork, in shiny blue applique. He bought a size small and figured he couldn't get any tighter than that, so he paid seven dollars for the T-shirt and felt pleased that he would have something new to wear tomorrow.

The next day, in the T-shirt, he felt as though he were putting on a show in the restaurant, slipping between the tables, with men watching him from all sides, and some of them flirting, trying to talk to him. Later, Curtis called Newell to his office and said, "You're really getting into this, babycake."

"I like it all right," Newell said, but he felt suddenly uncomfortable, knowing Stuart was somewhere in the dining rooms, watching all this.

"How long have you lived in town?"

"I just got here a couple of weeks ago, right before I came in here the first time."

"That's too sweet." Curtis's tone offended Newell, something about it he could not place, but he showed nothing except that he was listening. "Anyway, you seem like you're settling in all right."

Stuart appeared suddenly in the doorway, across from Newell, close enough to touch, and smiled in a brittle way. "You two look so comfortable together."

Curtis turned to face the wall, lifting a pencil. "Stuart, did you want to talk about something?"

"No, Curtis, I just wanted to find out how much you two have to talk about, you know?"

They were staring at each other now. Curtis had started to blush, and Stuart was about to start an argument. Newell figured it was a good time to leave, and so he did, with Alan waiting for him at the server's station, complaining that there was not even a pitcher's worth of ice in the bin, Newell needed to bring in some ice, where had he been anyway, the little nitwit?

Stuart and Frank tipped out and left the restaurant, Stuart lingering for a while to hover over Curtis, while Newell was still eating his lunch. He felt the comfort of his day's tip money in his pocket. Stuart kissed Curtis good-bye on the lips and left the restaurant, and Curtis hardly waited for Stuart to get out of sight before he sat down with Newell himself. He was watching Newell. Something hangdog in his air. "You doing all right, Newell?"

"Sure."

"Things are working out pretty good for you, here."

"Yeah. I like it."

"Stuart likes you."

Newell gave him a look.

"No, I mean it. He's fine about you. Look." He pulled his chair closer to Newell. "You could probably be a waiter, don't you think? Those guys pull down the real tips."

Newell felt something pressing on his midsection, a strange pressure that he had never felt before, a bit hard to breathe while Curtis was sitting so close, talking so low. "I'm fine with being a bus boy."

"But you'd like to make the real money."

He let that go. Curtis was still watching him. After a while Newell wiped his mouth with the napkin and laid it across his plate. "I like to make money, that's a fact."

"Well, then," Curtis said, but he was looking down at his plate. "I'll have to see what I can do about it."

"See you tomorrow."

"Why don't you sit for a while? Talk to me."

"I have something I have to do," Newell said.

"You sure?" Curtis asked, and there was something suddenly cool in his aspect.

"Yes. I have a friend coming over to my house."

Curtis nodded.

"See you."

Curtis nodded again, staring down at the table.

Umberto had been watching the whole time, and part-way through the scene brought Felix to the kitchen door to witness too.

Newell walked out of the restaurant with a sinking feeling, already dreading the next morning. On Thursday, Curtis sent Newell home after breakfast, because things were slow, he said. Curtis was off the next day, but Stuart was working, and it was clear that Stuart had heard something. He was cold and unfriendly to Newell all day, and that coupled with Alan's continual harangues made the hours nearly impossible to endure. The next day was Saturday, and Curtis was working though it was usually his day off, and he treated Newell distantly. But there was so much business in the restaurant, nobody had time to say very much to anybody. At the end of the day Alan left with the restaurant still full, Curtis interviewing people in the office, the rumor going around that Curtis was hiring another waiter.

When Curtis went out of his way to say good-bye to Newell in the coldest tones possible, in front of Stuart, Newell left the restaurant fearing the worst. In fact, it was as bad as he expected, because the next morning, a Sunday, a new bus boy was on duty when Newell came to work, and Curtis called Newell to the office and fired him very first thing. Almost a week's pay for the days he had worked since the last payday, plus an extra fifty for getting fired, as best Newell could understand it.

"What did I do?" Newell asked.

Curtis shrugged, looked down at his desk.

"You were too disruptive," Alan said, passing the door. "Nobody could get along with you."

"Was this because I wouldn't go out with you?" Newell asked.

Curtis never answered at all, going back to his books, and Newell asked, "Well, what am I supposed to do now?"

"Leave, honey," Alan said. "It's just that simple."

In a daze he headed back to his room. He went upstairs immediately and counted out two hundred fifty dollars from what he had. This was the rent; he put it aside. He had enough to keep him alive till he got another job. He had a couple of cans of soup and some crackers left from when he had been unemployed. Curtis could have fired him after breakfast, he could have waited that long. Could you really be fired because you didn't respond when your boss flirted with you? Newell ate a can of soup slowly to make it last longer, counted his money again, discouraged that the folded bills and precise stacks of coins added up to such a tiny sum. The hot soup calmed his belly, and he felt less anxious and tried to lie across the bed, but when he did, with the afternoon sun slanting across his belly through the slats of the blinds, when he drifted toward sleep, he felt his belly rumbling as if hungry and turned over on his side and counted his money again, worried that it would not be enough. He had meant to stay in the room but, with thoughts like these churning, he sprang up from the bed and splashed water on his face, folded the money into his pocket and went out walking along Bourbon Street. But whenever he saw a sign for help wanted, he first surged toward the door of the business and then away from it. Sunday, it wouldn't do any good to ask, most places the managers didn't even work on Sundays. His heart pounded, and he talked himself out of each opportunity, and walked away, and finally drifted toward the bars again.

He went into a bar and ordered one of the cocktails that had worked so well to dull his thinking before. He moved from bar to bar. Late in the evening, in the Bourbon Pub among a lot of men dressed like cowboys in flannel shirts, cowboy boots, and belts with ornate silver buckles, Newell felt a wave of nausea pass through him and sank to the barstool and hung his head down. There was a drink in his hand, somewhere distant, and he concentrated on that, because he knew if he failed to sustain the thought of it in his head he would drop the glass, and that would be unpardonable, to drop the drink glass, with the whole bar watching. The bar was spinning and the music was making him dizzy, but he thought he was okay sitting there, he thought the nausea was going away and he was acting pretty normal, he thought he blended in pretty well, until someone leaned into his face and asked, "Honey, are you all right?"

"I'm fine," he said, or tried to say, and some sound did come out of his mouth, but he was mostly focused on the kindness of the face in front of him, a flabby, pale, man's face, with big eyes made bigger by makeup, a line along the eyelid and mascara, but he was a man, needing to shave. Newell took a deep breath and said again, slowly, "I'm fine."

"You're about to fall off that stool, honey."

Newell nodded, and he could suddenly feel himself moving, though he had not noted this before.

"Do you want to go home?"

Newell tried to focus on the man again. "Yes. I'd like that."

"Do you know where you live? Do you think you can get home by yourself?"

"I live over the junk store," he answered, and he felt very clear that he did indeed live over the junk store, but he could no longer tell where that was. He looked around vaguely.

The man fretted, his face pale and fleshy with its narrow range of expressions. He took Newell by the arm, and Newell moved with him as if he had become fluid. Outside he gulped the fresh air and felt suddenly sick and leaned against the side of a building for a few moments, while the man watched him anxiously.

Louise had come outside to sit on the steps to the back gallery, looking up at the hazy summer sky. For hours she had been trying to sleep, but finally she left the bed, restless. She dressed and walked outside to the courtyard. The street sweepers would drive their trucks through the Quarter soon, with the jets of water and the spinning brushes, and she liked to be awake for that sometimes. She had no thought that Newell was anywhere but at the top of the stairs, in that little room at the end of the gallery, but soon he came staggering down the passage, accompanied by a pot-bellied, soft-faced man with a bald spot on the top of his head. Something like makeup had smeared around his eyes in the heat. He mostly carried Newell to the stairs, and Newell looked around and said, in a slurred voice, "This is it." When Louise stood and looked at him, he nodded to her. "Good evening, Miss Kimbro. I come home drunk."

"I see that you have," she said, and Newell passed up the stairs and into his room, leaving her alone with this stranger.

"It wasn't me who got him drunk like this," explained the pudgy man, and she had to look away from him, she found him so unattractive with his sallow, fleshy face.

"But when I found him he was all slumped down on the stool, so I thought I would help him home."

"He's getting used to the Quarter, I see." Louise had the feeling this was the right thing to say, though she didn't know why, and it embarrassed her so that she turned and abruptly walked back to the loggia, taking out her keys. "Oh, well, good night."

"Good night," answered the man, and waited till she had gone inside before he ambled, appearing almost aimless, down the passageway to the street.

In the morning Newell woke to a pounding head like nothing he had ever imagined, a feeling that his stomach was slowly wringing itself inside out, and as soon as he dared sit up, the flashes of agony in his head and the topsy-turvy state of his stomach sent him reeling to the bathroom, where he hung against the toilet and heaved bitter-tasting, yellow bile into the toilet bowl. After a while he rinsed his mouth and brushed his teeth and rinsed his mouth again, and he wanted to take a bath but his head throbbed with sharp bursts of pain. He had broken out in a sweat and hung on the sink looking at himself in the mirror, his hair matted in clumps of curls, his eyes ringed with shade, skin so pale it was almost blue. He drank a cup of water and waited to see whether his stomach would accept it, ran a tub of water and slid into it, sweating, into the hot water with his head throbbing.

He found his clothes from the night before and went through all the pockets. Laying out the money, counting all the bills and change, and adding what he'd left in the wallet, he had less than one hundred dollars. He'd spent the rest last night. How was that possible? Had he lost a bill somewhere? His heart sank at the thought, and he searched the pockets again, and came up with another dime and a nickel, and added them to his careful piles. Sitting there dumbfounded, he stared at the money as if willing it to grow.

A soft knocking sounded on his door. He tightened the towel around his waist and opened the door a bit, and saw a man standing on the gallery, no one Newell had ever met, he thought at first, with his head pounding from having stood so suddenly, but, with a renewed feeling of dull, nauseous weight in his stomach, he noted something familiar about the stranger, and said, "Hello."

"Hello. Do you remember me?"

A fat man, shorter than Newell. Round, sloping shoulders under a stretch shirt that swelled over his sagging stomach. Newell shook his head. The man smiled and explained, "I brought you home last night."

"You did?"

"You were pretty drunk. You were about to fall off that stool in the pub. Do you remember?"

Newell shook his head.

"You were pretty drunk," the man repeated, then stopped, and looked at Newell again. "How you feeling?"

"Not so good," Newell said, and leaned against the door jamb. "I need to go back to bed."

The man shrugged. "Sure. I was only wondering how you were. I wanted to make sure you were all right."

Newell shrugged. "Thanks. I'm okay."

The man ducked his head for a moment each time he spoke. "I'm Henry," he said, and to Newell it seemed that the man spoke his name as though it were the key to everything. He offered his hand to Newell as if to shake hands but instead gripped in his thick fingers was a small brown bag. Newell found a bottle of aspirin inside it. But by then it was already too late to thank the man, to thank Henry, who hurriedly climbed down to the courtyard with his socks showing at the back, threadbare where shoes had rubbed away the weave, and so Newell closed the door and swallowed three aspirin and went back to bed.

He slept through the rest of Monday, got up for a while, too depressed to do much more than eat chicken noodle soup.

In the morning, he woke up and bathed, his head still tender but no longer throbbing. He went to breakfast because he was starving from the day before and ate a big omelette and a lot of potatoes and toast, and he felt better after that, though the meal cost five dollars with the tip. He bought a *Times-Picayune* and read the want ads in his room. He sat on the front gallery with all his money in an envelope in his hand, and he listened to the sounds of the city in the hot morning, felt its strangeness and indifference, and this scrap of money in his hand was the only force that could protect him.

He slept for a while, real sleep, with the effects of all that alcohol finally gone, and when he woke he went for an afternoon walk and ended up, he never knew quite how, at Mac's.

This time of day the cool, high-ceilinged room was mostly empty, but Louis was nowhere to be seen. Mac himself slouched behind the cash register, a cigarillo in his fingertips, brown and thin, trailing a signature of smoke toward the drop lights. He had something on his mind and merely nodded at Newell when he passed, which made Newell shy, so he strayed along the shelves of magazines and scanned them. Standing in front of the magazines that had women and men on them, the women shoving their breasts toward the camera, bending over to show the creases and pinknesses of their inner parts, sometimes sprawled on a bed with a man hovering over them, a man with a pale, flat, white ass and a limber cock in his hand, and the woman staring up at him and pretending to have some expression on her face that somebody told her to try to have, and all the while the invisible camera hovered there, and their relationship was with the camera, and with Newell, and with anyone who wanted to watch. Newell thought this effect must come from the fact that the regular magazines were not made as well as the magazines that had only men in them, because the magazines with only men seemed very real and exciting to him. While these big-breasted women and sag-assed men were flat and lifeless.

"You like that stuff too?" Mac surprised him, walking over from the cash register, scarcely lifting the cigarillo from his lips.

Newell blinked and watched him.

"You like this stuff too?"

Newell shook his head. "Not much."

"I didn't think so."

They blinked at each other in mild surprise. They were suddenly watching as if they might know each other, in a friendly way, nothing too personal, and Newell became less nervous. He moved away from the racks of magazines with their rows of breasts, and Mac gestured to him. "Come look at these."

Mac lifted a stack of magazines to the counter. These had not yet been wrapped in their plastic covers and Newell lifted each one and smelled it and opened it. Every kind of magazine offered itself, magazines with thin pale boys, smooth asses, a little fat at the lower back; with tall lanky men in cowboy hats, sometimes with cowboy clothes on, maybe a vest or chaps or just boots; with men who were dressed like sailors in a cheap motel room, or what looked like a cheap motel room, though it might have been someone's cheap apartment, or even a room in a mobile home in Pastel, Alabama, and the sailor men taking off their clothes, and one was thickly muscled and one was thin and hairy, and they both had moles on their butt cheeks. But occasionally one of the magazines contained someone beautiful, and Newell felt his tongue go thick, and these he laid aside in a pile, as if by instinct, since Mac had only asked that he come and look. He spent some time sorting the stack into the magazines that he liked and the ones that he didn't care much about.

Now and then Mac would chuckle and say, "You like that one," or, "There ain't much to that one, right?" Pointing with the little cigar.

A couple of other customers came in, but Newell and Mac went on talking, even when Mac was taking the money, making change, answering the phone. Newell helped put the magazines into the plastic covers, tape them shut, and write up the price tags. He had heard Mac mention this sort of task to Louis, and knew he was up to something but wasn't altogether sure what it was until he had a thought, and asked, "Where's the guy that works here?"

"Louis? That fucked-up motherfucker? He don't work here no more."

"No?"

"His ass is gone back to Mississippi where he the fuck belongs."

"That's too bad," Newell said.

Mac fixed a look on him and chewed on the end of a match. "You want his job?"

"You bet I do."

"You want to start right now?"

A weight lifted off Newell, and he took a deep breath and took a look around the store. The fluorescent lights were humming in the sweetest way. "Yes sir."

"You ever cashier before?"

So Mac began to teach him how to work the cash register, and pretty soon Newell stood on the other side of the counter, and he relaxed, for the first time since

Curtis fired him, maybe even for the first time since he stepped off the bus that morning on Tulane Avenue. He learned the operation of the cash register without trouble, and soon he was making change or ringing up sales himself with Mac supervising, arms folded. Newell's first sale was a magazine called *Suck City* with women and men on the cover, and for the rest of the afternoon Mac sipped Barq's root beer and sat on the stool while Newell operated the cash register, made change, and checked in magazines from below the counter, ticking them off on a handwritten invoice sheet that he could barely read, then bagging them and pricing them and, with Mac's advice, moving them to the shelves.

That night, in bed, satisfied, having eaten two whole cans of chicken noodle soup, he stared at the shadowed stains on the ceiling and was aware of the ridiculous smile on his face, here on a day that had begun so badly and that was ending so well. Visions of naked breasts and stiff nipples rose before his eyes, and something in that parade of body parts pleased him, as if he had found something for which he was destined. He would have money now. He would be able to call Flora and tell her he had a job at a bookstore, and she would think that was nice, and she would not worry about him so much, and he would leave out the part about the exact type of bookstore, and everything would be fine. She would stop being afraid he was about to go bad. Like his mother, though Flora would never say that.

In the morning Mac greeted him near the movie

booths and handed him a cup of coffee with cream and many spoons of sugar. Newell accepted the paper cup without a word and wrapped a napkin around it, as Mac had done with his own cup, to keep from burning his fingers. He drank the coffee without a word. The store opened later than most of the other shops, at eleven, and this would be one of Newell's duties, to open up every day, count out correct change into the cash register, check to make sure the alarm buzzer for upstairs was working, and make the coffee in the drip coffee maker in the back room. He had to check the movie machines in the back to make sure they were working like they ought to, and this meant taking a few quarters and running them through each machine, watching snippets of the movies that were featured, women bobbing their heads over penises made blurry by the poor resolution of the viewboxes, men bending over other men and pumping them from behind like dogs astraddle each other in a farmyard. Mac led him through the whole routine of changing the movies, checking the machines, removing the coin boxes, and Newell kept his mind on his work but still felt a thrill at the glimpses of sex, the covers of the magazines, even the smell of the place.

The store took up most of the bottom floor of an old Creole town house, Mac explained, and Newell remembered he had read that word "Creole" in the book he had bought; aside from the main floor and the two sections of movie booths, there was a storeroom downstairs and more space in the entresol; there was Mac's office, a couple of bathrooms, a laundry with a washer and dryer, and a gallery at the back leading to a loggia and the big house upstairs. The girls had the upstairs, and Mac was in charge of that part of the building too, though he had some people to help him, like Dixie, Ferdinand, and Kelly. Mac showed the button for the silent alarm and explained that Newell had to press it to alert the girls upstairs whenever a policeman entered the store. Didn't matter if it was a city police or a county deputy or a fucking Secret Service agent. Visitors to the house traveled in and out the passage from Rampart Street, but Dixie liked to know whenever a cop walked in the front door, he said. Newell nodded as if this made perfect sense to him, as if he understood who the visitors and the girls were, and why it was sensible that they should be warned. After, Mac took him to the back room to show him where to find extra cash register tape and brown paper bags.

"Most of our customers want their bags taped shut," Mac said, and showed him how. Later, when the store was open and the first few customers had come and gone, Mac said, "People are ashamed to be in here."

Newell remembered how he himself had felt, how he had gripped the brown bag with the copy of *Brute Hombre* inside, how he had been certain people could see through the paper. Mac was watching him, waiting for something, so Newell said, "I guess it's only natural."

"Horseshit, it's natural," Mac snorted, and pulled his belt midway up his stomach. "I'm going upstairs to see the girls for a little while. You think you ready to handle this by yourself?"

"I think so."

"All you got to do is keep an eye on these fuckers and take the money and don't let nobody start slipping these magazines inside their drawers. You got it?"

"I got it."

Mac grinned at him and adjusted the hang of his balls inside his trousers. Newell found himself grinning too, warm inside at the beauty of it all, of Mac disappearing upstairs and leaving Newell alone in the shop with these shelves of magazines. He took a deep breath and stood there. The quiet that surrounded him contrasted with the noise and commotion of the Circle K.

Customers, nearly always men, stuck their heads in the door, crept in furtively, stood blinking as their eyes adjusted to the light, standing back from the shelves to study the covers. Sometimes it apparently took them a moment to realize these were pictures of the naked parts of people, the parts that were usually covered, and these people were doing things to one another that were usually hidden, all this out in the open. They would pause and look up from the shelves and the merchandise, and what Newell saw on their faces was not shame but hunger.

Some men stayed only a few moments, rushing into the sunshine loosening their collars as if hurrying for oxygen. Many more stayed longer, drifting along the magazine shelves, lifting a magazine in its plastic cover and turning it over to see the back, studying the magazine from all angles, carefully. When there were several men in the store at the same time, they all pretended to be alone and stepped past one another, pretending not to see. The ones who bought magazines or the other items that the store offered, like the little bottles that said "Rush" on the label, or the plastic penises, or packages of French ticklers, refused to meet his eye as he counted out their money and bagged and taped their purchases. Maybe one or two murmured thank you. But most of them looked through him to the calendar from Stony's Fishing and Tackle on the wall behind his head, a thick-waisted fisherman in hip boots and a flannel shirt lifting a helpless, gasping trout high over a river. Customers studied the fish and pretended Newell was not there, or so he imagined. They hurried into the street again, shading their eyes, looking one way and another, stepping into the stream of tourists and becoming, within a few steps, anonymous.

He rearranged the shelves to make room for more magazines, and right away showed a talent for it, according to Mac, who liked the way Newell grouped certain kinds of covers and titles together. Mac only had to change a couple of magazines that were displayed in the wrong sections, including one in the women's section that was actually drag queens, men dressed as women, according to Mac, and though Newell had heard of this before, the fact that these pictures had fooled him sent hairs standing up on the back of his head.

Beginning in the early afternoon, the movies drew a lot

of traffic, men disappearing into the mazes of booths on both sides. Most of these men seemed comfortable and eager, less sheepish than the men who had been through the store in the morning. The whirring of the movie players and the jingle-click of coins sliding into the slot provided background for the radio Mac kept tuned to a country music station. The section that had movies with women in them remained pretty quiet, only an occasional grunt or groan, but from the section where the all-male movies played came a lot more commotion, footsteps between the booths, muttered words, the sound of strange movements against the cheap plywood walls of the booths, the muffled grunts and groans, and Mac occasionally walking through the booth calling out, "I want to hear them quarters hitting them slots, boys, else you got to come out of there."

Near evening one of the girls, Starla, came down to mind the store. Mac still had to hire somebody for the night shift. Newell offered to stay, but Mac said Newell should go home and come back the next day at the same time, to continue his training. Newell left the store oddly disappointed that he could not stay all night, till closing time. But he picked his way home through the bright, noisy blocks of the upper Quarter, tourists emerging from their hotels for the night, and he had a sudden certainty that everything was going to be all right.

At home, when he was walking into the loggia from the passageway he heard voices and paused, concealed by one of the arches, seeing Miss Kimbro in the courtyard with somebody, embracing a girl who turned out, when he could see her, to be the girl who worked in the junk store. Standing in the shadows of the balcony of the slave quarters, slatted shadows across their faces, the young girl with a mocking look on her face, a low-pitched laugh as she pulled away. Miss Kimbro let the girl go as far as arms could reach, then called, "Millie," quietly, hurtled forward toward this Millie again, collided with her, and pulled her close, and the girl laughed—a ripple of plea-sure, that sound, and she leaned toward her with tanta-lizing slowness, kissed the woman on the lips, a kiss that melted across both their faces, and Miss Kimbro drew the girl back into the shadows, never aware that anyone had seen her, though Newell stood breathless till they were gone.

He followed along the loggia, crossed the courtyard in the shadows and stood where he could see into the room where they were standing. He felt no compunction in spy-ing, he simply watched as she stood the girl against the wall, slowly stroked her hair with long, curved fingers, kissed her face on all sides, but slowly, with careful pre-cision, as though she were reading invisible signs to learn where she should place her lips, and the girl gone rapt and sightless at the pleasure. Standing in the light of a torchère beyond a casement door, half open. Miss Kimbro kept them there for a long time; she was clearly the one in control, whispering in the girl's ear, touching the under-side of her throat with the tips of her nails. Newell watched till Louise closed the door.

Upstairs in his room he opened the windows and let fresh air enter, trying to get calm, but the memory of Louise and the girl stirred him up, no matter that he tried to think of something else. No matter that it disturbed him that two women together like that could excite him. The force that drew them together, the compulsion toward each other that draped over them like a mantle, taking them over. Louise and the girl who worked for her. Now he knew a secret. For everything about the scene had the sheen of something to be concealed.

But when he was leaving to make a trip to the Verti Mart for a *Times-Picayune,* he found Miss Kimbro waiting for him, or so it seemed to him, standing in the loggia near the stairs. When she saw Newell she beckoned to him, and when he was close said, "Well, why don't you come inside and we can have a drink," as if that were something special. But he followed her inside the same rooms where she had been fooling around with the girl earlier, a nice sitting room with handsome old furniture, including a low wooden table with curvy legs, where she had set up a silver tray and a bottle of bourbon with a black label.

"What do you drink?"

"Well, to tell the truth, I drink mostly beer. But I like vodka, too." He wanted to sound adult.

He settled on a beer, and she brought it and poured herself a bourbon in a plain small glass. She had a nervous way of handling things, of looking around the room, and he wondered why she had brought him here, whether maybe the room had become too quiet now that the girl was gone. Miss Kimbro had hardly been more than cordial to Newell before, so it was hard for him to figure why she would invite him inside for a beer. But he sipped it anyway and ate the potato chips with the sour-cream-and-onion fur on them, and by now he was accustomed to the flavor of beer and quickly finished his first one.

She brought him another one and sat down. She was wearing a long robe that tied at the waist, a silky fabric, emerald green, a delicate brocade running through it. When she sat, she sipped the whiskey with such intensity Newell was sure she hardly knew he was there at all.

"I just got off work," Newell said.

"Are you still being a bus boy?"

"Oh, no ma'am. I quit that job. Now I'm a cashier at a bookstore."

"Which one?"

He had never asked, and had never seen a sign, so he shrugged. "I don't even know the name of it. It's on St. Ann near North Rampart."

She blinked. "Why, I know where that is. That's an adult bookstore."

"Yes ma'am, it is. And there is stuff in that store you would not believe."

"I suppose there would be." She sipped her whiskey and lifted a kerchief to her lips. "Well, I suppose it's better than the restaurant."

"Oh, yes ma'am. It's clean. And the people are all nice.

I work the cash register and make change." He found himself watching her with tremendous enthusiasm. He liked her odd face with its sharp lines, and he sipped the beer, which had warmed some. "It's almost like an office job. My grandma wanted me to get an office job."

"Well, this is nearly like that," she agreed, though she was staring distractedly at something on the tip of her shoe.

"So now I can call her and tell her I have an office job, and she won't worry so much."

"Where does your grandmother live?"

"Pastel, Alabama. Near Pocatawny. I gave you the address, remember?"

"My husband had people up that way," she nodded. "Pretty country."

"You can't beat it for looks," Newell agreed.

"You grew up with your grandmother?"

"Yes ma'am," he answered, but he decided not to offer anything else. She watched him. Finally he asked, "You had a husband?" This surprised him, after seeing her with the girl.

"Oh yes. But he died."

They sat there sipping their drinks and refrained from any more questions. Miss Kimbro chewed the inside of her lip, the loose, softly wrinkled skin sliding up and down her throat. "Well," she remarked, "since you are so well employed, I hope you'll be staying in your apartment."

"Oh, yes ma'am. I like it up there very much."

"You can get you a window fan for when it's hot. I won't charge for the electricity."

"Yes ma'am, that's a good idea."

"You might even get you a television," she added.

But he could tell by the way she was watching him that she was thinking about something else. She had gone suddenly very far away. When she returned, she faced him and smiled. "You should be careful, working at that bookstore."

"I think it's safe," Newell said, "I think it's all right."

After a moment she added, deciding each word, "You have to be careful how you live, here."

When she began to clear away the glasses, he helped her a bit and said good-bye, decided to forget buying a newspaper, went upstairs and wondered what Louise had meant.

For the next few days, with the sweltering summer settling onto the city, he went to work early and left late. He learned about the bookstore and especially relished Mac's ominous hints about the mysterious barge that brought the magazines downriver from St. Louis and Chicago, its secret connections to crime, to a network of criminals spread throughout New Orleans. "There's people in this city would take one look at you and kill you and not think twice about it. You think I'm playing?" An image of a life full of nebulous danger. Now and then Newell thought about Louise Kimbro and the alcohol she had shared with him, and he wondered if this was what she had meant, he had to be careful how he lived; but he soon forgot when Mac presented the possibility of something else.

Mornings, while the traffic in the store was slow, Newell drank coffee with Mac and stood in the cloud of his cigarette smoke. Afternoons, Mac went upstairs to the girls, to do some business in his office upstairs, he said, and Newell tended the store by himself. The phone rang sometimes, and he answered it, mostly wrong numbers or people who breathed heavily or mumbled, asking about some magazine or other; occasionally a message for Mac. He dusted the shelves of dildoes and plastic vaginas with fake hair and the bottles of Rush, and he wondered what was the good of such a small bottle when it cost so much money, almost four dollars.

Often he was drawn to the racks of magazines, especially the ones that had only men on the covers, and he arranged them and rearranged them until the blend of faces and thighs and elbows seemed to him more harmonious, as if in grouping these hairy and pale, flabby and firm asses side by side, he were writing sentences in some picture language. He grouped the Stallion Studios magazines near the Eagle Studios magazines, at first through instinct, afterward noticing that the beefy men on the Stallion covers complemented the more adventurous covers of the Eagle magazines, on which the boys were piled on top of each other in poses that could not be mistaken for sports practice. The rest of the magazines were a blur of titles to him at first, *More Than Enough, Two Hands Full, Take Ten, Truck Stop, Marine Daddy, Three in a Barn, The House Painter, Navy Buddies, Beefcake, Muscle Love, Stag,* and their covers appealed to him when the color was good, the skin looking like skin, the pimples none too prominent. His discrimination, at first, amounted to nothing more than a feeling about each image that he saw, each magazine on the rack, each postcard of some oily-haired blond from the fifties posing naked with his thigh thrust forward to hide his penis, a feeling that these images were overpowering him in some way, were speaking to him.

He had started work on a Tuesday night and finished out that week on the day shift. Mac paid him at the end of his shift on Saturday, the end of his first week, Mac counting cash into Newell's hand, one hundred sixty dollars. Newell found himself surprised by the amount and by the fact that he was paid in cash. He could pay his rent and still have some left over to live on. Next week he would be paid one hundred sixty dollars again, and he wouldn't have to pay rent then, he would have all the money for himself. He gaped at the stack of bills and stood there tingling, then folded the money and slipped it into his pocket as if he always carried that kind of money. He grinned at Mac, who said, "You're doing a good job. The cash register hadn't been short once all week."

"I like working here," Newell said, and he truly did, from the bottom of his heart, but speaking the sentiment aloud disturbed him so he got busy dusting the dildoes, the big inflatable woman with the holes in all the right places that had taken Newell a good morning and a bicycle pump to blow up, and all the other toys that were displayed in the locked case beside the door.

Mac said, "You get Sunday and Monday off. People don't like it if you sell smut on a Sunday, so we close. And Monday you get off."

"Really?" Newell asked, as though this had never occurred to him, and Mac nodded.

Mac watched him for a while longer, without speaking, and Newell continued to work with that same cheerful air, as Mac marveled, though he himself would not have used the word; he marveled at the nonchalance with which Newell worked among the plastic cocks and leather harnesses and studded masks, as though this were some five-and-ten-cent store. Mac had been struck by this thought for most of the week while Newell trained on the cash register or answered the phone or stuck price labels onto the plastic covers of the magazines. Finally Mac said, "I told you to go home, now," and Newell grinned, stored away his dust cloths, and left the store just as the phone rang, Marlene from upstairs to tell Mac she was bringing down his dinner.

That night, Newell bought cologne at a drugstore on Canal Street, a fragrance called English Leather, which the cashier allowed him to sample at the counter; he also bought a new comb, and a conditioner for his hair, even though he did not know what a conditioner was supposed to do, and he bought a separate kind of soap for washing his face, and he priced a gold chain at a counter that also had watches and a few rings, but he would have to wait to spend that much money, nearly fifty dollars. But he could see himself with the gold chain around his neck, and he realized as he pictured himself that this gold chain would make him more similar to the other people he had seen in the bars. The cashier bagged his cologne and comb and toiletries, a word that he savored, having read it over the section of the drugstore where he found the soap, and Newell took the bag and his change and felt the bulge of money in his pocket and hurried home.

He got the rest of his money from upstairs and paid the next month's rent at that very moment, wanting to secure his room before he spent more money on anything else. He found Louise in the courtyard with a cat in her arms, stroking it down the spine and along the tail, the cat blinking in satisfaction. Someone at the back of the courtyard was singing, a young girl's voice; and Louise smiled serenely as if no sound on earth could please her more. She stood there as though she had been waiting for Newell, and she accepted the rent money when he counted it into her hand, and slid it into the pocket of her skirt. "Thank you," she said, as if she had been expecting him to come in at that moment and pay the rent, even though she could hardly have known he would do so; and he dipped his head to her, and smiled, and the voice from the back of the courtyard called, "Louise?" and she turned and walked away, stooping just a bit, letting the cat glide out of her arms to the pavement.

Upstairs, Newell heated a can of soup on the hot plate and ate it with a slice of bread. He had the money to eat out if he wanted, but he decided to spend it in the bars instead. Before leaving he spread a film of cologne behind his ears and along his wrists, the way he had seen his grandmother do before going to the Moose Lodge dances, and he smelled his fingers and checked his hair in the mirror. He wished he had new clothes and planned, briefly, to buy clothes next week, when he got paid again, at least a new shirt or new jeans.

But he went out anyway, wandered up and down the sidewalks looking all the men in the eye. He had lost part of his fear of them, now that he had a job, now that he knew he could stay. He went to Lafitte's, where the men congregated, some of them strong and masculine in their jeans, some emaciated, and others with large, round rear ends and thighs that tapered toward the knee. But he looked at them all and slid past the ones who lounged near the doorway watching the new arrivals and headed for a stool near the corner of the bar, beside the jukebox. Music came from the jukebox, though it was piped through the sound system, and so the music was changing all the time; but somebody played "Don't Leave Me This Way," by Thelma Houston, which was his favorite song, and then "I Love the Night Life," by Alicia Bridges, which was his second favorite song. So he felt as if this must be a lucky day for him, and he drank another beer for eighty-five cents.

Men were watching him from all sides, but this was nothing special, because they were watching each other too, and watching the door that led upstairs and the door that led to the street, and watching the bathroom door, and watching the bartenders and watching their own drinks, their own hands. If there had been a mirror they would have been watching their own reflections, he thought. With the music so loud hardly anyone was talking, though occasionally someone would lean to the ear of someone else and say a few words. A lot of men were alone, like Newell, so he hardly felt out of place, and the second beer went down faster than the first, helping any anxiety he might develop. He sat wondering what time this place would fill up, what it would be like then, because the other night when he had walked past the bar had been stuffed with men, hanging off the upstairs gallery and overflowing into the street.

He had ordered another beer from the bartender and turned to scan the titles on the jukebox when a voice spoke to him, from behind, close to his ear and soft, "Hello there."

When he turned there was Henry, wearing a red flannel shirt and a red handkerchief in his pocket. Newell remembered him at once and wished he would go away. He had been standing very close to Newell but took a step back, with an anxious look on his face that made Newell feel anxious too, and Henry's eyes seemed far too large and round, and what was he staring at? Irritated, Newell started to turn away from him, but instead noticed that other people in the bar were watching Henry talk to him, and this seemed to Newell more desirable than to sit there alone with the beer like so many of the rest, so he nodded to Henry to sit on the stool next to him, and Henry hopped onto it at once. He had a drink with a lime wedge floating in it, and he set that on the counter. The bartender came along and slid a napkin under it, and Henry and Newell sat there listening to the jukebox, which was so loud there was no way to talk except to lean one head close to another. So Newell leaned a little toward Henry and asked, "This isn't the bar where you met me, right?"

"No, that was the Bourbon Pub. Do you want to go there?"

Newell shook his head and sipped his beer. The music pounded the walls, the ceiling, the countertops, making everything vibrate, *raining men, it's raining men*, he heard the words and watched Henry out of the corner of his eye, knowing that Henry was staring at him, feeling odd because of that, feeling as if he ought to walk away. But he went on sitting there because it was pleasant to have someone watching him with eyes so avid, and he wondered whether Henry could smell the new cologne the way Newell could smell the sweet stuff Henry used. But Newell was careful to keep his eyes moving, ranging through the bar over the hard, round shoulders of the men, many of whom had torn the sleeves off their shirts, every color of skin, every texture. He wondered if his arms looked like that or if they could look like that. He surreptitiously squeezed a shoulder, a forearm.

"I like this bar this time of day," Henry whispered. The sound located him close behind Newell, invisible, speaking into Newell's ear. "Everybody comes here early. To get ready for the rest of the night."

"Then where do they go?" Holding himself perfectly still, with Henry's breath on his ear lobe.

"A couple of streets over to Travis's. Or over to the baths on Frenchmen. Or dancing. Or down to the waterfront, late. Then toward daybreak people eat beignets at the Café du Monde. Or cheeseburgers at the Clover Grill. Or else they drive to Susie's for breakfast." He spoke plainly, but his words drew a map in Newell's brain, and he looked around the bar again, at all the men, and he remembered the men on the street outside, and he wondered. Henry's description framed the whole event. Newell could feel a sense of preparation in the air, everybody sizing up everybody else, the evening about to unroll like some magic carpet. "I like this time of night," Henry added.

They sat through more songs on the jukebox, and Henry asked if Newell would like to go to the Corral, and Newell said yes and thought they were leaving the bar, but, as it turned out, the Corral was the bar upstairs; he felt comfortable there, in the noise and smoke. Henry and Newell found places for themselves along the wall, and Henry bought drinks and they stood there, sipping, Newell watching the other men linger, exiting, coming in the door, passing by on the way to the jukebox or the bathroom. Newell felt, as he had since he got the job at the bookstore, that his eyes had opened fully and he was really seeing what was around him for the first time. Where once he had seen only a mass of faces, now he could distinguish groups of men in the bar, and different types of men in each group. Some of them were lean and sullen and had a polished look to their skin, especially to the skin of their faces, like women's faces, Newell thought, though these were clearly masculine men. Some of the men were pale and soft, some slim and soft, and these soft men spoke with a lilt and stood with a slight curve to every part of the body, and spoke with soft curved arm gestures and tracings of the hand through the air. Some of the men sat at the bar and stared hungrily at the others, clearly here alone, stooping over their drinks with a furtive air. One of these men was wearing a business suit and had a wedding ring on his hand, a banker or insurance salesman, and Newell wondered if he had come here by accident, if he had failed to notice that there were no women here. There was one man wearing a woman's wig and polka dot blouse tied to leave his midriff bare, his hairy navel sunk in a few pale folds of fat. He had a lot of friends around him and laughed and slapped his hands on the bar and whooped and threw his hand up in the air and lit a cigarette on a long, thin cigarette holder with rhinestones at the tip. He stopped talking only to freshen his red lipstick and his friends surrounded him, chattering and laughing, and all of them looking around the bar to make sure other people were noticing their fun, their friend with the wig, the lipstick, and meanwhile the music from the jukebox pounded as three men in leather clothes stood over it slipping in quarter after quarter and choosing song after song. The bartenders whirled and slid along the counter slipping their hands across each others' backsides as they passed one another, with the noise so loud they had to lean close to the customers to hear what they were saying; two of them wore flannel shirts and the other a halter-type T-shirt that outlined the smooth curves of his body. Everyone moved to the beat of the music in some way, the bartenders neatly dancing in the little space they had, and the men at the bar tapping their fingers, keeping time with head movements or undulating at the hip, some of them singing along with the record, or appearing to sing along—hard to tell, since nothing could be heard except the music.

He and Henry stayed at the Corral a long time, where men were playing pool, with more men lined along the walls to watch them, and lined up along the walls in the other room to watch the bartenders, and lined outside the bathroom to watch each other there as well. This upstairs bar had a balcony, and Newell and Henry walked onto it, stepping out of the noise into the humid air that fell on them like a weight. They looked at each other and smiled, and Newell now felt curiously warm and grateful that Henry was with him, but still uncomfortable about it, especially when Henry stared at him too long. "I like to come out here for the quiet."

"It's cooling off," Newell said.

Henry gestured, and Newell looked at a group of shadows standing farther along the balcony, formless except that a point of orange light, a cigarette ember, hung in their midst, and Henry said, "People smoke joints out here. Nobody cares." At the same time Newell smelled the smoke, which he recognized from the one joint he had ever tried to smoke in Pastel, with his cousin Joel, one night in back of the cemetery in the bend of the river, the same smell of grass and earth, and it had thrilled him then as now because it was illegal, and yet here were these men on this balcony in the middle of a bar right out in the open, far more daring than Newell's taste of the smoke beside a moonlit grave. Next thing he knew, Henry was lighting one too and handing it to him and he took it, as if he had always taken such things, and he put the hand-rolled tip to his mouth and pulled in, and coughed and felt the rasping of the smoke along his throat, and wanted to cough again but refused. They passed the joint back and forth.

He would be aware through the rest of the night, at times, that the drug had altered his perception of the world, but since the world he was coming to know was itself a narcotic, acting on him in that way, he was never quite sure whether the night seemed so strange and long because of the drug or simply because of itself. They stood on the balcony in the warm breeze until the throbbing of music from the Parade, a block down the street, became insistent, and Henry asked Newell if he wanted to go dancing, and Newell nodded and they picked their way through the bar and stepped onto the street. Henry led Newell to the Parade where Henry bought a bottle of Rush and paid for the cover charge for both of them. From upstairs flowed rivers of sound, the same beat Newell had heard everywhere, on every jukebox, and they arrived at the top of the stairs to the dance floor, a sea of undulating heads and shoulders and arms thrown high; and Henry leaned into Newell's ear and whispered, "This place is my favorite, except for the waterfront," at the same moment that one song melted into something new, a woman with a trumpet of a voice singing, "It took all the strength I had not to fall apart," a song Newell had not heard before, but which caused a sensation on the dance floor. A crush of people carried Henry and Newell forward, toward the whirling lights and globes and the shifting mass of bodies.

They never made it as far as the dance floor. They danced under one of the arches beside it, and bodies pressed them from all around. Newell's head was spinning, and the music hardly helped him orient himself. Soon Henry had opened the bottle of Rush and shoved it under Newell's nose, saying, "Take a breath up your nostril." Newell did, and felt the harsh rush of whatever was in the bottle, a wind through his head and the feeling that the music was slamming at his bones, and he began to dance as Henry inhaled the stuff too and threw back his head and smiled.

The music never stopped, one song blending into the next, Newell and Henry danced, with Henry holding the bottle under Newell's nose and the heady, intoxicating scent flooding Newell, the music suddenly more intense inside him, his heartbeat like hammers, and Henry passing the bottle of Rush to adjacent dancers, faces that appeared in Newell's sight then vanished again, and parts of bodies undulating against him, the dance floor packed, and the feeling of unity with all the rest of them, their arms and legs rippling in the same wind as it coursed through them all, the music whipped around them like a storm, and everybody blowing. Everywhere he looked, men were dancing with men, everyone with everyone, while the music spun the room into a frenzy. A first glimpse of ecstasy rose in Newell, like a window opening, and he was amazed by the feeling and empty, completely empty of everything except this one moment, the beat of the music, the beat of his body on waves of it, and the feeling of a tribe around him, exalted.

At a certain moment he looked across the room to the center of the dance floor, and, as if the crowd had parted especially for that reason, he saw a blond man he had seen before, and recognized him in some way, an unmistakable perfection, his skin golden, his hair cut close to his scalp, such a look of strength and health, a perfect body in the light. For as long as they were dancing, Newell could hardly look anywhere else. But within a couple of songs, Henry took Newell by the arm and led him outside onto another balcony. Even through the closed doors the muted bass line of the dance music made their bodies vibrate. A breeze brought a scent of storm coming, a cool edge to the night. From far away came the lowing of ships passing on the river. Newell could almost see in his mind the curve of the river and the lights along it, the lights of the ships doubled in reflection in the river. He gripped the black iron rail of the balcony and leaned out over the street. Behind, doors opened and closed, and the music washed over them whenever the doors were open. Newell's head pounded. Henry asked, "Do you want something to drink?"

"No. I'm fine."

"It's going to rain," Henry said.

"Not for a while."

"How do you know?"

Newell shrugged.

"You tired of dancing?" Henry asked.

"Do you want to do something else?"

Henry looked at him with the tip of his tongue visible, just behind his teeth, and his eyes big and round. "We could walk to the riverfront. You ever been there?"

"You mean at Jackson Square? I walk there a lot."

Henry laughed. "No. I'll show you where I mean."

On the street again, they drifted toward the river along St. Peter, Newell following Henry's narrow, stooped shoulders among the other men. Newell realized with a start of surprise that they were headed toward the old brewery, to the deserted warehouses along the riverfront; soon they had crossed beyond the Moonwalk and hurried along narrow streets till they came to a loading dock, which Henry scrambled to climb, beckoning Newell to follow, at the top of which they slid through a door that somebody had propped open.

Into an eerie, shadowed space they walked, Newell staying close to Henry while his eyes adjusted. Newell thought, once or twice, voices were murmuring around him, as Henry led him to an open space where the lights of the opposite bank of the river threw the old warehouse into a dim twilight.

Shadows moved through the dreamy space, slipping out of darkness along the walls, appearing briefly as silhouettes in distant doorways, or slouched along the open bays leading to the quay. Pairs of men, or trios, or single men wandering from one place to another, and one warehouse opening onto the next, space after space, and the shadows moving and receding. Henry and Newell also wandered through the dark, listening to the soft sounds, the quiet voices, the low groans. They wandered through the labyrinth for what seemed like hours, Newell had lost track of time. Finally they came to a vaulted space with its riverside loading doors open and the river murmuring beyond, and Henry led Newell to a brick wall and stood him against it and lay his hands along Newell's hips. Newell was surprised by the touch and drew back, but Henry held him, knelt and pressed his mouth against Newell's zipper, and Newell stood there with Henry's hands gripping his buttocks as though it were simply an abstraction, these motions in this space, and Henry opened Newell's pants with clumsy tugs and took Newell in his mouth, a shock, and the stirring of Henry's lips and tongue that sent gradually thrills then shocks then fires through Newell, and he was aroused in spite of himself, and Henry guided him through the motions skillfully. But Newell leaned back into the shadows, against the cool bricks, and when he looked down he saw Henry looking up at him, round-eyed, solemn, and forlorn as a puppy. The distended lips and sad face struck Newell as ridiculous. He giggled and took Henry's face in his hands, pushed it gently back. "I don't want to do this with you," Newell said, and pulled up his pants and belted them and walked away a few steps, toward the river breeze.

After a few moments Henry joined him, and they began to walk again. Henry seemed all right, as though nothing had happened. They cruised the warehouses for a while, and Newell watched everything around him, the shadows of the men passing back and forth, the places where knots of men clustered, men with their arms spread wide grasping the edge of an old work table, a support beam, an old rope tied to a ring in the wall, groans of men echoing in the open space, in the alcoves, the labyrinths of little offices surrounding the loading area, a man wiping cobwebs from his face while another man knelt in front of him, head moving in and out of shadow. Henry and Newell walked for a long time, till Henry found another man for himself and those two went off together. Newell kept wandering alone, studying the faces, wondering if he had seen these men in the bars earlier, or on other nights; watching, at last, a group of men around an old packing crate, one man sprawled across the crate and another doing something Newell could barely see; it looked as if the standing man were slowly working his hand inside the one over the crate, as if to plunge his whole arm inside the first man, and that one groaning and shuddering in a way that shocked

Newell, who was suddenly frightened and wanted to leave. So he found his way to Elysian, the sight of familiar streetlights, the fresh breeze across his face.

For an hour or more he walked, too excited by all he had seen to sleep, with his headed swaddled in Rush and smoke and the smells of the warehouses. Snatches of what he had seen came back to him, in particular the last image, the one that had shocked him. Newell walked and tried to clear his head. He went to the Café du Monde for coffee and beignets, and it still felt miraculous to him, that he could sit there so easily, with money in his pocket now, with no worries, and he could order food and coffee and someone would bring it; and further, the whole thought of the night satisfied him, and he felt adult and in control of the world, having gone out for an evening to enjoy himself, having roamed the streets with Henry, having danced and inhaled the strange stuff, Rush, having smoked the joint, having done all those things; but still his thoughts kept veering from those pleasant places to the warehouses along Elysian, to Henry kneeling in front of him so clumsily when it had been such a nice evening up till then, and to the man on the packing crate, his face lost in pleasure, or in some feeling that had control of him that was like pleasure; though Newell could not imagine how it felt lying there like that, and he went a bit queasy in the stomach.

The strong coffee made his heart race, and he walked along the river for a while, along the levee. The briny, dank, rich smell of the Mississippi flooded through him, a hundred scents in one. A ship moved downriver, a tug following behind. The easy lapping of the river against the levee, the wash of water, mingled with the gentle sound of a few cars moving on the street behind him. At this hour the park at Jackson Square was closed and locked, but there were still a few people in the square, sitting on the steps of the St. Louis Cathedral, a name he now remembered, wandering among the benches. He could turn and watch the tall tower of the cathedral, dappled with streetlight and moonlight, or he could face the river and drink its darkness, its breezes, the hypnotic light along the black glassy surface; he could feel, inside himself, the rushing of his blood, the sound of it, the sensations of the drugs that he had taken into himself. He rested with a feeling of peace descending and enfolding him. *Don't leave me this way*, a voice was singing in his head, as he picked his way down Bourbon Street, moving among the tourists who were still stumbling along the lighted storefronts and bars and dance clubs that never closed their doors. He was proud again, in a vague way, that he had gone out and had himself some real fun tonight, that he had seen some things, and that it was all right to do so, because he had money in his pocket and a good job, and he was proud again, too, that he lived in the city.

The next morning was Sunday, and he woke to a peaceful light filling his room, the echoes of church bells from outside, near and distant. For a moment the sounds were like the Sunday mornings of Pastel, Alabama, and he thought he was back in his grandmother's trailer, in that small room where he had slept. But he opened his eyes, and he was in the room in New Orleans. The smell of rain drifting through the window drew him to it, and he studied the gray sky, the light drizzle of rain over the street. He stared at the roofs and chimneys as far as the eye could see, where this rain was falling, the city gone gauzy with fog.

Later, he stood on the back gallery at the top of the stairs, sipping instant coffee as the rain drifted round his head in tiny beads, hardly falling at all but rather floating toward him and lighting on him, a slow film of moisture. He stood there till the rain increased, till he could see actual drops, and the sky such an even slate of gray it looked as if it would rain for hours.

He went for a walk in the drizzle. One of the hot dog vendors had pulled his cart under the shelter of one of the cast iron balconies, and the steam from the wieners curled as it rose. The smell hit Newell like a weight, he saw it was that big man again, the one in the dingy overcoat who looked as though gravity were worse for him than for anyone else, and farther down the street Newell had to pass a one-legged man with the flap of his pants come loose and dragging in the wet street, the man on crutches, swinging carefully forward then standing, breathing, swinging forward again then standing again, a wet cigarette in his mouth, not burning but sagging a bit with the rain.

Newell walked as far as the cathedral, stopping at the

end of Pirate's Alley and sheltering against the wall, as though he dared not take one step more but must simply stand there and peer out at the square, at the fine old buildings along it, as though if he took that next step he would be transported backward to the world of long ago, but instead a woman was approaching him, her hair matted, strands of it clinging to the black plastic she clutched around herself to keep dry, and when she came close enough she spit something yellow and red and glistening that landed on the stone pavement of the alley and shivered there, and she shuffled down the alley with the plastic poncho rustling. Newell watched her go as the rain thickened and fell more fully over Jackson Square and the cathedral and the buildings the Spanish colonial governors had built that were still standing here. He was getting soaked, but he stood there for a while, happy to know something, to have facts in his head, and to be able to carry them around with him. He was happy to know, for instance, that these buildings were called the Cabildo, these fine ones here, flanking the cathedral. He finally shivered and hurried away, trotting under the balconies and awnings along the mostly deserted Royal Street. He bought a few groceries in the A&P. In the junk store, he bought a lamp and another book, dusty and sour-smelling, *Strange True Stories of Lousiana*, by George W. Cable, and when Louise saw it she wrote down the title carefully. "I never did read that," she said. "My mama had it."

"It looks like some good stories."

"I don't doubt." Louise listed the lamp as well. Checking to see if there was a bulb in it. With finial, she noted, in case Newell should complain later.

"Do you have any bulbs?" Newell asked.

"I got one I'll sell you," she sighed, "to keep you from having to go back in the rain." No one else in the store, anyway. She adjusted the necklace at her bodice, found the bulb, gave him a plastic sack to keep the lamp and book dry. "It leaks in that passageway. It'll wet you good."

The rain continued all night, soothing him even as he slept, and he dreamed he was still wandering in it, that he was walking in the empty warehouses with water dripping everywhere, other men slipping in and out of the shadows. He was following them, and every time he woke up that night he heard the rain and fell asleep and the dream began again, so that by morning he had lain in the dream all night and the rain still fell over everything.

Rain fell all day Monday, and Newell stayed indoors and read the new book. Strange, the world that unfolded in the words of George W. Cable, when the Spanish built the first houses, when German farmers lived upriver and sailed into frontier countries on flatboats to have balls and fetes with French people who had moved here because of the Revolution, which Newell dimly remembered from world history, the one with the guillotine and Marie Antoinette. A story about a woman in the Civil War who thought slavery was stupid and the war was worse, who lived through the shelling of Vicksburg. A story about a lady who tortured her slaves, kept her eighty-year-old cook in a neck collar chained in the kitchen, who chased a four-year-old slave girl out a fourth-story window, whose house was said to be haunted still by the ghost of all the suffering she had caused. Newell read that one over again, chilled by it, as if he were that old woman with heavy iron chafing her neck to blood, whose despair had become so great that one day she set fire to the kitchen to see if she could free herself by burning.

He put down the book at one point, went to his door, stood on the back gallery, looked at the slave quarters, which Louise had fixed up into such a nice apartment for herself.

The next day, rain was still falling, so he bought an umbrella on the way to work, and the rest of the way to work he smelled the new umbrella, the first he had ever owned. At the bookstore he shook it out and propped it against the wall behind the cash register to let the water drip into the trash can. Mac watched him and slowly drained the cigarette toward his mouth. "Son of a bitch of a morning," Mac said.

"It's coming down," Newell agreed. "Cools everything off some, though."

"That's right. And washes the vomit off the street. God bless the rain."

On Tuesday mornings they changed the movies in the quarter movie booths. There were fifteen booths at the back, in a dark room behind the curtains, and each of the booths had a door, but in fact if you walked behind the booths you could easily go from one to the other, and Mac and Newell changed the movies that way, before the store opened. Some of the films were still doing pretty well, so Mac said those could stay, especially the one with Bruno and the guy on the back of the truck, and the one about the two guys on the couch, entitled, "The Biggest He Ever Had." So far Newell had not watched any of the movies beginning to end, but that morning he became curious, and he noticed, as they moved from the men section to the other one, that most of the movies were about men being with men, and there were only a few booths showing movies that had women in them. He had never noticed this particularly before. Newell knelt at the side of each of the movie players, removed three bolts and opened the hinged back cover, and Mac held the new movie while Newell unthreaded the old loop from the projector, closed it in its case, then took the new one and threaded it through the rollers with exactly enough slack to please Mac, who supervised, pointing and directing without even bending to look at the machine.

"We got to get some of those new machines," Mac said, watching Newell struggle with one of the projectors, "I keep telling Philip."

"Who's Philip?"

"The owner," Mac said, and hitched up his pants, and took a long drag on his cigarette, and shambled to the front of the store with the exhale swirling around his head.

Newell watched one of the new movies before the

store opened, a short subject, in which a man dressed like a lumberjack caught another man looking at him in the woods, and came up to him and grabbed him, and then the frame stopped for Newell to drop in another quarter, after which the lumberjack pulled the other man, who looked shabby, like a tramp, pulled him down onto a log, and they straddled the log facing each other, the shabby man staring at the arrogant lumberjack, and the lumberjack took the belt out of his pants and looped it around the other man's neck and pulled him violently forward and then the movie stopped and the screen went dark and Newell fumbled for another quarter and quickly dropped it and the image blurred and came to focus, the lumberjack unbuttoning his red flannel shirt with his belt around the shabby man's neck, the man raising his hands, helpless, to run them inside the red flannel shirt along the lumberjack's body, and glimpses of the body, the layer of hard muscle cut with shadow, the two men pressing against each other, then the whirring sound, the light dying in the screen, while Newell held the next quarter ready. The scene changed when the screen lit again, and the lumberjack was naked to the waist and the shabby man was running his hands up and down the lumberjack's crotch, up and down, and Newell knew he had seen pictures of this in the magazines but this, the moving image, even this one, as blurry and out of focus as it was, showed him something. The shabby man pressed his pale fingers against denim, fumbling for the zipper and opening it, scene changing, the lumberjack jerking forward with the belt, scene changing, the first man was rocking his hips into the shabby man's face, both straddling the log and moving as easily with each other as though the shaggy bark of the tree were a comfortable cushion, and suddenly both men were kneeling on the ground, with the lumberjack behind the shabby man, with all their clothes thrown onto the grass and the lumberjack spitting into his palm, and Newell made a short, sharp laugh, only a moment or so, at the sight, but at the same time felt a tingling in the tip of his tongue. The screen went dark and Newell slipped the last coin in the slot, the last loop revealed the lumberjack collapsing over the shabby one and then some footage that embarrassed Newell of oozing dripping stuff and the film was over and Newell went back to the cash register in a daze.

Mac greeted him by saying, very simply, "I'll fire you if I catch you looking at them movies all day."

"Yes sir," Newell answered, and his eyes focused on the cash register as he took a deep breath, inhaling the scent of last night's dose of carpet cleaner.

But he had never seen anything like that movie before, and all day he was seeing it in his head, the man unbuttoning his red flannel shirt and wrapping his belt around the shabby man's neck, pulling him forward so viciously, accusing him of something with these gestures, and the shabby man so willing to let this happen, to run his hands over the bare skin, the broad shoulders, images that would rise up in Newell's head so vivid he might have been standing in the booth with the next quarter in his hand. A few customers came in and bought magazines, and as usual the men buying the magazines laid their money on the counter and looked down or away or up, while Newell slid the bright-colored magazines into a bag and felt himself embarrassed as much as anyone, because he was sure everyone could tell he was thinking about this movie, about these two men and what he had seen them do to each other. For it had become as vivid to him as if it had actually happened inside the little box with the screen on top of it, happened only this morning at the moment when he started to watch.

When the store closed, he balanced out the cash drawer in front of Mac, and it counted out to the penny as usual, but today Mac had mostly left him alone to run the cash register, and so the old man was particularly pleased with himself for having hired Newell. "I knew you was a kid with a brain. Most kids don't have a goddamn lick of sense."

"I know," Newell sighed.

Mac was counting the stacks of quarters from the movie machines, with the change boxes stacked beside him. "That movie you was watching made a lot of money today. People must like it."

Newell shrugged. "It seemed like it was all right to me."

"Maybe you have an eye for this stuff. What do you think?"

"Maybe I do."

Mac handed him a roll of quarters and said, "Go back there and look at the rest of them."

"I ain't watching the ones with the women in them."

"Well, no shit, I already knew that."

"All right," Newell said, and turned and headed to the movie booths, while Mac leaned his chair back on two legs, his pants hiked up past the top of his socks and his bald white legs shining in the light.

By the time Newell came out again, Miss Sophia had arrived and started to clean. He had seen her before, an older woman with a big-boned body, cheeks sunken, mouth mostly toothless, given to wearing wigs and old party dresses while she cleaned the store. She sometimes spoke softly to Mac but ignored Newell, and tonight he hardly saw her as she emptied the waste cans and sprayed the front of the display case with glass cleaner. He had stopped after four of the movies, as much as Mac's roll of quarters would pay for, and he had seen things he never thought of seeing before. Two of the movies were very bad, featuring thin, pale, unattractive people fumbling with each other and stripping off their clothes, when Newell would have preferred they keep them on; and he watched these two movies dutifully. But the third movie was about a carpenter, a short man with black hair and a moustache and a solid, thick, carved body, bronze skin, brown eyes, who met a younger, taller man at his worksite, and took the young man back to his truck, the carpenter grabbing the younger kid pretty roughly, making him straddle the ladder that hung down from the back of the truck, and straddling the kid himself, and this all reminded Newell of the other movie, the tree trunk and the two men facing each other across it, and the carpenter pushed himself into the lanky fellow, who made a face for the camera like something strange was happening inside him. He watched that one all the way to the end and decided to watch one more before he headed home.

The next movie was called *Night Crawler*, according to the sign on the door, and a picture above the words, torn out of one of the magazines, showed a man in shadow, back to the camera, hat pulled low over his eyes, a room of indeterminate size and shape, and the movie began exactly in that way, with the camera panning the room full of phantoms, then lingering on the bare back of the man, the curve of his deltoid, and when the man turned around, there was Rod the Rock, facing the camera, and Newell's breath left him and his heart began to thud against his ribs. He was grateful for the pause when he needed to put in another quarter because he could stand there, hardly able to believe it, before the image appeared, lagged, shook, steadied itself and became Rod the Rock again. Quarter after quarter Newell watched until he hadn't any more quarters, and he stood there with the whole tape, which he had seen through nearly twice before the money ran out, contained in his mind. But he refused to touch himself in the movie booth, because that seemed wrong to him, in some way. He waited till his excitement died down and headed to the cash register intending to ask for more quarters, until he saw the look on Mac's face, the expectancy.

"What did you think?" Mac asked, "which ones did you watch?"

So Newell told him that the first two movies had ugly people in them and that nobody would want to watch them, but the carpenter movie was pretty good. "But I really like *Night Crawler*. That's the really good one."

Mac chuckled and said, "That one's been playing for six months and it's steady money every week. People like that guy or something. I don't know what it is."

Miss Sophia had begun cleaning the store, running the vacuum along the carpet between the racks of magazines, wearing her favorite black wig, or at least the one that Mac claimed was her favorite, a big twisty high-combed number that made her look like a country music queen; she had wrapped a rag partway around her head, as she did sometimes to indicate she was on duty. She wore a white polyester one-piece pantsuit with flared bottoms and attractive white sandals, flats. Mac caught Newell staring at her, so Newell asked, "How old is she?"

"I don't know." Raising his voice over the vacuum, he asked, "How old are you, Miss Sophia?"

She flicked her hair back casually, wrinkled her nose, and went on with the vacuuming. Mac laughed, and Newell, embarrassed, said good night to Mac and nodded to Sophia on his way out. He was struck by the strong, harsh bones of her face and the pale fuzz on her chin. Her nose, thick and bulbous, shaded thin lips. Because of the hairdo, which was falling as much as it was rising, Newell could not see her ears, but the lobes hung down thick and fleshy, and long earrings hung down from the lobes and tangled in the hair; and while she could have been a woman with any of those features, Newell gaped at her in recognition. She bent over and he saw her cleavage, real as far as the eye could see, and he was confused again. So he left the bookstore with Miss Sophia in his head, instead of Rod the Rock; Miss Sophia with the body of an old woman and the face of an old man; and while he was walking away, he could not remember whether he had said good-bye to her.

July and August passed, and Newell settled into the routine of his job. He worked mostly on the day shift, running the cash register and helping with the stock. He made some changes in the store that Mac liked. At the entrance to the movie booths, Newell fashioned an attractive display featuring the titles of all the movies, as well as promotional photos when they were available. When Newell had watched a movie, he would write a short description of it on the sign, like "Hot lumberjack gets horny on a tree with bearded guy," or something like that. The sign drew a lot of attention, and business at the all-men movies picked up. So Mac had him make the same kind of a sign for what he called the titty movies, and Newell did, though he still refused to watch them and could not write any descriptions.

One morning, watching the usual game of men choosing a movie, he noted that two of the men eyed each other and moved into the movie booth section together. One of them looked like the dark-haired man Newell had seen before, Jack, in the courtyard. He wished he could guess which movie they were going to see together, and thought it might be the one about the house painter who comes in through the window and pulls down his white bib overalls to reveal a very large paintbrush. Newell had an instinct that the two men would choose this movie. Here was a force, in these magazines and in these movies, that drew so many people to go into the booths together. To do the same things in the booths as they were watching on the screen. To move from booth to booth, partner to partner.

Mac, who listened for a different sound, walked to the curtain at the entrance. "I don't hear no quarters falling into no machines in there. I hear a plenty else. You keep them quarters turning them movies, you hear?"

Back at the cash register he advised Newell, "You got to get so you can hear every coin drop in the slot. Else they'll stay back there and fuck all day and we won't make a dime."

The pay gave Newell a charge, every week, the same extravagant stack of bills in cash, the same white envelope with the amount written on it, and Newell pocketed the bills and added them to the stack he kept in his room, in the wallet Uncle Jarman had given him. He paid his bills and had a lot left over, more than he had ever imagined. So he had a phone put in his room and bought new shirts and colognes and a gold chain like the one he had seen and some nice leather shoes and a shirt made out of linen. The linen shirt, a soft lavender color with full sleeves and a narrow collar, felt so extravagant to Newell that he hung it in his closet and felt terrified at the prospect of wearing it, as though people would be staring at him and whispering, and so a couple of times he put it on, and felt self-conscious, and took it off and hung it up again.

One day in August, while he was counting the rolls of quarters in the safe below the cash register, a customer's shadow fell across him, and he looked up at the face of Henry Carlton, a five-dollar bill thrust forward in his stubby fingers. "Hey," Newell said as he straightened up, "you want some change, I guess."

"I didn't know you worked here."

"I been working here since June. I never seen you come in before."

"I haven't been by lately."

"You want the whole thing in quarters?"

Henry nodded, and Newell counted them out. Henry started to speak, then ducked his head and turned away, and Newell said, "Look at that one about the artist model and the artist. Everybody is looking at that one. It has Roger. You know. From Blueboy."

"Thanks," Henry said, and slipped through the curtains. Some other people were already in the booths, and more people went in while Henry was there, and Newell was steadily counting out quarters. People were buying magazines too, and Newell was recommending the new Rod the Rock magazine *Chain of Desire* to a lot of people. They were asking about the movie, but Mac never knew what would be available. Traffic in the bookstore remained brisk in spite of the rain, and Newell forgot about Henry until he appeared again, asking Newell what time he got off, and so Newell agreed to meet Henry at the Corral. When Newell arrived there, he pulled over an empty stool to where Henry was sitting, asking, "Well, did you like the movie?"

As Henry smiled, his face relaxed and he became suddenly very pleasant to watch. "It was all right. There was this man in the booth watching that movie you told me about, and I went in there with him, and honey, we had us a time." He spoke quietly and matter-of-factly and rolled his eyes a bit, as if to show what a good time it had been, and it reminded Newell of the way Henry had walked off into the shadows in the warehouses that night after they went dancing.

"But what did you do?"

"You mean, exactly?" Henry giggled. The music in the room had suddenly got soft, and Henry leaned close and told Newell, in detail. Newell listened and tried to picture it. He made Henry repeat certain parts and explain. Who had remembered to bring lubrication, for example. How did they have room for so much action in those booths?

"The only problem is remembering to put in the goddamn quarter." Henry arranged a series of matches on the bar counter in the shape of the letter N, and set fire to them, a flash of sulfur and flame. The letter burned into the polished wood of the countertop, where many other people had also burned their initials. The bartender, bobbing back and forth to the beat, came over to inspect the handiwork and asked who that was for. Henry pointed to Newell, and the bartender said, "Welcome to the brotherhood," dancing away again.

After that Newell went out often with Henry, which proved to be better than going out by himself. Each time, Newell felt something stirring in himself, most acutely when he happened to be in the same place as the beautiful blond man, whose face remained imprinted on Newell's memory, but at other times as well. Newell tasted the feeling and let it go, tasted it and let it go, again and again, while Henry hung out in the bathrooms and tricked in the stalls half the night. Henry was there for the night once he got started, so Newell went for air on the balcony upstairs, where a perfect stranger offered him a puff on one of the funny cigarettes. Newell held the smoke in his lungs till his ears were ringing, and when he let it out someone was shoving a bottle of popper under his nose and his head began to swim in circles.

Every time he went out with Henry he felt himself being pushed a little farther, and after a while he wondered how long it would be before he let someone back him into one of those stalls in the bathroom, before he let somebody get down on their knees in front of him, or else got down on his own knees, looking up at some stranger's face, as Henry so often did. But so far, Newell only stood and watched. So far, that was all he wanted to do.

Or did he want more? Did he know what this wanting was? This sheen of wanting that rippled across Henry's face in the bathroom at the Corral, this hollow place to fill with something inside? Maybe this was why Newell traveled with Henry, because his hunger remained so palpable? Newell followed Henry and watched him and learned.

When Henry came to the bookstore during the day, he would stay in the booths for a long time and come out and tell Newell exactly what he had done, and with whom, and often enough Newell could match Henry's description with someone for whom he had made change. Henry liked to do almost everything you could do with another man, including things he called rimming and going around the world, which had to do with sticking his tongue into someone's butthole, and he described it graphically for Newell one afternoon while Mac was upstairs with the girls.

"But doesn't it stink?"

Henry rolled his eyes. "That smell is heaven on earth, honey, you don't know what you're talking about."

"You're making this up. Nobody would do that."

"I'm not making anything up." Henry always spoke mildly, regardless of what he was describing or the effect the description had on Newell. "It's fun. You'll see. You'll end up with your tongue up somebody's asshole one of these days. We all do."

"Do you brush your teeth afterward or something?"

"Don't be stupid."

"I mean it. It sounds so gross. I would have to brush my teeth a hundred times."

Henry shook his head and shivered. "You'll find out."

He leaned against the shelf where the tallest of the dildos stood, and he looked Newell up and down for a moment, as though he wanted to talk about something else, then thought better of it, and instead said good afternoon.

In the disco one night, a man asked him to dance, a handsome man in good-quality trousers and a starched shirt, a sweater tied around his shoulders, and Newell started to say no, but the song was something he liked, *Oh, let me run let me run let me run*, a long, low moaning voice, Donna Summer sounding like a high wind, and a beat that coursed through him, so he let the man lead him onto the floor. Soon he was moving among the others, thankful for the music. When the song changed, the man kept dancing, and they stayed on the floor till late, the floor crowded by then, bodies pulsing against each other. Newell could feel it in himself, the change that was coming, that he was nearly ready now, that something would happen soon. So he kept dancing, till the beat was one long wave passing through his bones. When the man finally got tired, he tried to lead Newell to the bar, but Newell got his jacket instead and headed outside, and he never saw that man again.

He was falling toward that place in himself, he could feel his descent. The process was compounded by the movies he watched at the bookstore, the dreams he made up to stimulate himself in the dark. Now that he was used to the bookstore he could feel the furtiveness of the customers, their awe as they entered, their perusing of the magazines as if they simply happened to be glancing in that direction, the hand drawn slowly to touch one of the covers, to look at the back. A certain look on the face indicated whether the man would buy or not; a certain slackness came to the jaw and a keenness to the eye. The grip of the hand on the magazine would change. Men chose their movies with the same silence, the same fixedness, and Newell could feel them, drifting from booth to booth the same way bodies had drifted back and forth in the warehouses along the riverfront.

But he had never gone back to the booths for any reason other than the job. He had stopped buying magazines for himself. He felt himself drifting nearer and nearer a place in himself that would open out like a flower and cause the rest of him to be transformed, but the pictures and the movies were no longer what he wanted.

When he studied Mac, he wondered what the old man was like when he climbed the stairs, when Dixie or Starla or one of the other girls met him and took him into a room for a long, careful massage. He wondered what sounds Mac made, what his body looked like, moving with the flow of pleasure through his nerves. By now, Newell had seen enough pictures, enough movies, so that he could imagine almost anything, even Mac's white, soft body, his thin legs, and flat ass.

"This business will make you think about fucking all the time," Mac said one day, "to where you can't even stand it, to where you don't even want to think about a naked woman." But that same day, after hiring a new guy with a face like a rat for the night shift, Mac crept up the back steps to the massage rooms and disappeared for an hour and a half.

Louise said to Newell one evening, while they were having a drink, while he was licking the foam off the lip of the bottle, "You do know that I like women, don't you?"

"You like them?"

"Oh yes. I like them very much." She had flushed a bit and seemed suddenly younger.

"Well, I did see you with a woman in here, once."

"Oh, you're telling a fib."

"Yes, I did. But I couldn't tell who it was."

She blinked, then shrugged.

"Did you always like women?"

"Oh, yes. Even when I had a husband. But he was a very nice man, for a man."

Later in his room, alone, he spoke to himself in a quiet voice, and even though he was alone the words unsettled him, "I like men. Did you know I like men?" He said them aloud a couple of times and sat on the new chair he had bought, beside the window, where he could watch the street below.

He dressed carefully, imitating styles he had seen on the streets and in the bars. He wore a tight, white sleeveless T-shirt, tight jeans, and a flannel shirt. He inspected himself in the mirror and thought he had nice shoulders, nice arms. He combed his hair the way Chris, his barber, had taught him. He touched behind his ears with the cologne that smelled like cut clover, and he stuffed some bills in his pocket and locked his door. He thought he was good looking; he carried that with him down the steps.

He avoided places where he would have found Henry, visiting a couple of bars he had never seen before, then spent the late part of the evening in a bar called Blacksmith's. Men were coming up to him that night and talking to him, he had been talking to them, he felt easy about it, and he wondered what the change was about, though he had his suspicions. In Blacksmith's he had been sitting alone for while when a dark-skinned man approached him and started talking to him, and something about the moment made Newell aware of the man in a particular way, as though taking his scent. A strong face with a heavy shadow of beard, his nappy hair tinged with red, cut close to his head. He had a thick body, wide round shoulders. He was as old as Jesse, Flora's boyfriend, or maybe a few years younger than that, but his body was hard and lean, and there was something familiar about him, Newell figured he must have seen the guy before. He eased next to Newell at the bar to speak to him in deep whispers, drawing closer as he spoke. What stuff he said! You're about the prettiest thing in this bar. You got the prettiest mouth. Do you know how pretty you are? I come into town looking for something just like you. Can't believe there's a handsome thing like you sitting in here all by yourself. Can't believe you don't belong to one of these men in here, can't believe somebody doesn't already own you, body and soul. I'd be the one to take care of you if I lived around here. Don't you want to come with me? Don't you have somewhere we can go? Do you want another drink?

They drank another drink and another, and Newell stopped drinking after that, and listened, kept the man close, felt himself wanting to get up from the stool to go with the man, while the night deepened and the bar filled. His name was Jerry Thibodeaux, and he was an off-shoreman home for a few days. His wife wanted him to stay home and kiss her ass, but he had to go out. His wife probably knew exactly where he was, but he had no choice, he had to find out if there was somebody waiting, and now he knew. By now Jerry was pressed close against Newell, and when Jerry talked he sometimes leaned in so that his lips brushed against Newell's ear. The sensation was transfixing, worse than any alcohol, and when Newell laid his hands on Jerry's chest, Jerry sagged and sighed and Newell felt a force binding them, and when he moved his hands Jerry's eyes glazed, the power of it, all that power flowing in Newell's hands.

He had come to the point, and now he moved. They would not go anywhere, they would stay here. He un-buttoned Jerry's flannel shirt and slid his hands inside to ease it open, and it was like a movie as he moved, one of the good ones, his hands easing open the shirt, the tight shot of the hard brown body, the corded stomach, the thick, hairy chest, and then Jerry gripping him hard at the back and Newell relaxing, like it was being filmed and he knew what to do. He knew it really was a movie now because a space was clearing around them at the bar, as Newell opened Jerry's shirt and reached his hands in Jerry's pants; the movie was about the hard, lean, older man and his need for the tender, choice, young one in front of him, and Newell saw the scenes in his head, everything coming together, the man's ginger kisses and Newell descending along the lean body, sliding down Jerry's pants, taking his dark tender tongue of meat from inside, kissing it till it grew and everybody was watching, and in the middle of the action Newell saw himself as though he were one of the people watching, and he was amazed to see how much he had learned on the job at the bookstore, because he copied the motions perfectly. Jerry was sagging back against the bar with his hips going up and down, that tension so perfect, so urgent, the cock rigid in Newell's mouth, Newell moving on it, people watching and some of them starting to grope each other, but most simply rapt. Only when Newell had to swallow the stuff, or try to, did he falter, choking some and pulling back, then drying his mouth afterward with a napkin the bartender handed him. Jerry hung onto the bar while some friendly men moved affectionately close to him and ran their hands along his body, as if to thank him for what he had done. The bartender brought Newell a drink on the house. Newell washed away the peppery taste in his mouth. He sipped the drink, but felt his head clear, completely sober.

They would talk about the kid who gave the blow job at Blacksmith's last night, did you see that? Maybe some of them knew him from the bookstore. They were still staring at him now to see what he would do next.

There, in the shadows, even his boyfriend was watching, the boy he would meet soon, whose name was Mark.

Jerry was surrounded by his own admirers now, and Newell walked away without saying good-bye, without responding to anybody. He walked outside, rubbing a spot of drying semen from the corner of his mouth, sipping the liquor and walking to the Moonwalk, where he listened to the ships' horns till nearly morning.

The
Green Tree

Miss Sophia was glad when Mac moved Newell to the night shift, after the shiftless Ratboy was finally gone for good, because, of course, Miss Sophia cleaned the bookstore on that shift, and she had liked Newell from the first time she met him, although she never said so to him or to anybody else. For the most part she had very little to say to people. But Newell she liked, because of the look in his eyes when he stood at the cash register making change, while Miss Sophia wielded mop, broom, and sponge. She had hated Ratboy worse than anything, even worse than Louis, but she liked Newell. She studied him the first few evenings, and the very first night she noticed a difference in the way he held his body from the times she had seem him on the day shift. She thought to herself, he is getting ripe. He is starting to look nice.

Miss Sophia had the mop wringer to worry with and paid no more mind to Newell for a while, till that fat friend of his came in, the one with the swishy walk and the pot belly, thin hair at the top, which was often attractive on a man, but not on this man, who was far from a hunk or a stud in Miss Sophia's book. Right away Henry Carlton started in on Newell. Miss Sophia learned his name when Newell said it, and from that time on she thought of him as both names, Henry Carlton, a pale woodchuck, she thought, or even worse, a mole, a flat one, tunneling under the dirt looking for grubs.

Henry said to Newell—and he was actually moving his puffy white hands like he was digging, and Miss Sophia happened to be wringing out the mop nearby and listened—"I was looking for you at the Corral last night. Did you stay home?"

"Oh no," Newell said, "I went out," and told the story of what he had done, and Miss Sophia was nodding as he told the story of the big hunk in the Blacksmith's bar. All the men in the Blacksmith's bar were big hunks as far as Miss Sophia was concerned. She walked by there, in the way that she walked by many places, and at Blacksmith's men were hanging all out the doors all hours of the day and night. So she was hardly surprised Newell would go there and do what he had done, find a complete stranger and have sex with him right in the bar. Miss Sophia had seen this kind of thing happen very often in that bar and in other bars. But neither was she surprised when Henry Carlton became instantly jealous. Henry's brow furrowed and he started to grind his jaw. "We never go to Blacksmith's. You must have been drunk."

"No, I didn't have that much to drink."

"You knew I was waiting for you."

"No, I didn't."

"You liar. You know I'm always at the Corral waiting for you. And you went to Blacksmith's and sucked somebody's cock. Jesus."

"Henry, you do it all the time."

He fell silent, staring fixedly into the glass counter. "Who was it?"

"Some old man."

"Old?"

"Not as old as you are. But really nice. He was really nice."

"You sucked his dick out in the middle of the bar?"

"I sure did."

"You're trash," Henry shook his head. "I guess I ought to remember that. You're exactly the kind of trash that comes here from Alabama."

"You do the same thing in the bathroom nearly every night we go out."

"Well, at least, I'm in the bathroom."

Newell shrugged. He was writing the prices on the stickers for the new magazines like *Cock Lust, Babes Away, Mama's Got More,* and *Big Juicy,* for the corner with the big-breasted-women magazines that Miss Sophia found to be distasteful, though she cleaned that part of the store as carefully as any other.

"Alabama is a very nice state," Miss Sophia said, "though it was not one of the original thirteen colonies of the United States."

"That's right," Newell said, "there's nothing wrong with coming from Alabama, is there, Miss Sophia? You tell him."

But she already had. Henry Carlton was giving her such an ugly look, too, as though she were not welcome, when she knew perfectly well that she was, because she worked here, after all, and she had been working here for many years, so many years that really, she had no idea of the number, or when she had started the job, who had been the president at the time, or any of the questions they would use to interrogate her when they took her in, and this confused her, but the mop handle was heavy in her hand and it led her back to the floor, where she started mopping again, saying, "Franklin Roosevelt was the president," she said, "when I started working here. Franklin Delaney Roosevelt."

They were laughing, but she knew what she knew.

"That was the year I was Queen of Carnival," she said.

They could think what they liked. Newell said, though, and she listened because she had already started to like him, "Miss Sophia, it don't seem like you could be old enough to have worked here all the way since then."

She was walking the mop bucket across the store to

the novelties section, which would have to be dusted soon. "I'm older than I look. It's been that way all my life."

Henry Carlton left the store, but she had the feeling she would be seeing him again. He was one of them that looked at the ground while he walked, nearly slumped over. You had to have misgivings about a man like that, Miss Sophia thought.

Sometimes she could see the future, sometimes she only thought she could. That night, looking across the store at Newell, so pretty in his blue sweater, that nice neck rising out of the collar so touchable, she had the feeling something was coming. She had the feeling Newell was coming onto the night shift to bring a change.

All night she cleaned and watched Newell, his motion so neat, his hair combed just right, his slender fingers counting the quarters. The hunks and studs who came in the place to look at the dirty movies in the back, they were noticing Newell, too. "Where's that guy with the snout usually works here at night," one of the studs asked, or he might have been a hunk, "looks like a mouse."

"Ben didn't show up," Newell said, dripping quarters through his fingers, "so I'm on nights till we hire somebody. Six nights a week."

"You cute thing, you. Aren't we the lucky ones?"

Newell smiled and leaned on the cash register. "Next in line." Holding out his hand, the tender palm lightly callused at the base of the fingers.

She told Mac the next day, came in early to tell him,

wearing her white chiffon with the satin bodice, a ribbon tied at the back. Wearing her soft white flats, pretty little things, and so comfortable. She told Mac, "I like that boy on nights. You keep him there."

"You mean Newell, Miss Sophia? I was thinking to hire somebody else for the nights and bring him back to days."

"Oh no, you leave him," she said.

"You ain't getting any ideas about him, you dirty old man."

Miss Sophia waved her hand at him and headed away.

She dusted the novelty counters that night, the long Caucasian-colored dildos, the chocolate ones, the fringed plastic pussies with hair, which she dusted with the same care as the men's organs, because they were there and she was a professional. She dusted the novelties most of the night, each and every carton of French ticklers, every bottle of Rush, and the whole night she watched Newell work, and so did Mac, who stayed late himself, smoking cigarettes in the carriageway and keeping an eye on things from the background.

Late in the evening he introduced Newell to Gus and Stoney, the men who kept an eye on the passageways that led from the courtyard of this building to adjacent streets. Mac watched the customers perusing the books, lining up to get quarters, some of them lining up two or three times so they could flirt with Newell a moment, sometimes even the sad husbands and fathers who came to watch the titty movies, the lonely ones who could not get enough love at home, sometimes even one of the titty men would flirt with Newell a heartbeat or two. Miss Sophia saw, and Mac saw, or must have, since he announced to Lafayette, the man who looked after the girls upstairs during the evenings, "Newell is probably going to take over on nights from now on. You need to look after him when you're here. Let him know where to find you if he gets any trouble."

"He been on days for a while," Gus said.

"Yep. He's the most regular one I've had in a long time."

"Be nice to have somebody who can count."

"You're fucking preaching to the choir here," Mac pulling at a jet black nose hair. "That midget rat-head son of a bitch come up short in the register every goddamn night."

"Where you reckon he is?"

"I hope the motherfucker is dead in the bayou, that's what I hope. If he shows his Cajun ass around here, you need to hurt him pretty good."

It was a good thing Miss Sophia heard that part, too, because only a couple of nights later, Ratboy did show up, sauntering himself at the hips like he always did, like he even had anything to carry down there, and them jeans needing to be washed for a month. First he stood in the light near the dildo case and blinked like he could not believe his eyes, then he spit on the carpet like the common stuff he was. He went plunking across the carpet with that rabbit walk of his, that narrow ass riding against his tailbone; he stopped right behind the cash register and glared at Newell and said, "What the fuck do you think you're doing?"

"What does it look like I'm doing, Benjamin."

"You take my job you shit fuck?"

"I got stuck with your job after you left it, is what happened. I was on days till you stopped showing up for work."

Miss Sophia, heart bumping against her ribs, hurried out the back door, ventured upstairs along the back gallery, though she always hated walking up those stairs into funnyland, where the women did all kinds of notions with the big and important men in the suits and ties. She went past the rooms where the girls were laid out and groaning and performing every sort of mess you could think of, till at the end of the gallery she found Lafayette and stood in front of him and said, "That rat-head boy come downstairs."

Lafayette slid up from the chair, very broad-shouldered and tall. "Is that a fact?"

"Yes, sir. That rat-face boy. And you know what Mr. Mac said."

"He making trouble?"

"Sure is. All behind the cash register."

His dark face darkened. She had accomplished her mission. So she turned around and shuffled away, hurried downstairs to get a good spot, since she could trust a man like Lafayette to know which side of the bread to butter. To know to get right down here and clear Ratboy Ugliness out of the bookstore. Newell was standing between Ratboy and the cash register, and Ratboy was just bending down to get his knife out of his boot, the customers backing away from the register, confused at this turn of events, when Lafayette come rumbling through the curtains from the storeroom, pulled Ratboy over the counter by his shirt, took the knife out his hand, slammed him against a couple of walls, and then threw him right on the street. Good as any Western movie Miss Sophia ever saw.

The customers lined up to get their quarters, looking at one another like they had seen a good show. Lafayette stopped off at the counter to show Newell the alarm button under the counter, the one he already knew to use if the police walked into the bookstore. "Once is for the police coming in," Lafayette said. "Twice is if you need help down here. You got it?"

"Yes sir."

"I never knew a white boy to call me sir before."

Newell shrugged.

Lafayette clapped him on the shoulder in front of the person who was trying to buy a copy of *Hunk Rider in Motor City*, one of the new paperback porno novels displayed with the all men's calendars. Lafayette squeezed Newell's shoulder some, Miss Sophia noted this. Then Lafayette went back upstairs.

Newell seemed shaken to Miss Sophia, but she offered no sympathy, since all she might have done was to take his face between her hands and stroke it, or some similar touch of tenderness, and he would never have accepted this from her, so she said nothing to him, had no idea really if he even realized it was she who had fetched Lafayette, and in the end that hardly mattered. Newell seemed shaken, and Miss Sophia let him be.

When she was watching Newell rearrange the novelties in the cases after she had dusted, she realized that he was the one who had always rearranged the shelves when she cleaned, even when he was on day shift, and that he was responsible for the harmony of the arrangements of plastic sex toys, harnesses, straps of leather with metal studs, black masks and steel tit clamps, bottles offering sexual potency, Newell was responsible for the arrangements that Miss Sophia had always admired, and when she realized that, she respected him all the more.

That night in her bed in her two-room apartment on South Bunny Friend Street, she was picturing the bookstore in her mind, reaching for herself with her hands, that part of herself that was a man's part, which never struck Miss Sophia as odd in the least, that she had a woman's breasts but a man's penis, that she could still think of herself as she, even though she went to sleep caressing her penis with her hands. She hardly thought about that. What she thought about was all the men coming in and out of the bookstore, Newell at the cash register so young and ripe and pretty, his gentleness and care as he shelved the magazines, as he built a display of bottles of Rush inside the glass counter, and all those men lined up all night to give him green money and get quarters to play the movies, back in the rooms that Miss

Sophia would later clean, all those hunks and studs in the stalls making little messes for Miss Sophia to remove. It was a grand life. What had she done to deserve it?

She was bad to drink on a weekend, though. On a Saturday morning she would take the St. Charles streetcar to Martin Wine Cellar where the liquor was cheap, and buy two half-gallons of vodka, not the worst but not the best, and two big cans of tomato juice, Worcestershire sauce if she was out, Tabasco, and take the purchase to the register where several cashiers were arguing about what color fingernail polish was the best for the girl named Tyesha, who was Miss Sophia's cashier. Tyesha said, "Good morning, Grammaw, same thing this week, huh?"

"If it's a Saturday it's time to buy my liquor," Miss Sophia said.

"Where you get that wig?"

"I had this wig."

"I ain't ever seen you in it."

"I don't like to be a redhead on the weekend much," Miss Sophia said, "but I felt like it today."

"Where you get that dress?"

"Magazine Street. I might go down there shopping today. To get me something nice to wear for the Mardi Gras this year."

Tyesha elbowed one of the other cashiers and asked, "Miss Sophia, what ball you plan a go to this year?"

"I believe I might get invited to Comus."

The girls hooted and laughed and slapped hands on the tight jeans over their healthy thighs. Tyesha loved to hear Miss Sophia say she might get invited to the Comus ball. Funny every time, no matter what. Miss Sophia picked up her brown bag and said, "I'll bring you the invitation, let you look at it. But I don't know what I'll wear."

She rode back to Canal Street on the streetcar with the bag in her lap and caught the Desire bus to her stop near South Bunny Friend Street. She got to her apartment and set the bag onto the counter. Her hand was shaking as she pulled down a glass from the cupboard over the sink. All week she had nothing to drink at all. But she mixed a strong tomato juice and vodka with a big splash of Tabasco and drank it down like water, and the rush of the sugary liquor flooded her and filled her head with a roaring sound, and she was on her way again.

It was a good idea to eat before she got to the point that she ought not to be working the stove, so she got out the pot of gumbo and scooped out enough for a bowl and set it on the stove in the pot, and a hunk of French bread smeared with butter. She was weaving some as she stirred the gumbo, singing under her breath, "If ever I cease to love, if ever I cease to love," the same snatch of tune over and over again. "Used to be my mama could sing that song," Miss Sophia said to the pot.

When she had eaten and when the roaring in her head was sufficiently loud she went for a walk, most of the time winding through the neighborhood streets with some of the vodka in a flask, which she carried today in a nice patent leather purse, maybe a bit worn; she was dressed in a purple tulle cocktail dress with a brown stain down the skirt, and for the walk she put on one of her hats, a pillbox with a bit of black veil. Walking in the sunny day along the neighborhood with the fog in her head and people looking at her, making remarks about her, more than likely, but at least today there were no loud boys to torment her, to call her old hag or witch or mop woman or any of the names the boys used for her. For Miss Sophia was well known in that part of town, part of the color, and she herself was aware of her status, which she maintained by showing herself on the streets whenever possible, as drunk as she could make herself. That was her only trick. Not like Ruthie the Duck Lady, who roller-skated around the French Quarter, not like the Bead Lady, who would use a carpet knife to threaten a person who refused to buy one of her Lucky Beads. Miss Sophia was more genteel.

Up Ramparts she walked, a promenade along the boulevard, singing the song again, the world like some kind of flat image bobbing this way and that in front of her, past the bars where the studs and the hunks went, the boys the age of Newell. Maybe she'd even see Newell today. She waited at the corner of Bourbon and St. Peter and looked down at the church, that bit of a boa wrapped around her arms and her perky flat shoes so pointed at the toe, everyone was looking, all the gewgaw tourists with their flat Alabama and soft Mississippi accents pointing to her, noticing her. Nobody took a picture this time, but plenty of times people had taken Miss

Sophia's picture. "What is it?" one teenage boy asked another as they passed, and Miss Sophia thought a curse at them, not a bad curse really, just that they would both get old one day and that they would arrive at old age looking every bit as funny as she did.

He would start to think of himself as a he for a while, when he was drunk. He would remember that his real name was Clarence Eldridge Dodd and that he was a man inside this dress and these support hose, these shoes that he took such painful care of, these pretty baby doll flats that he loved to wear because the higher heels hurt his ankles. He couldn't strut around in those spike heels like he used to, oh no. He found himself walking to the church up Pirate's Alley, and his skirt was drooping, dragging into the gray, slimy water that in the French Quarter could be pretty much any kind of liquid known to man, this good tulle dress that only had one stain on it to start with, and now he would have to hand wash it and very carefully dry it, because he could not afford the dry cleaners and anyway they never took care of your clothes, you paid good money to have people ruin your clothes for you when you could easily ruin them yourself for free. Up here was the square where President Jackson and his horse were having the usual good time standing there with everybody walking around them. It was easy for Miss Sophia to get a good sip from the vodka now and again, and people noticed but they thought it was cute to see, a man dressed up like a woman getting drunk in Jackson Square, weren't these New Orleans drunks all so cute and colorful? But a man in a purple dress, you didn't see that everywhere, and real breasts, too. He could almost see himself as if he were outside himself, and the spectacle he made, the wig and dress and boa, the shoes, the purse, the liquor, the walk, the whole parade, that gave him a feeling of soaring over all the rest of these people, of carrying himself grandly through the crowd as if he were a procession all by himself, because he had invented Miss Sophia, after all, and she was far more interesting to inhabit than nearly anybody he could see.

Except for the prettiest. The boys. The beauties on the street. He would become one of them, if he could. But you couldn't buy that in a used clothing store, nothing to make you look like that. Nothing to make you look like pretty Newell, with his long, tapered fingers, with his pouty lips and fine, clear skin. No, but Miss Sophia will do, will carry you through, this runs through his head like a jingle in a commercial about himself, Miss Sophia capers drunkenly across Decatur Street singing Miss Sophia will do, will carry you through.

To the river. She had walked here all her life. Clarence had. Come to stand at the edge of the river, the muddy water so broad, the distant line of Algiers on the opposite shore.

By then he was good and drunk and everything was soaring inside him, as if it all made sense, a babble of voices, darling this and darling that and where y'at and by your mama's house and everybody your friend, a nice afternoon on the Moonwalk looking at the *Venture*

Queen sail past, her decks loaded with containers so high he wondered how the ship could float, the day easing down, afternoon already here, and him having only to go home now, nothing else to do, because he had the weekend like normal people, to do what he pleased.

In the morning he woke up with a cottony feeling in his head, not entirely sure where he had been or how late he had returned home, though he always found home sometime; he was Clarence for a moment before he went back to being Miss Sophia. She struggled out of bed with the feeling that her head was stuffed with something, especially behind her eyeballs, and she poured herself a glass of tomato juice and vodka and drank it fast to get the feeling to go away.

While she was waiting for that first slug of vodka to hit, she cleaned. She kept her house immaculately swept. "Anonymity produces pigdom," she said, to no one; a phrase which, when she had first thought it, made her laugh. When nobody is looking, we are apt to do anything, make any kind of mess, and leave it for others to attend to. A person who is apt to do anything even in front of other people is a psychopath, a further stage of anonymity than most people can achieve. But Miss Sophia used to read a lot of true crime magazines and felt she could spot a psychopath, where others might see only an ordinary person like herself.

Miss Sophia drank the tomato juice and dressed for church. Tomato juice to settle her stomach. For church she dressed as a man, as Clarence Dodd, whom she once knew, a lawyer who worked in a fine office on Gravier. In the Whitney Building? A fine attorney from an old New Orleans family, Clarence Dodd.

She put on his trousers and his coat. Without makeup and wig, she looked so much like a man, it was amazing even to her. It never occurred to her to question the logic of this, that she, a woman, should dress in clothing of the opposite sex in order to go to church, but even more deeply she understood that this was necessary, and at moments would remember that she was a man, that her name was Clarence Dodd, that she was he. Fine to parade the streets in a dress but for mass she wore a suit, no wig, dark socks, a neatly tied silk tie, and a white starched shirt perfectly pressed. She wielded the steam iron and spray starch herself, her head spinning from the night before, her throat dry. On the way out the door she looked at the bottle of vodka. She never drank before mass, except the one slug to clear her head. But she looked at the liquor.

Mass she went to here and there various places, often taking the bus to St. Louis Cathedral. She liked the ceremony, the Holy Sacrament, Jesus dissolving like a kiss on her tongue. Sometime she went to confession, too, and confessed to various things that appeared to confuse the priests, but she said her Hail Marys and counted the rosary but always lost track, even with the beads, and sometimes she forgot to bring the rosary anyway, so it was hopeless. But she said the prayers. Sat in the churches. Perfectly prepared for God to speak.

Afterward she went home and made a drink and changed into her clothes for Sunday afternoon. Today she wore one of her conservative outfits, a long brown skirt of fine wool challis, a cream-colored silk blouse that tied in a fetching bow at the front, a nice wool jacket that looked like she was riding in the hunt, fitted at the sides, black Frye boots and a fedora. She looked smart, especially with the little brunette Mary Tyler Moore girl-on-her-own wig. Never mind these clothes were all too young for her and fit on her ungainly body in an even more ungainly way. She drank another tall drink, the ice cubes chattering in her glass. She looked at herself in the mirror.

Sunday was God's day, meaning it was the hardest day to live through, when God's eye was most watchful, God who sees even what the psychopath does when alone, God who sees even the tiny penis balled up in Miss Sophia's panties. She had to be most careful on Sunday, especially toward sundown, and on the best of all possible Sundays she arrived at dusk so drunk she passed blissfully into unconsciousness until the crisis of God's eye passed. God's eye on her all day Sunday as she walked through the streets, looking somehow even more a spectacle in the lumpish new clothes she had bought off the rack, the nice wool skirt making the legs beneath appear mannish to her, but she walked on the legs in the good boots that she loved, walking walking, stopping now and then to sip from her flask.

Once on Sunday she had been courageous, rode the

streetcar all the way down to Audubon Zoo to look at the animals, the monkeys in the cage, the parrots in the cage, the lion in the cage, but she got lost in the park, among the live oaks spreading their enormous branches, old spirits hovering over the ground, she thought, tough old spirits risen out of the ground and flinging out their arms. She read about the great cotton exposition of 1884 that had been the occasion for the building of the park and of many buildings, she read each plaque carefully, word after word, but none of the claims made any sense to her. If someone had built such beautiful structures, where were they? If somebody opened a mercantile exposition and fair here at one time, where was it now? What on earth was a cotton exposition? What did you do, lay out a lot of cotton in a line and let people look at it? Ridiculous it seemed to her, but by then she was weaving badly, the day getting late. She found a bar, sat in it, drank a Dixie beer, found her way over to Magazine Street, took the Magazine bus to downtown, and changed buses for home.

Today she had the memory of her adventure in the park vaguely flitting through her mind, wondering whether she could find the zoo if she tried, and for a few blocks she did head down Bourbon Street toward Canal, where she could catch the streetcar, but pretty soon she got tired and sat on the banquette.

To keep still was to invite God's attention, that eye was sure to focus on you if you were still, so she took a short rest but kept moving. So much to see. She walked to the old Mint to where the Desire streetcar was on display at the end of the market. Miss Sophia thought it a fine thing to display a streetcar like this, right out in the open with no sign or anything to explain it, but people nearly all the time pointed and said to one another, "Look, there it is. It says 'Desire,' right on the front."

At the end of the day she felt its heaviness no matter what. She had outrun her liquor, drunk it up. Now it was time to go home, the sun going down, the dark descending, the hardest time of all, when she would have to go home, look at what was left of the vodka and slug it down and crawl into bed for the night.

But for just a moment standing outside the Café du Monde, powdered sugar on her skirt, she wondered what it would have been like to go to the Audubon Zoo again today, to read the signs about the long-ago buildings that used to stand under those trees.

Monday afternoon Miss Sophia put Clarence to sleep for the week, got herself out of bed and made a pot of strong coffee with chicory, took a long hot bath, did her makeup, and dressed for work. She had only two brassieres to hold up what was left of her flaps of skin that had been breasts, but she wore a bra every day, even at home. To remind herself who she was. Who she was supposed to be. Miss Sophia Dodd Carter. Widow of Clarence Dodd Carter, a soldier who died in World War II. With this in mind and her breasts in place, she headed off to work.

Mac was lazing against the counter with his hair

slicked back greasy, the unhealthy yellowish jowls hanging off his face. He grinned like a dog with a bone and asked, "Miss Sophia, were you up to anything interesting this weekend?"

This took her up short, because he rarely spoke to her in such a way that she would have to answer. His mind might be set on wickedness, she thought. "You're getting to look old, Mr. Mac," she said, and walked past him to her closet.

"Well, you can kiss my ass, too," Mac said, and sauntered back to his office.

Newell giggled and said, "Good evening Miss Sophia. I'm always so glad to see you come in, it means I don't have to be here all by myself in this big store."

"You don't do enough business for two people on nights," Mac hollered from the office.

"We would if you would stay open on Sundays and get rid of some of them titty machines," Newell hollered back.

"You don't know what you're talking about."

"That place down on Decatur Street stays busy all night, and they're open all day Sunday, and there's no women in those movies."

Miss Sophia had to agree. The titty movies just didn't do as well in this part of the French Quarter, you had to face it. Those booths stayed too clean to be earning any money.

After a moment came Mac's voice out of the office. "What I ought to do is tear out that back partition and put more machines into the storeroom. We ain't storing fucking shit in there anyway."

Silence for a moment. One of the clip-clop tourist wagons passing in the street.

"Well," Newell said, "why don't you?"

She could hear the change when he said the words. Could hear the wheel turn in Mr. Mac's head.

The next few days one of the regular black clouds passed over her and engulfed her, and she paid hardly any attention to anything except getting from one moment to the next. She felt the cloud settle over her in the early morning when she was thirsty for liquor and sleep refused to come. The emptiness of the apartment was hollow at that hour, had a ringing to it that echoed through her. Her own apparition in the mirror had a dead look, an old man's face, bald at the top, hair chopped off and uneven, damp like chicken feathers to be plucked, his tits of skin, his bony shoulders, the scars from surgery on his hips and knees. She sat on the couch and stared at her hands till dawn. She went walking and walked most of the day, one street and another, restless. But when she stopped, when her mind went looking for something to do, it settled on a wish that she could go home with a bottle of vodka and lie in the bed curled around it; a wish that she could drown in a lake of vodka. She kept moving through the day and refused to drink a drop except water, not even a sweet drink of soda or Barq's root beer, because sugar would make her crave liquor that much more. She walked in and out of her neighborhood around

Bunny Friendly Park, and then she walked into the Fauborg Marigny and up and down those streets, and then along Esplanade and down Ramparts and through the old Fauborg St. Marie to Lee Circle and down St. Charles Avenue and then into the Irish Channel through the Garden District, and then back up Magazine Street and into the French Quarter again, where she went to work early at the bookstore.

She cleaned in the storeroom, moving all the empty and half-empty boxes and breaking them down. The hard work was what she needed now when only a hard job would take her mind off the feeling that she was beginning to sink into quicksand. She moved all the boxes far to the back wall and mopped the floor and even in that blank, hollow place, she knew she had begun to do this for a reason.

But the cloud around her got thicker, and for the next few days, she moved by force of will from one place to another doing what she knew she had to do, but without thinking of anything or anybody, without thinking at all if she could help it.

A voice insinuated itself in her head at those times, unending streams of words she had heard before. What is there? What do I have? What can there be? What do I do now? What now? And then what now? I don't think I can stand this I have to stand it. And now? I would like to stand here perfectly still where I am without moving even a hair, still like that, and have this voice go away, but what is there that I can do? Why do I go on? Except I can't think of anything else to do. It will go on like this, nobody here with me. Why did it turn out like this? No way to stop the words except to keep the body moving, to work, or to walk the streets.

The faces in a crowd were the most soothing to her, the faces along Bourbon Street on a night of good weather, and this was September now, the heat still intense, but the evenings beginning to cool. She walked along the street from Canal to Dumaine, then turned and walked back, and while she was in the bright lights with the noise around her, while the faces of people passed in front of her, eyes looking into hers for a moment, each face registering some change because of her, because of her appearance, her clothes, her face, her makeup, her wig; the motion acted on her like doses of a sedative, and it was easier for her to breathe. She walked in the crowds till the wee hours and finally went to Café du Monde, where there were always people, too.

If she slept at all she slept during the daylight, refusing to lie in her bed, where the voice in her head became most intense; she lay on the couch with a pillow for her head. Sleeping some.

She endured the weekdays, but the weekend was hard, because she would not drink while she was in a cloud like this, for fear it would end like the last time, when she ended up in Charity Hospital babbling the DTs away. Strapped to her bed, with nurses pointing to her, telling one another that this was the one with the penis and the breasts. That's right, both. One of them twenty-four-hour girls from the French Quarter, probably used to work at them female impersonator places. She would lie in the hospital pretending not to hear. If Miss Sophia had not walked out of that place, there was no telling what the evil nurses would have done. Worth any price not to go back there. Worth even the nagging discomfort of refusing to drink.

She took the bus to City Park and took the rest of the Saturday to walk back to the French Quarter from there. On Canal Street the crowd began to thicken, and people noticed her again, and she felt the first stirring of herself, certain it was good to be Miss Sophia because everybody recognized her. She was the crazy lady they all knew.

Clarence could never have survived. Clarence and Miss Sophia both knew that.

One day the next week, she went to work and heard hammering in the back, in the storeroom. She followed the sound and saw Lafayette's cousin Leon, who said, "Hey, Miss Sophia." She dipped her head, and figured he was here to put in the new movie booths that Newell had wanted, and when she had the thought she realized that the cloud must be lifting, because it mattered to her that Leon was here, and she went up to him and said, "Mr. Mac paying you pretty good, I bet."

"Mr. Mac, he all right. But he cheap."

"Gerald Ford is the president," Miss Sophia announced.

"I reckon he is." Leon gave her a look of mild surprise.

"That's what they ask the crazy people in Charity. Did

you know that? What is the day of the week? And this is Wednesday, I bet. And they ask you what is the name of the president of the United States and that would be Gerald Ford."

Leon laughed, mellow and quiet. "I guess you could pass the test, Miss Sophia."

"I know I ain't crazy," she said to him and to herself, as she went to work.

Cleaning was good work, she could see the result right away. Mr. Mac needed the Hoover run in his office, and she plugged it in and pushed it across the carpet and pulled out the chairs and vacuumed behind them, and when she was done the carpet was clean again. She dusted the glass tops of the counters and washed the fronts with Schwegmann's brand glass cleaner. She emptied the overflowing trash cans in the store and upstairs where the girls worked, but no higher than that. Everywhere she went, she made things better by making them cleaner, and she could see the result and felt good. "I ain't crazy," she said to herself, looking at the store late in the evening when everything was clean and the customers were all lined up to get change for the movie booths, and there was a gang of the hunk types reading Newell's billboard for the movies, and in the back was Leon working on the expansion, working after his regular job and on the cheap, the way Mr. Mac liked it.

When Leon was finished, the bookstore would be bigger, would be a movie parlor, a maze of movie booths, filled with more men, who would resemble the people in the movies; the future was like a room to her, and she was standing at the doorway studying what she had not yet reached to touch. The movie booths would bring more people, and Newell would stand at the cash register and make change for them all. Miss Sophia observed Newell's pale arms, nice shape, his shoulders under the T-shirt, and she felt warm toward him and cleaned the station behind him especially well.

Mac walked through the retail floor swearing about the goddamn building code the goddamn city a bunch of goddamn morons with their fucking heads in their goddamn mama's asses, do this shit and do that shit, fill this the fuck out, some stupid goddamn prick and his fucking piece of paper, the fuck he would, the absolute fuck, and he knew who to call about it, too, by the living fucking God. He stalked into his office fumbling with the cellophane on a pack of cigarettes, closing the door, still mumbling beyond it.

With Mac in the shop late at night and Newell tending the cash register, slick as a snake on his feet, and a lot of people in the store, all warm and comfortable, Miss Sophia realized Newell had cranked up the music, somebody singing about he's the greatest dancer, the disco beat. She shook her head for the noise. She headed up the steps to collect the garbage, shuffling along the plank floor of the upstairs gallery dragging her plastic sack.

Emptying the garbage upstairs, she always had the sense of herself as floating above the ground, as if the house were in no way intervening to support her and she herself were doing the levitating, holding the bag aloft as well, emptying the wastecan from the pink-painted lavatory, installed into one of the old Creole cabinets for the use of the patrons to refresh themselves on the way out of the house. On the wall of the lavatory a forlorn flamingo, fading pink, as if it had stood outside on some radioactive lawn, its color baking slowly out of it. At night Miss Sophia was only supposed to pull the trash upstairs. Tonight she polished the sink fittings with a dry cotton towel and left off only when the faucet and taps were gleaming. When she was done, she closed the door of the bathroom, locked it, hiked up her dress, pulled down her drawers, and sat on the toilet, feeling that useless flap of flesh between her fingers, the part she had to aim and point, looking vacantly upward as the piss ran out. She could watch herself in the mirror perched on the toilet in an ungainly pose, one arm reaching between her legs. The sight made her feel distant from herself, sliding backward.

She had to work, she dragged the garbage downstairs, started to dust the magazine racks, kept at it even after Newell closed the store. "Are you going to be here all night?" he asked, when he was ready to go, and she acted as if she had not heard anything, went on lifting the magazines off the shelves and dusting behind.

She cleaned till the wee morning and went home, lay on the bed, and stared at the ceiling till daylight, then dozed in the haze.

She was old and everything hurt, old, and nothing felt

right half the time, and more than half the time as time went on. In her head ran a jangling of memories and nerves, a vision of a man she had been in love with long ago, though if she stopped to consider the face she realized that it was her own face she was in love with, the face she allowed to appear when she was drunk and would sometimes still allow herself to see; and the name that she said over and over again in her head was her own, Clarence Dodd; he was not some long-lost lover, he was herself, she was sure of it.

She sat straight up in the bed about two in the afternoon, hot and sticky, even in October. Her skin was clammy, the cotton nightgown clinging. She had slept in a wig again and it sat crooked on her head. She could feel it but there was no mirror to show her the fool she looked.

This would get bad unless she found some magic to perform. If she could focus herself on something, like a spell. So that night, at work, she went to work, and what caught her eye was Newell.

He had dressed better than ever, as if he were ready for an occasion of some sort. Had he, too, picked up the wave of the future that was flowing toward them both? The tight, black T-shirt hugged across the nice plates of his chest, and his arms had thickened some, he had put some meat on his bones. He was wearing blue jeans, only they were black, a style she had never seen before, and his ass sat up high on his legs like it wanted to talk. So Miss Sophia talked to it all night under her breath, mutterings and sounds and words all night, and she noted the sheen on Newell's hair, the gloss on his skin, and she was hardly the only one noticing, because all the big burly men and the little girly men in line to get change were elbowing one another and pointing to Newell and cutting their eyes at one another; and furthermore the news was going around the store that there would soon be more movie booths in the back, more places where the hunks could join up with the studs and have sex with one another in packs and clusters, and this thought, along with all the magazine covers, and the counters full of clean, shining plastic and leather and metal toys, all this had everyone in a jolly spirit. In the middle of all this, Miss Sophia went to the leather goods counter and got out a leather dog collar with big silver spikes around it, and she took it to Newell and put it around his neck and he giggled, counting out somebody's change, saying, "Miss Sophia, what in the world?"

"You need some taming," she said, and moved away.

He was still wearing the dog collar when she looked back, the slash of dark leather across his pale neck, the shine of the spikes, and him moving with the music, yowsah yowsah yowsah, with the front door opening and men coming in from the streets, disappearing into the booths, ogling the magazines.

He had been in love with her, had he not? At one time? Or someone like him? A slender man like him, all pale and buttery so you wanted to poke things into him, a man like that had been in love with her in her youth, when she was a belle, when all the beaux lined up to court her, as the story always goes, in her mind, the line of men and her wide skirt spread out maybe on the porch swing, the porch on her house when she was a little girl, painted dark green over light gray, both colors flaking. The line of beaux stretched down the street, handsome men, clean-shaven, dimpled down to the last cheek, fresh and well-dressed and beaming at her as she sat on the porch feeling faint from all the attention, the clear blue sky overhead on a day when all her beaux had come to court her, to ask her the same question over and over again, "Do you love only me?" This would take her into the mist, thinking this way, as if she were no longer in the bookstore, and, indeed, she might no longer be there, for all she knew; she had slipped through places before, had blanked out on leaving and getting home, had blanked out a couple of days at a time, transporting herself like this. It troubled her to think that she would find herself suddenly, when she was conscious again, not standing in the bookstore but lying in her bed with the blankets pulled up over her head and the sheets moist from her sweat, the hot night, the close room, that she would suddenly find herself there alone and about to plunge into something deeper and farther away. But no, she knew she was doing her job somehow, she knew her body was, and that it was her mind detached and floating slightly above itself. She had been in love with someone very much like Newell, and now she could not remember his name, but his face floated up in front of her at odd moments, at this moment, for instance, and blotted everything else out, and suddenly all the beaux standing in the line had the same face, and they were all Newell in the dog collar, the pale white of his throat so tender. She knew she had never been in love with Newell but with someone who looked like him, and tonight they were slipping together in some way. Or was that even true? Because she had never noticed that their faces were so much alike before. Maybe she couldn't even remember the face, maybe there was only something about Newell that reminded her of something, maybe Miss Sophia had never been in love with anybody, or maybe it was Clarence Dodd she was thinking of, maybe Newell reminded her of Clarence Dodd a long time ago, and when she thought about that, she wanted to stop thinking, because there was no way any longer to decide.

"I want a disco ball and some good lights in here," Newell said, to nobody in particular, and Miss Sophia was spraying glass cleaner on the counter and looking at the tender backs of his hands. "We could turn this place into something."

"You got too goddamn many ideas," Mac said, reaching into the cash register to do a cash pull.

"You just don't want to make money."

"You little shit ass. You already got me running all over the goddamn city hall trying to get a fucking building permit." He waddled off grumbling to his office counting the stack of twenties and tens. "But I had enough of that shit, I got friends I can call."

"It'll be worth it, Mac," Newell said, and Mac waved his hand at him.

Newell could bring good fortune. She had seen that light on people before, and she knew it was true. No need to try to help him, he would make his way.

She refused to go home after work but walked all night again, aware of voices and refusing to listen, the ones in the overhead who talked all the time, only sometimes she could tune out that station and sometimes like tonight she had no choice but to listen. She was getting bad again and wanted a drink. But not one dime in her pocket, smart, to leave the money at home and to walk the other direction. It was all right to have the thirst in her mouth, but if she satisfied it she would plunge into the underground, something like the bottom of the Mississippi River, something that would suck her legs like mud and drown her lungs like water. It was okay to have the thirst but not to drink. So she walked down St. Charles Avenue all the way through the mansions of the Garden District and uptown to Audubon Park, and she wandered under the live oaks from the streetcar line all the way to the river, the mighty muddy, and she was in sight of it when the first light of day started to show and she felt the vise loosen across her chest and she headed home, the long walk back to the streetcar, and then the ride to Canal Street and the change to the Desire bus.

At home in the darkness of the apartment she lay down on the bed with all her folds of clammy skin and turned on the air conditioner as cold as it would go, even though it was October now. She fell deeply asleep and dreamed she was flying in a department store that became a supermarket and then outside over a city that was not New Orleans but somewhere else; she was flying and that was the whole dream, that she could will herself to rise and feel the lightness of her body. Everyone was looking up at her. She flew, but never so very high that she lost sight of the people on the ground, and sometimes she swooped down close to the ground, and then soared up again. She woke in the middle of the dream abruptly and felt so sad she wanted to cry because her body lay leaden and heavy on the bed; she knew she could never will it to rise from here.

She smelled Newell's beau for the first time that day, caught the scent of him in the bookstore, a whiff of perfume sweet, a smell of a man's chin freshly shaved, the clean line of the jaw, a white-toothed smile, ripe lips, she had all that from the scent, she knew the beau was there, or had been there, from the moment she arrived that evening to begin cleaning. This was a Friday night. She could tell by the crowd. On a Friday, on all the Fridays lately, the magazine shelves were crowded with men, looking at every kind of magazine, as if the men were somehow comfortable with one another, no matter what each had come here for individually; as if the presence of the toys and the Rush and the movie booths were pleasing to all of them in the same way, amid the rhythm of hammering, the sound of the new movie booths going up in the back. When she went back to talk to Leon tonight he was gleaming dark and giving her the busy eye, too busy to talk to any crazy lady, smoking a cigarette, sipping from a flask from time to time. She was not one to defy the busy eye, she would talk to him some other time.

She had forgotten something, the scent of the something, the beau, the word had been in her mind for a reason. She parted the curtain and returned to the front of the store, sticking a finger under her wig to scratch. Walking into the glare of the store, she caught the scent at once and saw Newell again in the dog collar leaning over the counter alongside the cash register and someone talking to him. Jeans tight onto his butt, slutting that pelvis forward like he wanted to drag the ground with it, this handsome thing, honey color of hair, eye of gold, grinning a slow grin at Newell and looking him into the eye, deep down into the base of the pupil like somebody about to go for the high dive. She had seen it before, she had seen this coming.

She goes to clean. She bows her head to do it. To look at a toilet to bow the head to kneel on the knees and scrub, the stiff white bristles of the toilet brush, the yellow stain that never goes away.

She went upstairs to pull the trash. The city smelled half of rot in the night, in the warm wet air. Rain smell. She stood on the back gallery and leaned over, listened. The sound of a jet airplane. The low calling of its engine the sweetest line of white noise. She would rise up there and fly one day. Into the starry night, oh yes indeed. With the smell of that man in her nostrils, the one whose scent was still there, honey sweetness, the man who was now leaning over the counter after Newell, poised for the dive, suspended in midair.

Later she was stumbling home with no memory of the bus from Canal Street or the ride to Bunny Friendly Park. She held her wig onto her head with her hand as if Clarence Dodd were trying to escape. Out of her mouth like her spirit rushing, out he would come flying like the friendly ghost, and she would no longer have to be drunk to see him. She would be face to face, she would have her penis in her hand and she would be face to face with him. The sadness of it, that she had married him long ago and he was inside her and only came out when he was drunk, when he could bear to comb his hair. She saw herself in front of the mirror, not now, not tonight after she stumbled into the apartment into the shadows, but years ago, the first time she dabbed color across her lips, the first time he stroked out eyelashes long and curved from a tube, the first girl he made of himself, with a wig as black as a mousketeer's ears. A girl in a tight sweater with pointed cone tits. Long ago.

He stood there in front of the mirror. He was himself. He took off the dress. He took off the yellowed slip, the satin bra, the girdle, the garters, the support hose, the rest. What he had made of himself looked back at him, the flaps of skin that might have been something else, the tiny penis that might have been removed. He was alone in the house, and he looked at himself.

Catching a whiff of the same scent again, trying to find

how it had got in his house, the smell of the beau, Newell's new beau, the one from tonight, the sight of him so sweet it had made Miss Sophia vanish altogether, for now. Clarence stood in front of the mirror for a long time. He was sober, he was himself. Here he was again.

Louisiana
Purchase

Leigh had asked Mark for the merest cut. A trifle. She had draped herself on the settee and opened her robe. The skin at the top of her breasts beginning to crease in that powdery way, white as milk. Such a fine skin. "Just do touch it to the skin." Her breath moving her so the blue veins lifted and subsided, she added, "You have a delicate touch, it's in the fingertips." She pulled the robe below her shoulders. She and Mark looked into each other's eyes now, breathing together.

Through the open door, in the dim bedroom beyond, Jack coughed, one deep sound, his shadow moving on the wall. Mark lay the blade onto Leigh's skin, hardly touching her, drawing the tipmost edge of the razor over the fine white creases, Leigh's breathing changing and the insides of her thighs shivering. He could see the motion where her robe had come open. Her breath caught and a flush rose through her and she smiled in a glimmering that became for an instant some other expression. She was rolling her eyes back in her head. Red blood trickled in a line down her breast. "That's good," she said, pulling the robe onto her shoulders again, "I knew you could do it," but when she stood her eyes slid past him to the open door where Jack's shadow had stopped on the wall, waiting. "This is so nice of you." Standing, with a nod of the head, one only, she stepped past him. Currents of air, everything, including the light she shed, smelled of her.

She paused at the open door, the robe gliding off her shoulders. She went into the bedroom and closed the door. Mark listened for a while. He laid the razor in the marble bowl, a drop of red pooling at the blade tip.

He was supposed to go away now. Not supposed to open the door and go inside himself. Leigh had told him so.

When he headed for the streets, he was looking for nothing. Out the courtyard and down the long, dark passageway to Governor Nicholls, opening the wooden door and closing it, he headed into a night with a smell of rain. He could feel the edge of the trip, now. He liked these first moments of chemical sensation, the taste of metal in the back of his throat. The feeling that his stomach was rising onto his ribs. Mark Cascade, he thought. No. Mark Chase. Or Chace. Mark Stone. Mark Rampart. Like the street, like the sign, the word he liked in his head, and every sound rushing at him in full doppler, a feeling of something in motion passing and receding, gone, so precise, every sound passing, the world.

He felt as if he could not get his breath, there was something constricting his ribs, but he did manage to take a breath, easily; the feeling stayed that he would strangle but he kept breathing, and walking, and his head felt as if it were becoming detached from his body.

He wandered for a while, went into the Golden Lantern and sat with the mellow crowd, men looking at him, while he wished he could fade a bit for the night. But in the gay bars he had become a famous blond of the season. When he thought he had the drug under control, he went into Travis's, walked to the movie house on Decatur Street, but too many people had crowded there already. He headed back to Mac's place. The guy who worked there at night was too cute.

He had been upstairs at Mac's earlier that day, with Jack. Now the store was more crowded. At the cash register the cute man, in a dog collar, gave Mark some quarters from the cash register. Mark tried to watch a movie, but he was seeing something else in front of his eyes in the booth, he started to strangle, the room was spinning. Somebody was at the door, some man coming into the booth. Mark took a deep long breath and hissed past the guy, as if Mark were full of air under compression. He stopped when he saw the dog collar again, the night cashier, and stood at the counter in the harsh light, pretending to look at things, near the dark-haired farm boy, somebody named Newell in a studded leather collar that matched Newell's hair and made his skin look white as the top of Leigh's breasts.

Mark was not even thinking about what he had done with Leigh, about what Leigh had asked him to do, about what any of that meant.

He was talking to Newell about Leigh, for some reason. He already liked Newell, as if the guy was some puppy in a box on a street, wanted to pet him and smooth down his fur. He was telling Newell his family was descended from the king of Comus. Not the first one, who was a Jew. He couldn't say which king of Comus, you were never supposed to reveal a secret like that. But not the first one.

Here was a fellow who did not know what Comus was, and laughing, too, and Mark had the feeling other things had been happening, that this short conversation had actually taken a very long time, and that everybody in the room knew that he, Mark, had taken a drug, was under the influence of something, was fucked up. He was looking down into the counter and what looked up at him almost winking was a plastic vagina with hair. A voice whispered in his ear, "Are you all right?"

It was the sweetest voice. Echoes and the tingle of peppermint gum breath and all this multiplied and the voice distorted, bouncing.

"I'm fucked up," Mark said. "Take me home."

"I can't go home right now."

Mark sagged toward the counter and stared deeply into the artificial pubic hair. He stood there for a long time mesmerized, and before he knew it Newell was leading him out of the store and the lights were turned off. He had been standing in front of a woman in a wig. Or maybe a man in a wig and a dress. Standing in front of this woman, who was sniffing him as if he gave off a scent. Newell came along exactly then, led Mark out of the bookstore, and Mark realized some time had passed; Newell still wearing the dog collar and a light, long-sleeved shirt. The night had a touch of chill.

"What are you fucked up on?" Newell asked. "Are you going to be all right?"

"I'll be fine."

"My apartment is not too far," Newell said. "I have some instant coffee."

Mark laughed. Newell gave him a puzzled look and he headed down the banquette. Mark's hand slipped between the collar and the throat and tightened and Newell coughed and shoved Mark backward and Mark laughed and Newell pulled him out of the boxwood in front of somebody's house and Newell was red in the face and said, "What do you think you're trying to do?"

"I'm trying to kill you. We should go to your house."

"That's where I was taking you, you asshole. Did you know you were choking me?"

"I can't breathe."

"Yes you can."

"I'm fucked up."

Mark wanted to go. He reached for the collar again. "I won't choke you this time."

His hand, however, was doing it already, and Newell made a sound and it shattered all around Mark, the sound splintered and broke and echoed and something huge, a fist in Mark's gut sudden and hard, all the air blew out, Newell slammed Mark, the wall came up hard at his back and he was bursting, wondering what to do, he could not seem to remember how to breathe.

Newell, close, said something, but Mark was deaf. Newell's lips were moving but no sound came out, and Mark grabbed Newell by the shirt and pulled him close and stroked him till he calmed down, lips at Newell's ear close enough to touch. "I want to fuck you. Take me home. I'll be good. "

Sounds from all sides were fluttering as if passing through a fan. Mark waited for the moment to pass. They were both leaning against a wall, cars passing in the street.

"You're crazy."

"I know. Take me home."

Newell unfastened the collar, took it off. Mark laughed.

They fucked on a bed with wire springs like rock 'em sock 'em robots, waves rushing over Mark's skin, rushes and ripples of sparks. It shouldn't be so easy to get hard like this with so much drug running through his head, but he was a steady drill sergeant, he was ready. He was fucking like the Marquis de Sade in the shithole the place of exhale; he was fucking against nature, against god.

With his body jerking and him barking hoarsely in somebody's ear, in the ear of this guy named Newell, who said, "Jesus, you know how to do this."

"I'm wired for motion."

"That hurts," Newell said, when Mark reached around to pinch his nipples, and then they were silent and licking each other and Mark jumped off the bed.

"Do you go to college?" Mark asked.

"Nope."

"Do you go to high school?"

"Nope. I finished. Then I moved here."

"From where?"

"Alabama."

"Do you know Leigh?"

Newell furrowed his brows and laughed. "You sure are on something, aren't you."

"I'm tripping. On the same acid Charley Manson likes. You know who he is?"

"Sure. He killed Sharon Tate."

"Killed her like the Marquis de Sade." Mark laughed.

Newell rolled off the bed, went to the bathroom. Mark stood in the door to watch him pee, to smell it. The warmth of the scent, the slight hint of some spice he could not name, and he walked outside, onto the front gallery, took a breath of the chilling air.

Leigh. He had finally done what she wanted. She had been asking for the longest time. And he had finally done it.

There was a story in Mark's family, too old to know if

it were true. The first Duval to leave France for America, the one whose accidents of sperm led to Mark's eventual existence, found he could no longer remain in his home country during the years of the Terror. Aldonse Duval, to shorten the name to its republican form. On his last evening in Paris he walked aimlessly through the chaos, the dirty ragged faces of the poor, the squalid filth of the neighborhoods. Hungry himself, having eaten little but bread for days, he walked to forget his belly. He would be leaving the country very soon, he already knew it, so his walk must have been tinged with the certainty that soon he would be far away from Paris and likely would never see the city again. He had been walking since before dawn, and his route took him near the Bastille just as the sun was rising. Guards were forcing a prisoner from the gatehouse to a closed carriage—a fat, white-skinned man the color of a moth. He was dressed in a nightshirt that clung to the back of his gelid thighs and carried nothing at all in splayed hands, his fingers moving like the legs of a dying spider. Face frightened, flushed. He walked unevenly and weakly, as though he were unaccustomed to bearing his own weight. When the guards had shoved his bulk into the carriage, Aldonse asked one of them, "Who is this man? Where are you taking him?"

The guard, one-eyed, scarred down the cheek by an old cut, spat green mucus onto the cobblestones. "This is the Marquis de Sade, a famous madman, and we're taking him to the nuthouse where he belongs."

Peering out from the carriage were the frightened, dark eyes, the white face like a moon. Even Aldonse Duval had heard of Sade, who had poisoned prostitutes or sliced them in the ass with a knife for his jollies or maybe had killed some girl by torture. All this from such a fat, frightened man.

Nearly dawn when Aldonse watched the carriage pull away. He stood in the shadow of the prison, the stink of the streets beginning to rise in the morning light. He could see shadows moving on top of the prison towers, activity in the gatehouse. Movement in the streets, sounds that began to frighten him. That morning he began his travels, heading by hired carriage to Marseilles and embarking from there a month later on a ship bound for Mobile, though he would find himself restless there, and would finally settle in New Orleans.

He tried to tell that story to Newell with his pale white hands, his shapely thighs, and sturdy shoulders. But each time, as Mark tried, the story itself dissolved; and by then they were touching, starting to have sex again, and Mark asked Newell to slap him across the ass with the flat of his hand, sharp smacks that Newell was eager to give, Mark feeling the rush of the stinging pain on his bare cheeks and noting Newell's sharpened gaze, his curl of the lip.

"You don't know anything about history."

"No. What the fuck do I care about that for, now?" Newell on top this time, sinuous as a snake.

"You should know about things."

"Then teach me, you stupid son of a bitch."

The fullness, that unbelievable nut of Mark over which Newell was riding, Mark feeling as if he were compacting only to explode. The sheets already damp from the last time.

"You never did that before, did you?" Mark asked, when they were done, lying on the bed.

"No."

Mark slid to the edge of the bed, headed to the bathroom, a dingy place, the claw-footed tub, old fixtures, the silence of the room ringing in his head, the sound of water running distant in the pipes of the house, the sound of traffic, Newell humming, Mark frozen in mid-step looking down at the tub. He had been thinking about a bath. About soaking in the water. Now the water was running into the tub, filling it, and Mark could feel the heat.

"You are so fucked up. Do you do this a lot?"

"Every chance I get."

"Well." Newell leaned over, adjusted the water, felt for the hot, adjusted again.

Mark shivered and looked down at the young man's shoulder, hearing the country lilt in his voice. Newell had become Leigh, Mark could see her bending down like this, filling a tub with water, stepping into it. Leigh letting down her hair, before, when she had long hair and kept it in a twist at the back of her head.

Water in the tub, Newell in the tub, pulling Mark there too, the men sitting face to face, legs wherever they would fit. The grimy tub under his butt, the gray cast to the light in the room. For a moment Leigh had been here, and Mark lay back and closed his eyes.

"What are you thinking?"

"You don't know Leigh," Mark said.

"No, I don't. Who is that?"

"A woman. She's kin to me, some way. She was in the Court of Comus a few years ago."

"What is Comus?"

Mark closed his eyes and felt the shimmering, the shivering world, ringing in his ears, the pressure on his ribs, the water. Breathe, breathe. "The queen of Mardi Gras. Leigh's from an old family. I don't even know why I'm talking about her."

"Because you're fucked up and talking about all kinds of things."

"That's right. That's why."

"What kind of drug are you on? LSD or something?"

Mark giggled. "LSD. LSD. Shit. Oh shit."

"That stuff is supposed to mess up your chromosomes."

"Who knows what the chromosomes bring?" Mark asked. "Nobody knows."

"And you have flashbacks."

"You don't have them enough, you have to take more acid to get the good ones."

"Acid."

"That's what it is. L-something, lysergic something. I don't know. You want some?"

Silence for a moment.

"Sure."

"Then we have to go to Prilla's." Mark stood in the tub, swayed and slipped but caught himself, and Newell helped brace Mark till he could step out of the tub and reach for a towel. He rubbed it over his hairy legs, his arms; he admired his own body very much. Soap on his skin, but he couldn't remember washing. Newell standing too, drying with the other towel.

After a while something occurred to Mark, and he turned. "You don't even know who Prilla is."

Newell giggled. "Well, no, I don't."

"You don't even know who I am."

"You're Mark."

Mark was trying to find his clothes, to dress, but he kept getting tired. He found his underwear and lost his energy and sat on the edge of the bed holding the briefs. The floor had begun to ripple and wave again, the whole world was waving and rippling in every direction. A horn sounded, a ship passing on the river, a long, low, moaning horn that made him shiver up the spine. "Put on your underwear," Newell said, and Mark obeyed quickly without thinking about it.

Step by step. Mark would stop upon completing a gesture, fixed on something new, a miracle the way light fell from the open bathroom door, spilling across the dark room, making long shadows of everything, but nothing holding still, nothing solid.

"We have to go," Newell said, and held out Mark's shirt.

"You're in love with me."

"That's right. Put your arm in there."

"You like this."

"Nothing else like it in the world," Newell said, but by then Mark had forgotten what he meant. They walked out the door and down the back gallery through the loggia. A cool interior courtyard. On the way to the street they heard the voice of a girl and a woman, *You don't need to treat me like a baby*, the girl was saying. *Then don't act like one*, the woman was saying. *I'm so tired of how you act, well I'm so tired of how you act.* Back and forth like that, till the sound faded to nothing. Nothing else like it in the world.

"Where are we going?"

"I don't know. You were the one who said we had to go."

"To Prilla's. That's right. Say it."

"To Prilla's."

"In case I forget again."

"Who's Prilla?"

"My aunt." Though this was false. Prilla was not part of his family. "She's not there right now. On Governor Nicholls."

In the brisk night air he was feeling more like himself, more capable, the world less runny and squirmy than indoors. The sensation of wind on his cheek felt like the most tender kiss.

Times like now when he was tripping he could see ghosts on every side in every window, some in midair suspended behind windows that no longer existed, echoes of past houses that had burned down or fallen down or been torn down. By now he had become convinced the ghosts were real. He always saw them, though he was never frightened—as if he had become assured of their distance. Echoes down the long corridor of the past, images that remained impressed on the air itself. When Mark was very young someone told him the story of Aldonse Duval who met the wicked Sade on the way out of Paris, but no one would tell him anything about Sade except that he liked to eat children. From then on he had gathered family stuff in his head. His study of history had begun from a suspicion that the story might be fiction. That same Duval married a girl who was raised by the Ursuline nuns, Emilie Aimée Beauchantesse, and he built a house for her on St. Ann. Emilie was an orphan whose parents had died in the fire of 1788 and who had inherited a large tract of property in *le carré de la ville*. The nuns gave Emilie to be married to Aldonse in exchange for what? A woman was a valuable commodity, especially a pure heiress raised in chastity by religious sisters. Mark was sure that if he walked along St. Ann near the corner of Dauphine he would see the outline of the windows of the old house, which had burned in a later fire; but tonight the house would be there, Emilie in one window and Aldonse in another, him with a glass of whiskey. Aldonse liked his liquor, liked other substances as well, like the opium that sometimes made its way to the port. He liked good food and grew quite fat. He invested his money well in brickworks, real estate ventures around the city, and at one point owned a sugar plantation and two dozen slaves upriver near Germantown. He had four sons and no daughters by his wife and two daughters by his mistress, whom he kept in a little house in the Marigny fauborg. She had been his slave when she mothered the girls, though he freed her when he died, in his will leaving her the ownership of her own daughters as slaves. So many facts in Mark's head, so many papers to turn over in his fingers.

"Why are you trying to tell me this?" Newell asked, and Mark realized that he must have been talking this whole time.

"It would help me if I understood where I came from."

"Do you go to college?" Newell asked.

"I did."

"Where?"

"Right here. Tulane. I studied history."

"Are you some kind of teacher or something?"

"I might start teaching one of these days."

"Well, I still don't understand why you're trying to tell me about this guy who ate babies."

"Turn here. This is Governor Nicholls."

Smells coming from all sides, vomit and piss, spilt liquor, spices from somebody's cooking. "I just wonder if the story is true," Mark said, fumbling in his pocket for a key to the courtyard gate. Even he was no longer certain if that was the reason, however, and he simply looked at Newell.

The main floor of the house was Prilla's apartment. Cool, calm rooms painted in pinks and yellows, tastefully furnished in the style of an uptown decorator. Somebody Father had hired. Four rooms, a back gallery with cabinets on either side, and stairs in one of the cabinets leading to the attic, where Mark led Newell.

Mark's room was there, neat as a pin, and the sense of order made him happy. He had kept a room at Prilla's house ever since he finished graduate school, and he stayed here more often than he stayed at home. He sprawled across his bed and stared up, the room spinning.

"This is a nice house."

What did he mean by that? Why was his face so flushed? Or was it flushed, was it actually shimmering? They had come to do something. Newell was watching him. Newell still smelled like sex even after the bath. That was all Mark could smell now that they were inside. But Mark's cock felt sore and tired. He would not be able to do anything no matter how excited he got. He sat at the desk. He had moved there for something, to get something, and Newell sat politely and waited.

"You're supposed to be getting me some of this drug. But you keep spacing out."

"Right." Mark turned to the desk, opened a metal box. Tore off a tab with a red rooster stamped on it. "You think you should take a whole one?"

"I never did this before. What did you say it is?"

"LSD. Man, what a farm boy."

"I never lived on a farm."

Mark handed the tab to him. Tip of finger to tip of finger. The tiny white square. "Chew it up good, till the paper is soft. Then swallow it."

"It's paper?"

"It's blotter acid. They drop it onto the paper, one drop."

"That's it?"

"Believe me, that's enough."

Newell shrugged, touched his finger to his tongue, drew the tab of acid inside his mouth and chewed.

Satisfaction warmed Mark through. To watch this child of the country now, to look into his eyes and watch the change, the secret of the chemical and the secret that the chemical would reveal. *How long does this take?* Newell asked, but Mark could only nod at first, so taken was he with the thought of what he was privileged to witness, on the same night that he had drawn a razor blade lightly across a woman's breast, now to watch a soul cope with the knowledge that consciousness can be adjusted like the tuner of a radio.

"Did you hear me? How long before I feel this?"

"Maybe an hour. Maybe sooner."

"That long?"

"You have to digest it."

Newell nodded. Sprawled in a soft chair nestled under the sloped ceiling. Trusses ran the length of the room.

"You read all these books?"

"Sure."

Newell ambled in front of the shelf reading the titles. "How do you say this?"

"Nee-chee. He's a philosopher, like Sade."

Newell shook his head and put the book on the shelf again. "I thought you said you studied history."

"I did. I took a lot of other stuff, too."

"You like school?"

"I did." He turned away. Newell had begun to sound thickheaded, stupid, to become boring, but a moment later Mark had to look at him again, to see the creamy skin, the dark hair, and eyes. Maybe just the acid making him see too much.

"I liked it, too," Newell said.

A moment later, Newell in front of him and the touch of Newell's hands on his thighs sent him backward and before he knew it he was on the bed, not in the chair, lying back along the bed with the quilt pulled smooth across it, the bed neatly made because that was always the first thing he did when got out of it, like a monk or a boy scout. He lay back and let Newell have his body, slow sensations so liquid along him, as if the sex were a puddle he lay in, as if it immersed him. Oh, oh, he said. Oh, oh. Otherwise the room was quiet. The top of Newell's head moved up and down, up and down, such a careful man.

Yes, Newell, yes, this is a worthy journey we are undertaking, yes, as I strive to rise to the challenge of the moment, and yes the flesh is weak and less than willing at the moment, pleasant to receive such ministrations, my dear Newell, but maybe a little frustrating for you, since nothing happens, really. But you are starting to feel something, too, aren't you? A change in your eyes, a cast of seeing inward. Of looking suddenly inward at an open door.

"My stomach," Newell said. "Wow."

"That's where it starts."

Newell had a look in his eyes as though something were blossoming inside him, as though a space were opening in his gut, as if he were about to rise off the floor. A light of wonder and an edge of fear. "How long does this last?"

"A long time. You'll feel it really strong for about six hours or so and you'll feel a lot of effects till tomorrow about this time. Or even longer, depending on your brain."

"Oh, this is weird." Newell touched his stomach as though something were inside it. "I have to work tomorrow night."

Mark wanted to say, you'll be fine by then, wanted the words to come out, but there was suddenly some need to grind his teeth, to close his eyes. He made a low sound and realized he was still lying on the bed, shirt shoved up his belly, his pants tugged open and his soft wet cock feeling like a flap of string. He had been lying here like this and Newell had turned away now, was drifting in the room, reading the titles of more books, humming some sound, making some rhythm under his breath, and Mark sat up to listen.

"I can tell an Eskimo's cold," he was singing, "all you got to tell me is go."

Mark tucked his shirt in, fastened his pants, between each gesture feeling the lag, the need to stop moving.

"Let's go for a walk," Mark said. "You should be outside when it hits you the first time."

"I don't know." Newell was already somewhere different, the light in his eyes, the glow of his skin.

"You'll be fine. We'll be together."

"This is so strange. My feet feel so far away."

Mark laughed, and heard the sound echo. Newell turned to him puzzled, drifting past to a Mardi Gras poster on the wall, a fabulous mask trimmed with feathers and sequins, with blank, cut-out eyes.

"Let's go walk," Mark said. "I want to sit at the river."

That time, when Newell looked at him, a feeling in Mark, something turning over, the memory of Leigh, that Newell had metamorphosed into Leigh once already tonight, in the bathtub, and that he might do it again. Might become Leigh again. Crazy. But the skin was the same, smooth as cream, without the creases of age that had begun to change Leigh.

Before they walked out of the room, Mark slipped another tab of acid onto his own finger, contemplated it, the fuzzy white paper that could alter the way he saw the world, and he ate it, to make the night go stranger still.

At times he would forget he was walking with Newell, the cool late-night air on his skin, the passing traffic and noise of horns, walking past an open door from which music was rushing out, pooling in the street, a dim interior, figures lining a bar. Shadows waiting for a drink. Walking under the galleries trying to imagine two hundred years ago, when the streets were mud and the houses hardly ran much farther out than Ramparts, named for the place where the fortifications used to run. Walking under the galleries, peering into the carriageways, occasionally seeing someone following him out of the corner of his eye and, recognizing Newell, remembering. "I love the way the streets are," Newell's voice distant and echoing oddly, as if he were speaking in a bottle underwater. So much noise all of a sudden—they were walking by the Bourbon Pub, all the gallery doors open and the dim lamps burning inside, the beat from the upstairs disco like a pulse. One of the songs he liked to dance to, "Contact."

The sensation in his head became overwhelming and he had to remind himself that he was all right, that more than likely he was walking without any sign of the drugs in his head, more than likely nobody could tell that the smell of the hamburgers from the Clover Grill, the smell of the potatoes frying in grease, made the top of his throat go tight. But he was still breathing, in spite of the feeling of a weight on his ribs, the sudden smell of vomit from the gutter, somebody growling words from a shadowed entryway. Still Mark kept on breathing and walking, people passing, some of the men looking at him as usually happened in this part of town, but looking at him so fiercely in the wash of the drug. Newell said, "It feels like the top of my head is about to come off."

"Oh boy."

"But we're almost to Jackson Square. Pretty soon we can sit down."

"I need to," Mark said.

Newell took his elbow and steered him. The Café du Monde was full, the sound of voices lively, a tired, big-boned horse standing in front of a carriage at the curb. They crossed the strip of land where the oyster sellers used to set their tents in the early days of the city, crossed the levee and looked across the batture the river had formed over the years. Mark smelled the dusky scent of the Mississippi, feeling the breeze pour across the water, rippling and dark, the river riding low.

"I need to sit down," someone said, and it was Newell, sitting, blinking, and Mark noted the change in his demeanor.

"You all right?"

Newell nodded his head, looking at something. He never bothered to answer.

But Mark was watching Newell's creamy face, turning lazily to look Mark in the eye, Newell gritting his teeth, working his jaw muscles. Throwing back his head to expose his white throat, the skin alive with some energy that rippled across it, Newell sitting up, eye to eye with Mark again. "I never had anything like this before."

"You like it?"

"Oh," Newell said and shivered, "too much," and

leaned forward and stared into the river, where the lights of a barge were moving.

"Just take a breath when it gets like that," Mark said.

Newell was staring, though, in a halo of soft blue light, and when he took a breath the sound was low. He had begun to smile.

"You like to try things," Mark said.

"Try things." He ran his fingers through his dark hair. "Yes. This is nice."

"New sensations."

"Shut up," Newell said. "I don't want to talk, I just want to look at the river." And Mark laughed and shut up and looked at the river, too.

"Shut up," Leigh had said to him, in the same tone of voice, the same languid heaviness to her lids. "You do nothing but talk and I get so tired of it. Just pour me a drink."

He had been telling her about the research he was doing. Papers inherited from two maiden great-aunts, sisters of her grandfather, not even named Duval or directly related to Mark at all, who had lived in modest houses in Metairie side by side, identical houses in identical yards. They died within months of each other, and Leigh was heir to both, Aunt Kit and Aunt Tit, she called them, and laughed, and never would explain the reason. With boxes of papers in the attic, family archives dating from the nineteenth century and even, as he found, some fragments of the Duvals in the eighteenth, a copy of a letter to Aldonse Duval from an uncle in France who wanted money, a list of household expenses from 1794, a news clipping from a paper of the day about a fire in the French Quarter. She had showed him the boxes of papers stored so carelessly with a slight curl of the lip, and every time he came to study them she gave him the same look. The more he learned, the more he bored her—she told him so in dry tones. "I'm tired of talking about it, sweetie. Really, I am. My family is so old sometimes I feel like I'm its asshole dragging the ground behind."

She had barely consented to meet Mark at all when he first got in touch with her, but once they came face to face she spent the evening telling him what a handsome young man he was and seemed actually surprised by that.

"The men in my family were never very good looking. But they were all named Robichaux, not Duval. I was glad to get married to a man who could give me a more interesting name. Pendergrass. In fact, I liked marrying a new name so much I did it twice more. And now I have three more names than when I was born. I think that's very interesting. And I believe I changed into a different person every time my name changed. The differences were subtle, but a person who knew me could tell."

"Is Jack your husband?"

"No."

Jack wants things. Asks me to do certain things. Acts of courage, is the way I think of it. Acts of personal responsibility and moral courage. He feels a certain responsibility to vary the course of events, he says. He has a way of making you want the same thing he wants.

You'll see when you meet him. I promise I'm going to let you do that. Introduce you. I want to be there the first time you see him. I know what your taste is, Mark dear.

Newell said, "I think I can walk now."

"Walk."

"Didn't you want to walk somewhere?"

"Are you enjoying yourself?"

"Oh, yes," Newell said, "I've found a new best friend."

"Can you move? I'm not sure I can move."

This melting self was what Mark loved, this feeling that when he closed his eyes he was sliding farther into darkness than usual, that the space in his mind was beyond mere consciousness and had become something else, a newly unfolded universe. Every time he closed his eyes he felt as if his eyes were dissolving, and at the moment before the darkness, the world transformed into something more. This was the effect of tripping that he craved, the feeling of a darkness within himself, of rooms constructed within the darkness, of a self elaborated through all these rooms, random lights across his retina shifting and swirling, an aurora of the interior. A field of shimmering lights. Standing in the dreaming place but awake, with a sense of knowing the world as though he had constructed it himself.

Leigh had given him the acid and watched. She liked to watch his skin flush with color, his eyes go radiant, as the drug immured him; she told him so as he was chewing the first of the small white tabs. Jack had picked up the acid earlier from Mac in the French Quarter, along with the black beauties that Leigh liked, and cocaine for Jack, and pot for them all. But Leigh had made Mark drop his first tab of acid in front of her. Because she wanted to witness the change. It was like watching a light come on, she'd said, but very slowly.

They talked for a while about a movie she had seen. After that she said, "I want you to do me a favor."

By then the lining of his stomach had become a fluttering inside him. The first edges. He knew already the nature of what she wanted. "What you talked about before?"

"Yes." She described what she wanted, showed him the slightly creped skin at the top of her breast. "Very lightly, that's the trick."

He saw a frail white scar, not even that, a thread of white. Nearly healed. "How often do you do this?"

She smiled, touching the scar herself. "It will disappear completely after a while."

Mark tasted a hint of metal, and the sounds of the room, the traffic outside, became suddenly velvety, and suddenly he was ready. The room was expanding and Leigh was ready and he did what she had asked.

At one moment, when Leigh's eyes were cast down, when she was shivering, as Mark lifted the razor blade and positioned it carefully in his fingers, through the open door Jack appeared, stood where Mark could see. Jack dark-haired, skin like copper, wearing a robe open at the front, the shadow of his body. Jack's bare calves below the robe seemed obscenely naked, his bare feet with a smattering of black hair across the top. Mark flushed and took a deep breath and Jack stepped out of sight.

"He likes it."

"Why?"

Leigh had shrugged. This was weeks before. When she first began to talk to him seriously. "I don't know."

Mark shook his head. "I doubt I can do this."

"I know you can."

But on the river, the person who kept becoming Leigh in the night, the one he had met in Mac's place, the face of Newell, a languid look of knowing, a thread of sound coming out of his lips. *I think I'm gonna be sad, I think it's today.* What a pretty face this was. What a fresh smell. Newell gritted his teeth and shivered, the drug flushing through him. This was what Mark had wanted to watch, the change of consciousness, the suddenly rich world of internal and external sensation, sounds pressing close, a breeze ruffling the skin one nerve at a time, every sensation minute, everything new.

Newell's nostrils flared. Flushes of color crossed his skin, or else the illusion of that took place in Mark's perception. The pupils of Newell's eyes slightly dilated. Slow, languid movements of the orbs. Small, precise gestures of the fingertips, as if Newell were making signs. Blowing out breath in an early morning that had become cool. A moment later, a sound began, and he turned his head to hear it, the cathedral clock striking three A.M. over the Place d'Armes.

He was trying to talk to Newell again, though at times he felt distant from the effort. "It's about Leigh," he said.

"What is?"

"What I'm studying."

"That Sade guy, you mean? You're studying that for Leigh?"

Mark shook his head. He would try again. "We're in the same family. Leigh and I."

"You already told me that."

He nodded. He had, of course. "But we're not close."

Newell nodded, looked away at the river. But that wasn't what Mark had meant to say. He gave up.

In the papers from Leigh, Mark had found a packet of yellowed pages, one packet among many. Most were ordinary letters, ordinary papers of the type he expected, records of the mundane affairs of people's lives only made valuable to him by their age, by their connection to some idea he had of his past. But in these pages was something else, a puzzle that might even become a mystery if he were to pursue it. A matter of history, even, if a minor one, and more legend than history. In the pages that unfolded he read what purported to be a journal kept by one of the neighbors of Madame Lalaurie, the owner of the infamous haunted house on Royal Street about which George W. Cable had written, about which Henry C. Castellanos had written, in their books about New Orleans. The neighbor had been a witness to the fire that nearly destroyed the house, and the later riot that did demolish it. Mark had been transcribing the pages ever since he found them, up to the moment today when Leigh handed him the tab of acid; he had even gone to Leigh's apartment today, hoping to tell her about what he had found, this apparent treasure, or very evident hoax, whatever it should prove to be. But the moment he saw her, the moment he knew Jack was in the house, he understood she would pay no attention. So he had taken the tab of acid instead of trying to tell her about what he had found, and now he was sitting with the words running through his head, written by a woman who had lived here, only a few blocks from the place where Mark and Newell were sitting, watching the river.

I was not aware of any alarm or signal that there was a fire anywhere in the neighborhood, but when I went out walking in the morning what else should I see but smoke billowing up from the direction of the river, close enough that I could guess the street. A crowd was rushing through the streets already, headed for the fire. Right away I got Marie, and we went together to see the excitement. I think Marie already guessed what we would see; she was wearing the new shoes I had bought her and vain of them, trying to walk only on the banquettes and never in the muck.

We found the fire on the corner of Royal Street and Hospital Street, the Lalaurie house, where Tante Emilie and her husband have had dinner many times. The Lalaurie woman has been married three times, and they say she is very fast with men and got very rich from her husbands when they died. I thought it was all a lot of talk until that story about the little girl she killed, the African child, threw her off the roof, I heard. But that was years ago, and of course she paid her fine, when the story came to light, and the child was a slave, after all. Decent people still eat at her table, though I would not. Because she has been married so often she cheapens the institution, or this is my view, and I have heard she is unkind to her stepdaughters. Anyway, it was her house on fire, and the streets were full. The firemen were everywhere, but their equipment is not the best, a shame, since we live in a city that threatens to burn down every year or so. We watched for a long time while the firemen tried to get the blaze under control; people started to whisper that the fire was winning, when the firemen climbed to the roof of the house to break through it and fight the fire from that direction as well. Another pump wagon arrived from the Marigny fauborg, and already it appeared to me the fire was coming under control, when I noticed for the first time the crowd, its hostility, its coldness.

I am writing this two days later, so I am prone to get ahead of myself. We knew nothing at the time except there was a fire, and when it was under control we had started back to the house when suddenly we stopped, Marie and I, at the same moment.

There was agitation on all sides. That woman, the Lalaurie woman, was in the streets. I glimpsed her walking in the muck with that large African footman of hers paraded at her backside. She is a loud, brassy woman with hair braided and coiled about her ears, thought handsome at one time, though her figure is too thick for my taste and her way of dress too assertive. She was directing people getting the goods out of the house, but I kept losing sight in the crowd, and Marie is not much taller than me, and so we waited and listened and tried to hear what we could not see; rumors were running through the crowd on all sides.

The story that chilled me most deeply was that the fire had been set by the cook, who was kept chained in the kitchen with her neck an open sore from the iron collar that confined her. We heard that story in bits and snatches, and that made it all the more awful when I understood.

Firemen were climbing on the roof of the house. We watched them breaking through the timbers. I kept thinking to myself, I should go back home, I should get out of this crowd, I'm not strong enough for this, but the scene had me spelled to the spot, I never felt such a fixedness in myself. We stood there, Marie and I, letting the crowd move us this way and that. I saw Dr. Mossy at the baker's shop and he said it was an awful thing, wasn't it? He'd talked to a fellow who'd looked in the upstairs windows, climbed up in a tree to look, and saw the most horrible sights, a table laid out with instruments of torture, and a man chained in the room, wounded and gored and dripping with blood. He spoke in a fever, nothing like the calm Dr. Mossy who comes when I have a complaint, who hardly speaks at all, and I couldn't make out half what he said myself, I had to ask Marie what he was talking about. When she told me, I thought he was making it all up, but then the doors of the house burst open, and the firemen began to bring out the slaves one by one.

One of the women was the cook, two white men helping her, an iron collar sharpened at the edges still gripping her at the neck, she barely able to walk, her neck, wrists, and ankles scored with wounds, and other ghastly bloody marks on her body. Everyone in the crowd was murmuring that she was the one who had set the fire.

She died that day, I think. The crowd fed her and gave her all the food she wanted right there, and she died of the kindness. She had been starved so long, her body was too tired to take in so much food.

The old paper was faded, fragile, the ink faded. He had held them carefully his hands that same afternoon, the smell of age, old dust that is in fact old skin. The skin of this woman had dusted over her papers, her smell reduced to its last essence.

"I could sit here all night," someone was saying, a voice was saying, and suddenly the whole shimmering night in motion, a ship sliding by in the dark, headed upriver to the new docks, sailing calm and even with towers of containers on deck. The lowing of the horn, a long full throbbing note, a hoarse high sound surrounded by plush, a sound so tangible it tingled across Mark's skin.

"I could sit here all night and watch the river," this guy was saying, this cute guy, the one Mark was supposed to be watching, studying, to see the effect of the acid on the untested young mind, except that Mark himself was strung on a thin wire, was seeing a brave new world of his own, a ship gliding by in the night with smells wafting off it, the dusky river.

"We are sitting here," Mark said, and Newell started to laugh, was laughing at him, and Mark looked away.

"But how long have we been?" asked the face.

"I don't know. Why are you laughing at me?"

"Laughing," the face said, "but I don't mean it."

"I don't know how long we've been here."

"You could look at your watch."

The ship's horn sounded again, the shivering sound filling the air along his skin, the breath of cool, and when he moved his hand, trails of his hand moved along behind, as if he were moving very slowly or seeing very quickly, or as if the hand left a taste of itself, colors, in the air where it passed. Mark looked at his watch, the thin metal hands splayed on the face; it made no sense to him. He looked at it again.

"We've been out here a long time," Newell said. "I want to stand up. Do you want to?"

"Stand up?" Still staring, though, at the face of time.

"Yes."

"I don't know if I can," Mark said.

"This is amazing. My head feels so clean. It's like there's a window in my head and there's a wind blowing inside."

"After you stand up."

"No, we have to stand up together. Come on."

Suddenly rising, he wondered if Newell were lifting

him somehow, and there they were standing, side by side.

"Can you walk?" Newell asked

"I don't think so."

"You sure?"

Mark shrugged, but by then, he had already taken a step and found that he could. A surprise, that first moment, moving, but now they were crossing the levee, looking down at the shadows of the grass and the trees, ahead the quiet of Jackson Square. Newell stopped to look back at him, on the landing of the steps, no one else on this side of the street, a few people still in the Café du Monde, sounds, though, from everywhere, the air, the river, the voices behind them and the traffic passing.

"Do you want to eat something?" Mark asked.

"I want to go dancing," Newell said.

We stayed in the street most of the day; I knew my husband would be angry (and he was) but I couldn't tear myself away. I'm one for a spectacle when it's to be had, and anyway, it was not much later than we usually set out for a walk along the levee or a drive down the Bayou St. Jean to the lake; in fact, it was exactly that hour. The crowd had been growing all afternoon, every color of skin and every shape of eye, all of us shameless, and I had come out of the house without a pair of gloves, though at least I had a hat. The Lalaurie house was locked up and the women were inside it, so we understood; some men had dug up two bodies in her courtyard, the skeleton of an adult and a child, and everyone guessed this was the little girl she had flung from the roof. Everyone around us was talking, we were all sharing the news, watching the comings and goings. The sheriff would be here to arrest her before nightfall, this was what we understood, but we waited and waited and he never came.

A carriage pulled up to the front of the house, and anybody who drives on the bayou road in the evening would have recognized it as her own, driven by that same sleek footman, who went to the front door and knocked. The door opened at once and Madame and her daughters descended instantly to the street, mounted to the carriage and closed it up too quickly for anyone to react, and the horses were off before people understood what had happened and started to shout.

Oh such a fury, such a commotion! I can't say I liked it, and I can't say I ever want to see it again. People took off after her, and pretty soon carriages were trying to push through the crowd. Marie and I were nearly trampled, and finally I told her we would have to go home. I spoke very firmly, and for once she had nothing to say. We had to fight our way the few blocks distance, and the whole way people were talking of nothing but the awful scene on Royal Street.

But the crowd was all moving to the jail, and we followed, Marie and I, because we heard the Lalaurie slaves were there, wounds on display, and we wanted to see, and we did—seven of the slaves, though the old woman was already sick and dying, though still out in plain sight. Her neck pitted, worms crawling in the wound. The instruments of torture were laid out on tables for everyone to see. I can't bring myself to describe more than one or two. A collar for the neck with the inner ring sharpened like a barber's razor. A device for piercing the breasts and nipples of a woman. Only two of dozens of such devices that these people kept and used.

Everyone is acting surprised that such monsters could live among us, but my opinion is that there are many more like Lalaurie. We are keeping slaves, after all. They are under our power, we may do with them what we like.

Even if she had stayed, Lalaurie, I mean, would she have been punished? Last time, she was barely touched, and all her slaves returned to her, after she flung a little girl from the roof of her house, and that's the story I believe, I tell you, no matter how many times I'm told the child fell while running away from Lalaurie, trying to escape a beating, because in my mind it amounts to the same thing, whether it's true the one way or the other.

They headed into the Bourbon Pub, the sound falling around them and pressing against them, music throbbing, but instead of walking to the stairs that led to the disco, Mark led Newell to the back room and they stood in the dark for a while, Mark pressing against Newell, the two of them touching each other, people in the room but so what? Newell's hand sliding inside Mark's clothes, Mark sliding his hands inside Newell's, the whole process amazing, so slow, both of them, lingering, the light low and the shadows shifting, the two of them moving small and precise and seeming quaint and almost private with each other, though they were at the center of a ring of spectators. They were mostly lost to the fact that they were anywhere at all.

Later, upstairs, dancing, at first with some inches of space between them, then belly to belly, their bodies rippling to the beat. The disco mostly empty, a few bodies drifting among the pillars, looking at reflections in the mirror, the lights whirling, the heat making them cling together.

They danced till sweat poured down them, and sometimes Mark heard every detail of the music, but on two different occasions he stopped hearing anything at all; he could see the beat and even feel it in a way, but he heard nothing, as if he were dancing and holding Newell in a bubble of silence, something perfect and unutterable, the shuddering of a heartbeat, the heat of breath.

In the back room Newell knelt and took Mark in his lips, teased him, touched him here and there, each move slow and deliberate. In Mark's perception the process was slowed and teased by the drug, the slowing of time to a trickle, every touch of the mouth intense. Later in his memory it would blend with the dancing, this long interval in the dim lit room moving his hips against Newell's face, Newell's hands sliding inside Mark's shirt along his back, the circle of silence around them. Mark felt as if he were melting along the wall, draining into Newell.

A mob has gathered in the streets, I'm frightened out of my wits, and Marie and André and Louise and the kitchen help are all begging to join it, so I've said yes, get out, go do it, I don't care, but get back here before my husband gets home. Mind me you do that. And they swore each and every one they would be back. But they know my husband's with his mistress in St. Jean tonight, he may not come home at all. So they hurried away and left me here with old madame. They joined that crowd in the street. You know that house is just around the corner from mine. Well, practically so, anyway. And I can hear the sounds now, there are thousands of people in the streets and they're tearing the Lalaurie house to pieces.

The papers pulsing in his hand like a rainbow, sheets of colored fire, and the smell of talcum, a velvety odor with an aftertaste of four o'clocks. Like sitting in a garden. His vision of the past became so acute sometimes. While getting a blow job in the Bourbon Pub, he was thinking about the existence of the self, its construction. The fact that he could alter it and yet remain, or even become more intensely, a construction. To feel more intensely the construction of the picture in his head, the running picture, himself the moviegoer. When he closed his eyes it was all so sweet. Getting a blow job in the back room of the Bourbon Pub on acid with a relative stranger at the helm down there in the murk, and Mark himself bemused at the thought of history. A perfect moment in the search for the good and the beautiful.

Outside in the French Quarter of 4:30 A.M., they wandered a long way, toward the riverfront. They walked together, and for a while they were holding hands.

Singing, music in Mark's head, sensation ringing through

him. *I have walked past the Lalaurie house today. It sits an empty shell, as though the woman and all her cruelties had never existed, or as if it required so complete a scouring to cleanse the crimes away. I never saw anything like it. They say the mob took it apart board by board. The Lalauries have not yet surfaced anywhere that I have heard about, though there are rumors she fled to France. I believe she should be brought to justice, but she never will be.*

Newell said, in the lower part of the Quarter, "Let's slow down, this is too fast."

"Okay."

"I can't go so fast, everything is moving."

"Okay. Are you all right? It's not much farther."

Newell nodded, as if he knew where they were going, though Mark hadn't said. "I feel like my head is flying."

"You said that."

"I can see everything."

"Come on. We're almost there."

"Where?"

"Leigh's house."

"But Mark, it's five A.M."

Mark grinned, feeling suddenly clear about something. "She's awake. She's with a friend of hers. Come on."

Newell seemed reluctant. Mark took his arm. They walked down Dauphine and turned on Barracks and Mark buzzed the gate and after only a little while somebody buzzed him in. They headed through a lush courtyard.

The front door was open and they went upstairs, Mark leading, heading into the sitting room, when Newell suddenly stopped. "I don't want to go in there."

"What?"

"I don't want to. I don't know who they are."

"They're my friends. They're doing the same drugs we're doing. We're just being friendly."

"What do you want me to do?"

"Meet them."

"I feel so funny in my stomach," Newell said.

Mark took his hand, knocked on the door to the sitting room.

"Come in." It was Leigh's voice, but Jack opened the door.

Jack took one look at Newell. Only one. Mark flushed with jealousy toward both men, and watched Jack, a glaze of fascination in his eyes. Newell hardly noticed, stepped into the room past Jack. Jack asked, in the deep voice that Mark could feel on his skin, "What have we here?"

"He's my friend. Newell." Mark added, "He works at Mac's bookstore."

"The famous Mac," Leigh said.

"I never saw you at Mac's." Jack was standing very close to Newell. "You gave him some of the acid? He gave you some?"

Jack and Newell locked eyes.

Leigh was on the settee again, she had been reclining but now she sat up and was shaking herself alert.

"I got my share," Newell said. "My head is way beyond."

Jack laughed. Mark took Newell's hand, led him to a couch. He motioned Newell to sit down. Jack was watching the whole time, but went to Leigh, who relaxed when he slid beside her.

"You're the cutest thing," Leigh said to Newell.

"He was wearing a dog collar," Mark explained. "At Mac's."

"You tried to choke me in it," Newell added. "I didn't like that."

Jack smirked. "You didn't?" They were eye to eye again, Jack and Newell. Jack's broken nose, thin lips, hard eyes.

"No."

"Mark's just pushing your limits."

"You could be right." Newell ran his fingertips along his scalp again. His eyes rolled back, no longer aware of Jack. "He pushes really nice."

Mark laughed. Newell stood from the couch. "I want to go." He smiled at Leigh. "We just came to visit."

The room was quiet, water dripping somewhere. They looked at one another as if they had been having dinner together.

"You don't have to leave so soon," Leigh said, but she was pleased, and giggled.

Mark waited by the door. Now Jack was looking at him, at Mark, for the first time, because Newell wanted to leave with Mark. Now Mark could be pleased with himself. But Jack went on sitting beside Leigh. Who was smiling quietly, holding the top of her robe together with her hand, the robe spotless, the lightly wrinkled skin of her face, her throat, so fine. Her freshly colored hair, honey brown. Mark's father said she was one of the beauties, her year, one of the great ones in the ball circuit, because of that skin; Father remembered Leigh, after Mark had written her. One of the beauties.

Jack was looking at Newell, and said, "You should come back."

"I just need to walk right now."

"You should come back for more." Jack was displaying himself, offering something. "Of the acid. We have more."

"I have enough," Mark said, and Newell had already stepped through the door as if no one were talking to him.

"What a night it's been," Leigh said. "Take care." She turned to Jack as Mark closed the door.

Newell stared into the courtyard. "Your friends are nice," he said. "They must have money."

"Leigh does. Jack has Leigh."

"She's beautiful."

"She was famous in New Orleans as a debutante. Do you know what that means here? Mardi Gras, and all?"

"No," Newell said, so Mark explained as they walked, a sentence at a time, but soon gave up, and Newell said, "You can tell me later. It will make more sense."

"You want to go back to your apartment? We could go to bed. But I don't know if I can sleep."

"Yes."

But yes to what? "I should have got a joint from Jack."

"He was full of shit."

"Jack?"

"Yes. He was so full of it."

Mark laughed.

"What's so funny?"

"Just things. Never mind. Do you have anything to drink in your house?"

"Yes."

When they went into the courtyard the older woman and the young one were outside again but in nightgowns and the young one was screaming, "Why are you acting like this? You won't let me sleep."

"Please, Millie, I'm sorry."

"You should leave me alone." The young woman, Millie.

"Come inside. Please."

"I don't want to come inside."

"Please, come in the house."

Both were silent when Newell stepped into the loggia, Mark beside him, Mark staring at the women in the shadows, who were looking at the ground now, pretending no one was anywhere near. "She's crazy," Newell whispered. "That girl is young. Her daddy is going to find out."

"Who is she?"

"Louise is my landlady. Millie is the girl. Her daddy works for Louise. Lord."

They headed inside, their whispers echoing in the high ceilings. No light, but everything was visible in the spill from the front windows. When Newell closed the door they stood apart and alone in the quiet. Mark sat on the bed and Newell sat beside him.

It was like being in love. Like falling that way. Not that, but like it.

I was in the mob myself for a while, hanging outside the courthouse waiting for news the day of the trial. We had been hearing more and more about the story, and what I kept wondering was how easily it could have happened to me, when my husband was keeping Leitha. Leitha was the one who lived in the back cabinet, not me, but she came close to behaving as if she were the wife of the house at times, when M. was away especially, after he would sleep in her bed and get out of it for his breakfast and take a carriage to the train for business in St. Louis or Memphis or Birmingham. At one point I wondered if he would put me by and bring her upstairs, I really did, though Marie was constantly telling me that my husband would not lose his senses like that, his own people would turn against him if he did. But here was this woman Pauline, a slave just like Leitha, who shut up her mistress and her children in a room and beat them and nearly starved them. And that poor woman and her children so abused, her husband the author of the whole affair, through his unwholesome relations with Pauline, through her unnatural elevation to a place of authority over the wife of the house, and to my horror I find I can remember Pauline's name but not the name of the wife. I was picturing myself, and Leitha with the whip. I suppose I do this to make myself feel better for the fact that I am the mistress, but am chattel at the same time. Though the truth is I'm well aware M. built Leitha a house in the Fauborg, and now he has a family there as well, a nice daughter of mixed blood; and as far as I know he may have other women; there's a lot of money, and it all goes somewhere; and, anyway, I knew when I married him that he was too fond of women for his own good.

Pauline will be hanged. I think I will watch her die.

The history roiled in his head, words to say to Newell, to explain the look on Leigh's face, the somber acceptance of strangeness, of a small scratch at the top of her breast. But why explain to Newell? What could be the purpose? What was it that Mark was feeling that made him want to tell Newell exactly what he meant? What was it that would change in Mark if he could recite the history perfectly, even once?

Louisiana was purchased from the French when Napoléon needed money. He had not yet killed enough people and wanted to kill more. Without money it was harder to pay for the war he wanted, and the colony was irksome anyway. *Le nouveau Orléans.* So he sold the whole continent to a man who only wanted the city. Thomas Jefferson bought the Louisiana colony for ten million dollars and was called a visionary for it, when

224 / JIM GRIMSLEY

really, who would have passed it up, a deal like that? As good as getting Manhattan for a handful of beads, any day. Mark studied the past because he felt confused about the present. About who he was. Though it was silly to look so far back for an answer, wasn't it?

Louisiana had been purchased from the French, the very ground he was lying on sold from one nation to another. What kind of price for it today? What price to sell land that doesn't really belong to you anyway, the nationality of the land, the sovereignty of it? What price?

Eight hundred dollars in the year 1834 would buy a human soul after all, or at least the body containing the soul and all the labor that could be forced out of the body during one lifetime.

Three dollars to go into the Parade disco for the night, dance as long as you like, and one drink included in the price of the cover.

"You're not even thinking about this, are you?" Newell asked at one point, after they had gone to bed, and the question took Mark out of his head.

"What we're doing? I'm thinking about it some."

"I feel the same way."

"Do you?"

"It feels good. To lick you and stuff. But at the same time I could stop."

"I know," Mark said. They lay together in the quiet. "I'm thinking about some things right now."

"What?"

"Strange true tales of Louisiana."

"I only know the strange true tales of Alabama," Newell said.

"Alabama, right. But you don't live there anymore."

"No, I don't."

Already slowing down in his head, the head space diminished in the time it took to notice and still diminished more. Mark wondered what he would keep of this feeling, looking at this fresh face on the pillow, the white skin, the dark eyes. Newell watched back with the same calm seriousness, when, in a kind of revulsion, Newell disentangled himself, stood and went to the gallery.

In a moment Mark would say, "You need some plants. We should get you some plants today. For the balcony." He could feel the thought in his head, the words in his mouth. He would let himself say them, if only to cause Newell to turn his way again. If only to cause Newell to wonder. As if this were the beginning of something.

*Pleasure
for Pain*

On Sunday, two days before Halloween, Newell was sitting in his room reading the *Times-Picayune* front news section when somebody knocked quick and light on the door and opened it. Millie walked in and closed the door behind her. He had spoken to her only a few times in the junk store and had seen her in the courtyard now and again, lately, talking to Louise.

"I'm sorry to bust in on you, but I had to get away from her, I swear."

"Hey, Millie."

"She will not leave me alone, Newell. What am I going to do?"

"Who won't, honey?"

"Louise."

She had tears in her eyes. Her hair needed washing. She must be sixteen, he thought, if that old. She had a smell to her like socks, but cold.

"Sit down, right there." Newell brought her a glass of water and a wad of toilet tissue to wipe her eyes. She took the tissue and dabbed at herself.

"I told her I don't want to mess with her anymore, but every weekend when I work she finds one reason and another for me to come back to her rooms. We don't even open the store till one o'clock on Sunday, but she wants me to come here in the morning so she can get me alone."

"I thought you liked it."

"I did, but it wasn't right." She folded her arms across her simple chest, pulling at her pink sweater, taking it off.

"And you told her you don't want her to do it anymore?"

"No. What I told her was it makes my skin crawl just to hear her voice. But she still won't quit trying."

"You really told her that?"

"Yes." Holding one elbow in one palm, she swung from side to side as if she were waiting her turn at jump rope.

"When?"

"Last weekend. And first thing yesterday morning she starts asking me to help her with some boxes in her house, and I says all day no, I can't, and lucky we had customers all day and I found plenty to do. But this morning I knew what she wanted and sure enough as soon as we got in that apartment she was after me again."

"She was after you?"

"Touching me, and . . . ." She breathed out in a long sigh. "Things."

"Did you tell her to stop?"

"She can't stop. She can't control herself." Millie sipped the water.

A knock on the door again. Millie froze.

Before Newell could move, the door swung open and Louise stood there. She reacted palpably to the sight of Millie. "What are you doing here?"

"We're talking," Newell said. "She came in my room and we're talking."

"Come on downstairs with me, Millie, you have work to do."

"Louise, you can't come in my room like this without my permission."

"I knocked."

"But I didn't say, come in."

They squared off at each other. "So you're telling me you want me to go?"

"I'm telling you that Millie is welcome here just like you are, when I say you can come in."

She stood there for a moment, head hanging, looking at the floor.

Mark appeared behind her on the gallery.

"I should go." Louise, embarrassed, fled down the gallery.

Hurried steps, tip-tap tip-tap, Louise descended the stairs in quick tiny hops. Newell closed the door. Millie started to giggle at the table where she was sitting.

"What's going on?" Mark asked.

"Millie came in here to get away from Louise, and Louise followed her."

"She's gone crazy," Millie gestured at Mark with her hands. "She worries me all the time like that."

"Does she try to force herself on you?" Mark asked.

"Does she what?"

"Try to. You know."

"Try to lick you and touch you and stuff," Newell explained.

"Oh. Sure. I used to let her, but I don't want her to do that anymore." She blinked at the two of them. She had taken her sandal off, was cleaning under her toenails with a match.

"So she tries to force you to do it."

"She tries to get me to want to. But I don't."

"You need to tell your father," Mark said.

"What?"

"Your father can make her stop. He can tell her to stop."

"But then I have to tell him what I was doing."

"Maybe."

"Unless I lie. I could lie."

Newell stepped behind Mark, nearly touched him. The grace of Mark's shoulders in a gray wool sweater.

"You probably shouldn't do that."

"I could say Louise has been asking me to do stuff but I never have. Done it."

"But what if Louise tells him something different."

Millie laughed. She was on her feet now. "What's she going to do, tell him she had sex with me? I don't think so."

She was finding her shoes, sliding them on her feet, pulling on the sweater, beige skin, a nice enough face, a soft round chin, heavy lashes over dark brown eyes. Her breasts were bigger than had appeared when she was sitting, full under the tight dress.

"Listen, thanks," she was pulling at the back of one sandal, plump feet bulging over the leather. "Thanks for letting me come in here and stuff."

"Sure," Newell said.

She showed no more reluctance to face Louise, leaving as soon as she had pulled her cardigan down over her dress. She closed the door with a quiet, emphatic click.

Newell locked the door and turned to Mark, who was sitting on the bed. "Oh, Jesus."

"She should tell her father."

"Her father works for Louise."

Mark had to think about that. Newell went to the bathroom and pissed and brushed his teeth and watched Mark on the thin chenille bedspread.

"Are you angry?" Mark asked.

"No," Newell answered, though the question irritated him. He went to the door, opened it, walked onto the back gallery and stood looking over the courtyard. Forlorn in the damp chill, on the southern wall climbing roses were still blooming, pink blossoms tattered. Louise and Millie had disappeared, but he could hear their voices. Newell went inside again and closed the door.

"Are they in the courtyard?"

"No. They're in the apartment. I can hear them fighting."

"That's sad," Mark said.

"What are you doing here?"

Mark flushed and lay back on the bed.

"Answer me. What are you doing here? I thought you weren't coming back."

"You never give me a break, Newell."

"You're the one who broke up with me, Mark. You're the one who told me we weren't compatible socially."

"You never let me explain what I meant."

"I know what you meant. I didn't go to college. And you're all educated."

"Look," Mark said, sighing, "Leigh wanted me to come invite you to her Halloween party, that's all. Okay? We can go together if you want to."

Downstairs in the courtyard the two women had come to stand at the plantain tree, and Louise was listening as Millie began to sing, not in melody but in complaint. Louise stood listening with her shoulders sloped, feeling, as she had been feeling for weeks now, slightly sick to her stomach, which was at the same time knotted with anguish that she could no longer face. Millie's face flushed that horrible scarlet-blue color, her voice a shriek, "You sick old hag, what did you want to ruin my life for, why are you treating me like I belong to you? I don't belong to anybody!" More at the same volume and pitch, so that after a few sentences Louise could stop listening, though still repulsed by the corded stretched ligaments at the base of Millie's throat, the pretty skin all creased and flushed with blood, those shapely shoulders tensed with her passion and her hands clenched to fists. Nothing more to hear, only Millie screaming again, and Louise turned and walked into the house, surprised herself at this movement, since she rarely walked away from Millie, or even turned away from her. It had become, for a while, her greatest joy, to have Millie in her sight.

The rags of a Halloween costume littered the kitchen. Millie had torn the witch's dress into so many separate pieces, Louise wondered if she would ever be able to put the dress together again. She began to gather them together in case Millie should come back inside to start the fight anew.

"You're a goddamn sick old cow," Millie shrieked in the courtyard. "You've ruined my life." She broke into tears that appeared theatrical and false. The moment slowed to a crawl for Louise. In turning to leave Millie alone in the courtyard, in realizing she no longer trusted Millie's behavior to be real, Louise understood Millie no longer mattered. She could no longer care for Millie. Quietly stacking the pieces of the dress, the torn sleeves, the rags that had been a skirt, Louise felt herself becoming herself again, regaining the piece of herself that she had given over to this girl.

This was what Louise saw: Millie standing in the courtyard as rain began to fall, the water streaking through Millie's hair, causing it to collapse against her face, to cling to her cheeks, on which was the most delicious fine, white fuzz that Louise had loved to lick, and the rain coming out of nowhere as it was apt to do even in October, sticking Millie's dress to her plump lower belly, her small breasts, her thighs so round and big at the top. But now as Millie stood in the courtyard sobbing, the rain streaking her body, causing that lovely ripening shape to emerge, now watching, Louise felt miniscule. Such a feeling of ash and waste inside, as if Millie had run through her like a bonfire.

Millie kept screaming the same thing in the rain, "You sad sick cow, you sad sick cow, you wait till I tell my dad," and turning and running and stopping to slip off her sandals, loose at the back, so she could run in the rain, nearly falling in the mud of the courtyard then splashing away as Louise watched from the door, while upstairs, on the balcony, coming out of Newell's room was that boyfriend of his, the blond with the biceps, stepping onto the back gallery with the rain pouring over the gutters now, coming down so hard his image wavered behind the rain, but for a moment Louise and the blond looked at each other.

Millie was soaked through, running in the street, the feeling in her belly a bursting sensation, a knot of solid substance. She would tell this time, she would. She had torn up the dress for good this time, she had ruined the costume and Halloween, and now she would ruin Louise. Millie ran in the rain seeing the black dress come to pieces in her hands, feeling the force of the argument that had passed through her. She had pushed Louise so far now. She had torn up the pictures Louise had taken of their secret weekend in Gulfport, ripped them up shrieking the words she had wanted to say all along, that she had hated spending those two days with Louise, hated walking on the beach with an old wrinkled woman, belly sagging, thighs shaking as she walked. Lately, Millie had hated every moment she spent with Louise. But that would all change today when she found her dad, when she finally opened her mouth. Yes, she would tell, and Louise would pay, for whatever crime this was. Louise should have known better. Look what she had done to poor Millie, who had never meant to. Who was not one of those. Louise would have to pay for this, whatever it was, that had made Millie hate her.

Henry Carlton passed Millie on his way through the gate. A pale girl running in the rain, her dress so thin she looked naked, a sight that made no impression on Henry at all. He had been married for a while, when he was eighteen and knew no better, and his wife was seventeen and moist and ripe like that. He turned to watch the girl splash away in the rain, then opened the iron gate and walked down the passageway to the courtyard. *Hallelujah it's raining* in his head, a snatch of the disco song, *it's raining, Hallelujah it's raining men.*

By now he had washed away any trace of Eugenie,

whom he had called Genie, had washed every molecule of her touch from his skin through countless evenings along the waterfront, in the back rooms of the Bourbon Pub or TT's West, or like last evening when he spent all night in the baths on Frenchmen Street. He liked the dingy rooms, the low light, the multitude of body types, nobody perfect with their clothes off except, of course, the ones who were always perfect, the flawless ones, the flawless faces, a god walking down the corridor, powerful buttocks moving as he walks, nodding from side to side to his worshipers, drinking the desire like nectar, his only food. The perfect one in the baths last night had been Mark, Newell's boyfriend, or, rather, his ex-boyfriend, and so this morning Henry had gotten out of bed early with the anticipation of this visit, Henry rushing to Newell with the news that Mark had turned out to be exactly the kind of slut Henry had predicted, throwing up his legs for everybody in the place and in particular with this one hairy man who was bigger than him, who was all over him.

Climbing from the loggia to the gallery, Henry was still humming when what should he see or rather whom should he see, coming out of Newell's room.

Mark, without the hairy brute beside him, Mark all by himself with his clothes on, come crawling back to Newell, wouldn't you know? After a night like that, on his hands and knees on the floor in that tiny room in the baths, with that man at his backside, these hams of but-tocks pumping away at poor Mark who was all twisted around, tongue out of his mouth trying to get a look at what was happening, trying to be the camera of his own porn movie, and Henry at the door making sure he took in the whole scene.

"Well, good morning," Henry called, and waved, making sure to flail the hand a bit, knowing it got on Mark's nerves.

"Hey, Henry," Newell said, "look who showed up and is just leaving."

Mark flushed, in the middle of saying something, only now seeing Henry, and the part that galled Henry was, it was clear Mark hadn't seen Henry at all last night, didn't remember him at all. "I'll call you later," Mark called out.

Newell stepped to his doorway again, hand on the knob, motioning Henry inside. "Do whatever you want."

"I'll call. I really will."

Newell shrugged, looked at him a moment, and Henry was trying to maneuver to see Newell's face, to see if there was any affection in it, any weakness that Mark could possibly exploit; but Newell turned away in closing the door and so Henry never saw.

"I can't believe that son of a bitch," Newell said.

"What does he want?"

"Dumps me flat on my ass and then wants me to go to a party. With those stupid friends of his."

Henry sat on the edge of the bed, one leg crossed, ankle tucked under his knee, a posture that made him feel safe. "Maybe he wants to get back with you."

"Please. I can't stand him."

"He's really cute."

Newell walked to the front gallery with a glass of water, stood sipping it. Standing in front of a brown potted plant, completely dead. Newell looked down at it and poured the remains of the glass into it.

Coming back inside, he said, "He's not cute enough."

"They were following him all over the baths last night."

"He was at the baths?"

"Oh, yes, honey, he was the biggest whore there. He gave out more sugar last night than Belle Watling."

Newell gave out one snort of a breath, in contempt. "That's fine, I don't care where he goes."

"What kind of party does he want you to go to?"

"A Halloween party. With some friend of his."

Henry curled around the bedpost, leaning over, feeling the thickness at his midsection. "If it was that friend he was with last night, you better go."

"Henry, I already told you I don't care that he was there."

"This good-looking hairy man with a dick like a donkey."

"The friend is a woman," Newell said. "The party. This rich woman that he knows. I don't know why he wants me there."

"But you're going, aren't you?"

"I don't think so."

Henry stood. "You want to go to the tea dance today?"

"I have to work." He looked at the clock beside the bed. "Right now, as a matter of fact."

Henry walked with him. They had become comfortable over the past weeks, settled into a relationship as French Quarter sidekicks. Henry felt he himself was being very mature. He had enjoyed the drama between Newell and Mark as a spectator, noting that sucking Newell's cock appeared to be a fairly short-term proposition, whereas sidekick status was more durable. He liked Newell a lot, because of his face. Newell always appeared to have something on his mind. With an ordinary cute person, Henry never wondered much about what the guy was thinking; with Newell, Henry wondered all the time.

No wonder Mark would come crawling back like this. For Henry, it was almost as delicious as if it were happening to him.

He decided to go to the bookstore and get some quarters from Newell, prowl the booths there for a while. Since the new booths had opened, a lot of men were going there instead of patronizing the other movie houses. This afternoon the bookstore was full, people lined at the register when Henry followed Newell inside, Newell heading to the office to talk to that old flabby man who smoked cigarettes all the time. Glaring at Henry already was the world's ugliest transsexual, Miss Sophia, and her outfit for the night was a one-piece pants suit with flare bottoms, one of those bright, flowered sixties fabrics nobody would touch anymore, along with a pair of white vinyl boots that zipped on the side.

Henry stood in the line for the quarters, bought two whole rolls, figuring to watch the new Falcon movie a couple of times and see who showed up in there, but on the way to the booths he checked the marquee, the display of what was playing where, with Newell's descriptions of each movie printed on index cards in black fine-tip marker. "Hot action where this painter's model shows off himself and then the painter gets turned on, Roger is so fantastic!!!," "First the blond goes down on Hawk and then they get into the back of the Jeep, Hawk is just like this guy I knew in high school on the football team!!!" and finally, "Bruno visits his next door neighbor who is Roger!!!! and they go at it right on the patio!!!! Incredible!!!!!" Judging by the number of exclamation points, Bruno's was definitely the movie to see.

Henry was proud to patronize the bookstore as Newell's friend because this had become, in that ephemeral way of fashion, a good place to prowl between drinks at Travis's and dances at the Parade, the kind of place Henry was drawn to without any premeditation. Newell was someone to whom Henry could talk, publicly, in an intimate and friendly way, and Newell had become a star here, so that to be in his company, to be favored with his attention, was a mark of increased status, like being the pal of a bartender at Lafitte's.

Standing beside the marquee, Henry hooted across the counter, "Newell, this sign looks just fabulous," as Newell was checking out the day cashier, another young queen and pretty cute, too, Henry thought. He would have to be introduced.

"That movie with Bruno is great," Newell said. "I watch it every night after we close."

"He is so big, he scares me," said the day cashier, glancing at Henry, this dishwater blond with almond-shaped eyes and a spray of moles over both cheeks. "Honestly, honey. A man can be too big."

"Henry does not agree with that, do you, Henry?"

"Oh, no."

"And that Roger," said Dishwater. "Honey, if he came after me with that thing, I would have to scream."

"So would I," said Henry. "With pure appreciation."

He went through the curtains into the twilight of the booths exactly on the beat, a perfect exit. He had a view of himself that was like theater, as if he were on stage and in the audience as well, and at the same time he was the play-by-play announcer, the critic, and the judge who awarded the prizes. As, at this moment, narrating to himself, *He swept aside the curtains and walked into the dark space. He listened to the sounds from all around. He had an uncanny awareness, walking forward, looking for the door with the gold number seven on it, somebody already inside but who? He looks inside. He moves with such grace. There are two men inside, comparing erections, one of them is holding a quarter in his hand, the other is holding his penis, rubbing it, like Bruno on the movie screen, and the two look at him and at once he understands, he has great perception, this is not the pair to interrupt, so he backs away with a glance at the pair in the room, a glance that says to them, I know you want to be alone with your change and your erections, I'll just find someone who's alone, like the man heading into the door marked with the gold number five, the black-and-white movie that is supposedly Chuck Connors the Rifleman doing a jerk-off scene for the camera, a sad, desperate film that Henry has seen, an attractor for the solitary. A lonely man this one must be, and not half bad to look at, judging from that glimpse of his retreating backside, so Henry followed and their eyes met in the booth as the man reached into his pocket and jingled coins.*

Henry can slip a coin into a slot so easily, dropping it neatly so the coin never touches the sides, the clean click of the coin engaging the electrical connection, the fluttering image reappearing, Henry's precise, neat fingers reaching to adjust the focus, smiling at his neighbor in the booth, who has already unzipped his trousers. Another amazing performance, keeping the man and his apparatus engaged at the proper velocity all the while watching poor Chuck Connors abuse himself and wondering, again, if it really was the actor, poor fellow, but nicely hung, and readying another quarter to drop at the proper moment when the projector sputtered and stopped, at moments like these Henry knew himself to be a fully engaged human being.

Lafayette hung around in the bookstore now that it was busy. He liked to be near the register, to jive at the counter while Newell kept the music going, listening to

Newell rag Mr. Mac, trying to convince the old man to buy some decent disco lights and maybe a mirror ball for the store, to make the place more festive, Newell said, a word the kid had started using lately. Lafayette made a rumble of a deep laugh in his throat and cut his eyes at Newell. A thing had been on Lafayette's mind, lately, nothing to put in words, but a willingness, if anything were ever to start itself, after work, for instance, if Newell were ever to approach him, say Newell needed something like a woman sometimes did, and he approached Lafayette. There were times when, thinking about it, wondering, looking at the sinuous way Newell moved to the music behind the cash register, moving those hips those thighs those lips. Sometimes Lafayette wanted to reach his fingers through that dog collar and pull a bit, grab Newell that way and let him know, but that would be the wrong way, as if Lafayette were the one who was wanting something, and he was certainly not, but on the other hand if some evening after the store closed Newell were to approach him, to touch him on the biceps, say, if Newell were to touch him there.

Not that he needed, not that he wanted . . . There were plenty of women to be had, there was no need for a man to reach, to ask, to lower himself, but on the other hand if the opportunity presented itself, if it should happen, what would be the harm in saying yes? Lafayette would be a part of it, yes, but not really, because he was only doing what he would have done with a woman anyway, receiving this lovely dust of pleasure over himself, he could picture it that way, and so the bookstore for a while became interesting to Lafayette, and Lafayette became interesting to the people in the bookstore.

Mac was sitting at his desk late that evening, stacks of rolled quarters everywhere, piled on the desk, on top of the filing cabinet, on the shelf next to the Mr. Coffee machine, stacked up on his extra shoes. He was going to have to buy a fucking safe on top of everything else and where the fuck to put it. Maybe hire Leon to build him a room in the back, a good stout room, and build a safe in it. Why fucking not? if he was going to have to keep so fucking much cash on hand. Jesus Christ, these faggots bought turns in the quarter movies like it was nothing. Lately he had to empty the machines in the middle of the day, stuffed with change already, and him just finished rolling up the goddamn quarters from the night before. Simpler to keep rolling the goddamn things himself than to hike back and forth from the fucking bank. The new booths had been open nine days, and the movie business was bigger every day, nearly double what it had been before. Now Newell had room to keep a good movie as long as he liked, and in fact he was having trouble keeping stocked. Mac supplied his store from a wholesale house in Algiers, a very quiet operation, and one to which Mac had been reluctant to introduce Newell; he would have to keep an eye on the kid for a while longer before taking a step like that. Maybe one of these days he would drive Newell to the warehouse with him, take a look at the whole range of available merchandise, most of the stock having come down from Chicago, novelties and fuck magazines and fuck movies, one-hand bullshit he liked to call it, his stock in trade, part of it, along with Dixie and the world upstairs.

Tonight the Owner was having a party upstairs, being a person whose name is best left out of this, for the good of all parties involved. The Owner was upstairs, maybe with Dixie in the parlor, or maybe he had already gone into one of the rooms off the gallery with his nephew Jack and a couple of the girls. The building always felt so much smaller when the Owner was in it, and tonight he planned to be here all evening, though if Mac was lucky he could avoid the ugly old son of a bitch, face that looked like a fucking skull with fucking skin stretched over it, lips like pieces of sausage, what a miserable ugly old motherfucker he was but with more money than the pope. Too much goddamn time to think, counting out these fucking quarters. He shook a cigarette out of its pack, lighting, puffing, and heading to the office door to stand in it, looking across at Newell. "There has fucking got to be a better way."

"What?"

"I have counted motherfucking quarters till my thumbs hurt."

"I bet you Schwegmann sells a machine."

Mac nodded, face veiled. Why was he thinking of that bastard anyway? Son of a bitch never came around here, sent his accountant sometimes but more often these days Mac had to fucking deal with the goddamn bookkeeping, too, had to go upstairs once a week and sit with Dixie and make her run a fucking tape on the goddamn adding machine, and the tired cunt half the time counted some fucking number twice or forgot to write through a no-show in the book, some such shit as that. "Fucking Schwegmann's."

"You drop the quarters and they fall in this funnel into this tube with the wrapper on it."

"I didn't know there was any such goddamn machine. Why didn't you fucking tell me? Me sitting here counting these goddamn things half the fucking night."

"I can't stand here talking, I have customers, Mac."

"Let fucking Maurice take the customers."

"His name is Lawrence."

"He looks like a freak. Where did he get a ring in his nose?"

"People like it. People are already talking about it. He's from Philadelphia."

"Fuck Philadelphia. Tell him to get that nasty thing out of his nose. It ain't sanitary." None of this was loud enough for Lawrence to hear, lost in the disco. Mac was grinning and Newell was grinning.

"We making a lot of money?" Newell asked.

Mac looked at him. "We're doing all right."

"You want Lawrence to do the quarters? I can run the cash register."

"Fuck no. The little son of a bitch is probably a thief."

"His pants are too tight to hide a whole lot of change," Newell noted, and Mac snorted cigarette smoke.

"They get any tighter they'll crush his balls."

"Let me know if you want any help," Newell said, wandering back to the second register, a fucking second cash register, would you fucking look at it. Mac puffed up big at the sight, brand new since two days ago, for times like this when the line was too long for one person. Mac listened to the drawer-bell ring every time the register completed a sale and opened the magic money drawer. Mac could see it in his mind, he no longer needed to be standing over it. Sweet cash and coin. Everything on the rise. Because with the movies doing a booming business, there were people in the store nearly all the time now, and with that kind of cruising going on, there were a lot of people buying magazines and novelties, rubbers with ticklers on them, cock rings, he puffed his cigarette, thinking about the stacks of money in the office, and he closed the door behind him, locking it.

Mac wandered through the back, behind the thin wall that was this side of the new movie booths; beyond he could hear the occasional muffled sound, and he wondered what these filthy motherfuckers would think if they knew he was only the thickness of a piece of sheetrock away from them, just on the other side doing some horrible strange kind of shit to one another, and him right here puffing away on a Camel. There was plenty of room back here. He could get Leon to build him a room. Buy a safe and build it into the walls. He wouldn't need to get the fucking city's permission, either, just pay Leon in cash and tell him to work at night and keep his mouth shut.

In the courtyard he felt a pain in his side and figured it was his liver; he guessed it was turning into a rock. A petrifying tree. One cell at a time, the liver tissue replaced by sharp painful bits of stone. He figured it would kill him before the smoking would, so he lit another cigarette and blew smoke into the leaves of the plantain tree.

He was eating a lot of benzedrine and drinking to take the edge off it. Black beauties, what the bikers liked to call them. Bought them buy the thousand, sold them to the girls upstairs, to some of the johns, and to the Owner's nephew Jack, a sordid motherfucker, a sick piece of shit, according to the girls. Mac was grinding his jaw. His nose ached from the line of cocaine he had done before leaving the office; he sold that, too, though it was harder to get in the quantity he wanted. These were businesses he conducted in the back cabinet upstairs, his little office, by appointment. The house was safe; the Owner paid for the right kind of protection. Safe as your sister's pussy, Mac liked to say.

Lafayette's friends were hanging out in the courtyard, that one named Milford, sitting at the table playing cards with some buddy of his. Mac gave up trying to remember all the names. Lucky to remember Milford, who was one fat dark motherfucker with forearms the size of hams. Mac wandered that way but not too close, enjoying the balmy night.

The loggia of the old house had been closed in long ago; a narrow door led to stairs to the gallery on the next level. Somebody came out the door, Dixie, stepping into the floodlight where Mac was standing; she had dyed her hair red again, that bright red with a hint of pink that gave an odd air of dissociation to her face, lined and creased with age, but her hair fluffed and groomed to perfection. She could have been a country-western star in the right outfit, but she was wearing a low-cut dress showing a moist ravine of cleavage. She was wobbling some in the high heels, either from the scotch or the pills or the combination. Her green eyes were surrounded by creases and folds of flesh; it made him sad to see her looking old like this; she had been such a pretty thing. "Mac," she said, her dusky voice raking his arm along with her manicured nails, "come upstairs. Jack wants to see you in your room."

"He knows I'm here?"

Dixie shrugged.

"All right," he said, shuffling toward the storeroom again. "Let me tell Newell where I am, I'll be up in a minute."

"He ain't going to want to wait."

"I ain't planning to make him wait, Dixie."

She blew out a long breath, touched the tips of her nails to the outer halo of her hair. "I hate it when these bastards come, anymore."

"You and me both."

"You don't have to lick his ass like I do."

"Well, not literally, I don't."

She tossed her head as if that proved her point.

"Tell Jack I'll be up."

"He's a sick bastard, too."

"Dixie, do you want me to come upstairs or do you want me to stand out here and fucking talk to you all night?"

"Oh, fuck you, Mac. Tell Newell I said hey."

When he left, she was lighting a cigarette, not looking as if she minded keeping Jack waiting a bit.

A few minutes later Mac puffed up the stairs, tightness in his chest, remembering when he leaped up these steps two or three at a time.

Jack was waiting for him, slouched in Mac's chair in a white starched shirt, perfectly pressed, the top button unbuttoned, dark trousers and shoes that shone in the dim light. He had lit a cigarette. Dark beard under his pale skin. Women went crazy for the son of a bitch, whores same as all the rest, till they found out what he was like. At one time or another Jack had bought every kind of drug Mac could find. Dixie's girls were afraid of him.

"Hey, Mac." That easy voice. "You look like you're working hard tonight."

"It's hot as fuck for October." Mac mopped his face, cool with sweat.

"Feels pretty good to me. You're just getting old. Heart's about ready to give out."

"Well, fuck you, too, Jack."

Jack laughed, drew his feet off the desk. He stood aside to let Mac stumble into his chair and put his legs up, the aching lower part of the shin that felt like it wanted to explode, Mac letting out a long breath. "You all right?" Jack asked.

"Yeah, I'm all right. Those motherfucking stairs. Takes me a minute to get my breath."

"You need to get more exercise."

"Fuck exercise. The only exercise I want is for Dixie to get one of the girls to suck my cock now and then."

They transacted their business cleanly and efficiently. Black beauties, a half-gram cocaine, a half-pound of good pot. Jack wanted more acid and Mac had part of a sheet left and sold him thirty tabs. "There won't be no more of that for a while."

"No?"

Mac shook his head. "Can't get it. Can't find the motherfucker."

"Who sold it to you?"

"Hell's Angel I know. He does the beauties and he had the acid, too, but he don't like it and he don't get it regular."

"Oh, Mac," Jack shaking his head.

"I don't like the shit myself. Makes the world puke purple to me."

"Give me the rest of what you have."

"Naw, I got to save some for Dixie, now."

"Give me as much as you can."

The acid was in a freezer in the pantry of the main house, padlocked. Mac unlocked it. Unrolled the tabs of red roosters under the dim light and cut off the twenty tabs he needed to save for Dixie. Jack counted out his cash. "How come I don't get a discount?"

"You don't need a discount."

"I'm a poor son of a bitch, Mac."

"Who never spends his own money." Mac laughed, shook his head. "I don't know why I even talk to you."

"You like me." Jack stretched, rotated an arm taking the shoulder through its whole range of motion, like an athlete checking himself, like a cat. A grin spread under his broken nose. He closed the door.

Mac sat with the lamplight spilling over his spotted hands. His knees in the polyester trousers made a sharp angle, as if there were only bone and no flesh.

Outside, Jack, instead of climbing the stairs to the attic, where the studio and the women and his uncle were in the midst of their evening, walked downstairs and into the bookstore by the back entrance, something he had done only once before.

He wanted a glimpse. Tonight the love child was wearing a better collar than before, thick brown leather with a ring of sharp spikes projected outward, a soft T-shirt that clung to his shoulders, his nipples outlined under the shirt. Jack watched Newell and felt in his gut that he would go after this child again very soon. Maybe tonight. Newell, moving unconsciously to the music, smiling and talking, glancing at Jack, once, followed by a moment of recognition when Jack smiled, Jack thinking to himself, Soon, very soon. Newell was watching and his color was rising, a line of rose out of the black collar of the shirt, lovely, the print of a hand in that soft skin, Jack pictured it, the print of a hand drawn sharply across that smooth cheek.

Somebody spoke to the love child, Jack lingering a second longer to make sure, yes, Newell was still watching, had returned to watching Jack, and this was enough for the moment. Jack ducked out the door into the courtyard again.

The big hoodlum in the courtyard stopped Jack under the plantain leaves. "Now, sir, you know Mr. Mac don't like the folk to use that door from back in here."

"I just got turned around," Jack said, raising both hands, heading for the loggia, bounding up the steps.

Where he saw, in its final stages, the artistry of the incomparable Leonora, in high black boots, black panties, breasts shaking with each lash, whipping a bundle of canes across the flaccid cheeks, the white and crumpled buttocks, the old man, Jack's uncle, gasping, his little leathery slip of cock straining to crow again as he made a high-pitched, yelping sound and reached for himself. Ghastly, his shivering white thighs, the stretched skin puckering over his skull, his forehead, his lips gone slack, drool in the corner of his mouth, old uncle in the height of ecstasy, or nearing the height of it, as Nora wielded the canes and screamed at him. True, her obscenities were not the most original or degrading, but her stroke-work with the canes was masterful, and the old man, to his fierce cloudy-eyed delight got hard as a tenpenny nail for a few moments and came, the end of the evening.

Lawrence, the new cashier, had seen that handsome man staring at the cash register and figured the stare was for him, nudged Newell, "Look at that one, baby."

Licking a fingertip, running it over his eyebrows. "The hottest man of the night award."

"He looks like somebody I know," Newell said.

"He's looking over here like he wants to eat me," Lawrence said.

"He is staring," Newell agreed.

Dark hair, almost jet black. Eyes the color of coal. A heavy jaw and beard, a face that would have looked homely except that its bolder touches—the heavy eyebrows, the deep olive tone to the skin, the strong nose— made such a masculine ensemble. The kind of a man you saw in the French Quarter no more than once or twice a week. For a few moments Lawrence hardly saw the customer in front of his face, that friend of Newell's, out of the booths for more change, looking like he had crawled on his hands and knees, his shirt stained, his beltless pants a mess. Booth trash, Lawrence thought, and when he looked again the oh-so-handsome man was gone.

"Did he go out the back?" Lawrence asked.

"Who? Your new boyfriend?"

"Who else? Oh, I can't believe I didn't see him leave or give him my number or anything." Lawrence shut the cash drawer emphatically.

Henry said to Newell, "You going out after work?"

"Maybe."

"You want to have a drink at the Corral?"

"I might walk down there," Newell shrugged. "I don't know what I'm going to feel like."

"Well, at least walk through the Corral on your way home, so I don't sit there all night."

Lawrence walked away from that tiny drama, wanted to snap his fingers in the air. Go on, fat man, go back to the booth you came from. You are too homely to hang around the counter as much as you do. But, as he reflected, everybody has a fat friend; his own friend, James, for instance, love handles the size of a life preserver. Lawrence ducked behind Newell, called back, "I need to potty, sweetie," and hurried to the back.

He stepped into the courtyard, lit a cigarette, and took a long drag on it. The courtyard was empty except for that black man who had been introduced to Lawrence as a security guard, with a friend of his. He was sitting at a table in the middle of the courtyard, looking up at the galleries of the house as if he were keeping watch. Lawrence was beginning to suspect that something was going on upstairs, that maybe this was a massage parlor. He stepped inside before the security guy could get suspicious. That handsome man was nowhere to be seen but Lawrence was sure he had left this way.

A man like that could make you wet for days. In the bathroom Lawrence ran fingers through his hair that some accident of the peroxide had turned a pale orange-sherbet color. That motherfucker Chris, his barber, could fuck up a hairdo in a heartbeat. Short and close-cropped, as was becoming the fashion, admittedly a good cut. But that color. Still, it was getting attention, like now, when Lawrence stepped into the bookstore again, the disco music enfolding him.

Wishing he would see that man waiting at the cash register, but never mind, Lawrence saw Henry was still pouting, watching Newell, who smiled at Lawrence as he passed. "That was a little too long for a bathroom break, Lawrence."

"What?"

"You don't get fifteen minutes to go to the bathroom. Unless you want that to be your break."

"What are you talking about? That wasn't any break."

Newell spoke coolly. "I'm just making a point, Lawrence. You don't get fifteen minutes to pee."

"Oh, kiss my ass, Newell. There's not even anybody in line." Though of course there was, by the time he got the words out of his mouth. What really pissed him off, though, was how much Newell appeared to be enjoying this confrontation. Newell sauntered away to Mac's office, hovering in the doorway there, while Lawrence glared at him.

Lawrence was thinking he should have taken the third-shift job at the doughnut place, making cream-filled and jelly-glazed doughnuts for the morning rush hour crowd, but here was another man in line, looking too cute to ignore, and Lawrence forgot about Newell, leaned forward over the counter and asked, "Now, how can I help you?"

Newell had gone to look at his face in the mirror. Touching fingertips to his skin, soft and supple, not so much silky as downy, a texture that wanted to be touched. He combed his black hair again and afterward roughed it with his fingers to make it appear less arranged. He had developed a habit, lately, of standing in front of the mirror and looking himself in the eyes, admiring the moist lips, the graceful shape of face and neck and shoulders, the muscles that were thickening on him through no apparent effort. When he had taken stock of himself in that way, he took a deep breath.

Outside, Lawrence was still hanging over the cash register with something to say to every customer, and Newell wondered if people coming into a dirty bookstore to sneak into a booth and have furtive sex in front of flickering movies really wanted to be chatted up like that. Newell's thoughts were confirmed when he stopped at Mac's door and Mac said to him, frowning, "That little cocksucking queen out there never shuts up, like a goddamn magpie."

"I've been listening."

"You better set him straight. People come here to look at some pussy in peace, they don't need all that jabber."

"Some of it is all right."

"When I have to hear it all night long it's not."

"I'll talk to him."

"Tell him to shut his mouth and make change."

"Yes, Mac."

"That is all the fuck I want him to do. What the fuck does he think this is, a goddamn church social?"

He could picture the scene that was coming, of course, when he pulled Lawrence away from the register to tell him to stop the chatter with the customers, to turn down the flame a notch or two, or else next time he could hear it from Mac. Weighty words from the night shift supervisor, which Newell had begun to turn over in his head as what he was, in fact, though without anyone saying so. For a moment he had a sense of satisfaction, and figured he would picture Lawrence as Curtis, the restaurant manager who had fired him, and say the hard words to Curtis instead of Lawrence. He liked having the power and being the one to cause the pain. It would be a good feeling, to be the person who could say, you're fired. Newell would have to say it to Mac, of course, and Mac would do the firing, but that, too, was fine with Newell, and it would all amount to the same thing. Watching Lawrence across the store twisting his tail this way and that like it was something to see, and him skinny as a chick, with that awful color to his hair, like an orange soda. He was lucky Newell wasn't like Curtis, in fact, that Newell wasn't trying to get into his pants; though, on second thought, Lawrence might not have minded.

He wanted to ask Mac what happened upstairs, with Jack. He knew it was Jack he had seen, he knew Jack was a customer of the upstairs business. But looking at Mac, Newell knew better. Since he wasn't supposed to know about the room or the business Mac did there. But it was Jack; Newell wanted to know about him. Newell's appetite was roused. Was it only vanity to think Jack had something in mind? That his appearance tonight was not precisely accidental?

Trying to put that out of his mind: Jack watching him from the back door, stepping into the store and standing there, watching so coolly, Jack, who might as well have been Rod the Rock stepping right off the cover of the magazine, down to the burning looks, the way he held his lips tense at the edges, like a predator tasting the air, letting nothing escape his senses.

Lawrence thought Jack was interested in him! But it wasn't true.

Newell said to Mac, "All right. You want to handle the cash register while I take Lawrence out to the courtyard and talk to him?"

Mac lurched forward, already reaching for a cigarette.

Mr. Mac suddenly appeared out of nowhere at the cash register, thought Miss Sophia, who was dusting the new display of French tickler condoms in seven edible flavors, and at the same time Newell took that sassy new boy to the back, that Miss Priss with the flapping mouth. Here Miss Sophia was dusting the showcases in the main room, but just at that moment she needed a clean dust cloth from the back—the one in her kit would not serve another minute—and so she marched to the cleaning supply closet, which was next to the toilet. There, with a clear view of the courtyard at the open window, she heard the spat that followed. Tussling outside like two cats, that sassy one hissing and spitting, Newell with his arms folded, standing perfectly calm, but in Miss Sophia's mind's eye his tail was slowly lashing.

"I don't talk any more than you do," Miss Priss was saying.

"You keep the line too long. Mac wants you to keep the line moving."

"Then why doesn't he tell me so himself?"

"You don't want Mac to tell you," Newell said. "He is nobody to fuck with, and he would probably end up firing you. So just listen to me, please, and tone it down some."

"You put him up to this, I know you did."

"Why would I do that?"

"You want to get rid of me."

"Oh, right. And work by myself again. Grow up, Lawrence. Some of these people don't want to be talked to, they just want their magazine put in a bag and their quarters handed to them all counted out right."

"I'm just trying to be friendly."

"If you want to be friendly, go to work in a bar. This is a dirty bookstore."

"Oh, fuck you." Lawrence waved his cigarette and sashayed into the store again. He had cultivated a liquid, curvaceous walk of the type Miss Sophia had once employed, and had herself been quite proud of, though she was certain she walked with more flair in her prime, even on the occasions when she was a man.

Newell stood in the courtyard for a while. When he had been alone a moment, somebody slid toward him out of the courtyard, from behind the big hydrangea bush, and stood in front of him and started to talk. A big, dark figure, Miss Sophia could not make out the shape, whether it was Lafayette or somebody else, but it was definitely a large man, taller than Newell, and they stood together for a while.

Something happened between their bodies, some moment of tension, a change in posture, and then Newell was turning, heading back to the store. One moment the two shadows merged, as if Newell were pressing against the other man, but she had seen no movement, she had only felt the charge. The man stood there for a long time and Miss Sophia waited, too. When he moved she thought he was a black man, but when he passed by the window she thought he was a white man. He climbed the stairs, and she wondered if it could have been Lafayette, and decided the footfalls were not his, the weight of the step not the same. A moment later, there was no more sound, and she could no longer be certain of anything.

She hurried to the store and resumed her dusting, but Newell was nowhere to be seen, most apt to be in the bathroom, collecting himself. Once she had opened the door on him when he forgot to lock it and there he was, standing in front of the mirror, arms spread around it, looking at his face. Cool contemplation, as if he were counting a stack of money. Blushing, he ran water and washed his hands when Miss Sophia apologized and closed the door again; and he had never forgotten to lock the door since. She could picture him now, watching himself in the mirror, as she was watching herself in the surface of the glass counter, her lovely red wig styled in the Carol Channing manner, and her lips a thick swath of red, her hands veined and spotted and her nails yellow. Dusting this, dusting that, wandering through the booths on occasion, to listen to the sounds.

She felt herself sliding at moments, into the floor or the

glass counter, sliding down, almost falling over, and yet she would come to her senses and realize she had not moved at all.

So she focused on objects, moving ones, like Miss Priss at the cash register, lips curled tight, making change and counting it out with stiff, stricken movements. Newell stood nearby checking a stock invoice, eyeing Lawrence the way a cat eyes something it has caught, something that offers new possibilities of what seems like play, to the cat.

That friend was with him, still hanging around, the one that looked like living lard. She dare not notice what he was wearing, his outfits were shamelessly uninteresting. She had long ago come to the conclusion the friend, Henry Carlton, had never developed a sense of self, not even of one self, let alone more than one, as some people were forced to cope with. But tonight the sight of him still here in the store made her angry, so she ran the mop bucket over the toe of his shoe. She had mopped the bathroom and needed to walk the bucket to the booths and the other cleaning closet, which meant she had to pass right by the counter where he was leaning with his tasseled loafers sticking out like duck feet, and Miss Sophia hardly saw it coming herself but walked right over to the bucket, grabbed the mop handle and steered the same as she always did. She could have run a slalom course with that thing, she was so accustomed to the physics of it, but a woman of her size never has a problem appearing clumsy in heels and so, when she rolled the bucket over

Henry Carlton's toe, oh, she knew his name all right, when she ran the bucket over him, he let out a yelp and jerked his foot and the bucket sloshed on his pants a good lick, Miss Sophia having the sense to dodge her part of the splash, and Miss Sophia waddled away looking down at the carpet and performing one of her favorites, mumbling to herself, making sounds that might have been words, deep in her throat, a ploy that always frightened people. She steered the mop bucket into the booths, into the cleaning space, and stood there for a while, in the paradise in which she worked, the hunks walking past her on all sides and the studs in the shadows watching the hunks, sizing them up for later, all this beauty in one place.

Miss Sophia had a theory about the space inside her head, growing on her recently, added to all that she had understood about herself and Clarence Dodd. One person could not be in two places at the same time, but two people could be in the same space, namely, the one inside her skull, and even more could fit in there, though she had only noticed the two; and this led her to wonder about the head space of others. Was it sufficient to hold more than one personality, more than one soul? She felt that the answer was yes, that many people, in fact, already had such compartments of themselves as she had developed.

For instance, Mr. Mac, she felt, might possibly have room for five or six different personalities inside his head, for his skull appeared mighty roomy to her. Whereas

Newell, she felt, most likely had only the one person in his skull, not for lack of room but because in his case he was possessed of a larger personality than usual. A singular personality, which would not accommodate the kind of mental company that Miss Sophia, for instance, was forced to endure.

She found Newell at the door to the bathroom, about to enter, she guessed, but he stopped when he saw her. "Do you need in here?"

She shook her head. He was still standing there, though. "Lord, Miss Sophia, it has been one night."

"That new boy is nothing but sass and ass," Miss Sophia answered.

Newell burst out laughing, hung onto the door jamb. Nodding his head, "Yes ma'am, you got that right."

"You'll learn him how to act."

"I'm not worried about that. But I was thinking, just now, what if my grandma saw me in this place? And all that stuff in the counters. What if she found out I worked in a dirty bookstore?"

Miss Sophia shrugged.

"It's no harm in any of this stuff," Newell said, looking through the door at the end of the short hallway where the customers were still milling through the store, "I guess that's the truth."

She felt he was not telling her the truth, quite, that he had something else on his mind, but that this subject was somehow related to that other one. She went on standing lumpishly, aware of herself as impenetrable, having decided long ago that her best course in most cases was to pretend she understood nothing. Newell was listening, waiting, and asked, after a point, "Did you ever do anything dangerous, Miss Sophia?"

She looked him in the eye.

He went on, "Did anybody ever ask you to do something dangerous, and you really wanted to say yes?"

She went on waiting. Trying to let him know that he had the attention of at least half of her head space.

"Something like you see in these movies." His voice trailed off. Shaking his head. "I ought to know better. But I don't."

Miss Sophia drew herself up, time to go, enough. "Time was, I would do most anything," she said, sliding past him, speaking, that time, and for the first time in the store that she could remember, in the voice of Clarence Dodd, as if he had been listening, too, inside her. As if he were answering, too.

Newell slipped into the bathroom, closing the door.

When he called Flora, later, from Mac's office, she was hardly surprised. She had been thinking about Sweet Thing all afternoon and that was usually a sign he would call or she would hear something from him. When the phone rang, in fact, she looked across the dinette to Jesse and said, "See what I told you?"

"You ain't never wrong, I know," Jesse dragging a long hit on his cigarillo in the fancy plastic holder.

"Hello, honey," she said into the receiver, and Newell said, "I just got lonesome for you, Gramma, that's all. I'm still at work."

"You miss your Gramma. Ain't that sweet."

"You know I do."

"You still working at that bookstore? Seems like you would get a vacation by now, and come on home to see me."

"I'm still at the bookstore," he said, and from the echo on the line she thought maybe he was listening to somebody else, too.

"You still like it?"

"Yes ma'am."

"They treating you good?"

"I'm the night supervisor, now. Our business is so good, lately."

"What kind of books you sell?"

"Picture books, mostly."

"I never even been in a bookstore," Flora said. "Well, honey, you sound all right."

"Oh, I'm fine. I'm just a little lonesome."

"Well, I tell you what. All you got to do is come home."

"I thought you and Jesse were coming to see me here one of these days."

"You know Jesse don't go nowhere. He's setting here right now in the kitchen chair happy as a dog with a bone. Long as he's got a beer and something another to smoke, he's fine."

"Tell him hey," Jesse said, waving the brown smoking cylinder looking like some kind of Hollywood fruit with that plastic holder.

"Jesse says hey, honey. I told you he was setting here.

He's took up smoking cigarillos. He looks some kind of sissy, let me tell you."

"Leave Jesse alone, Gramma."

"I ain't bothering him."

"Well, listen, I better go," Newell said, and Flora had the feeling he was listening to somebody again. "I just wanted to hear your voice a little bit."

"You come on home to see your grandma, now, if you're so lonesome. I promise I'll let you go back."

Newell's easy laughter always made Flora happy. "I tell you what, I might do that," he said, and added a good-bye, and there she was, alone in the glare of the kitchen light with Jesse again.

"I told you he would call," she said.

"I know."

"He misses his nana."

"You'll be all on your high horse, now."

"Oh, shut up. Give me one of them cigarettes."

"It's not a cigarette," Jesse explained patiently, but she waved her hand at him and took it by the holder and lit it. She realized Newell hadn't asked about his mother for a change and, oddly, was happier still.

"I think these things is for women," Flora said, inhaling the fragrant tobacco.

"Oh, shit."

"I mean it. This looks to me like it was made for a woman."

Jesse, patient, began his explanation again, that a cigarillo was different from a cigarette due to the quality of the tobacco and the fact that it was rolled in tobacco, like a cigar. He had already told her several times since he bought the first pack last week, a pretty good explanation, he thought, though he had no idea whether it was true or not and had made it up, in fact; and he knew he would have to say the whole paragraph again, probably for as long as he smoked the things. So he pulled another one of the little faggot sticks, as Flora had termed them, out of the pack and lit it and sat there grinning at Flora, and thought—as he often did when he was grinning at her and she was giving him that look, her head lowered some, her bedroom eyes, she called this look, one of her front teeth darkening, giving her a sinister edge—she's a handsome woman, he thought, I'm lucky to have something that nice, son of a bitch that I am, and with this much gut hanging over my belt.

Even after Newell called Flora, even after he stood in the bathroom to calm his nerves, all he could think of was Jack in the courtyard, the words he had said.

After work Newell met Henry in the Circle K and had something to eat. This happened by chance; usually they met in the Corral after the bookstore closed, but tonight Newell happened to walk past the restaurant, maybe because he had thought about Curtis earlier, and there was Henry in the window, eating, and he waved to Newell, and Newell went inside to join him.

In the restaurant was Alan and in the door to the kitchen, Umberto. But they were busy talking, and Newell slid into his seat without their noticing. Henry grinned at him and said, "I had to get something to eat after that bitch wet my pants."

"Miss Sophia is not a bitch. She just doesn't like you."

"Well, I'm not exactly feeling like her best friend right now, either."

"You do hang around there a lot."

Henry made a gesture with his chin that meant he would ignore the remark. "I hadn't ordered yet," Henry said, examining the laminated menu. "I just got here." He turned to signal the waiter to get another menu, and the waiter who responded turned out to be Alan.

Imagine Alan's surprise to see Newell at the table with that tired old man. Alan had helped to get this cute thing fired, and look at him now in that leather collar and those leather bracelets, that black T-shirt, oh my. Had he gotten bigger? Alan laid down silverware in front of Newell and their eyes met and Alan acted as if he had just that second recognized Newell, slapped Newell's shoulder then squeezed it some, what a nice springy texture the flesh had. "Hello," Alan said. "How are you? We've missed you around here." He acted as if he and Newell had always been the best of friends, and the performance drew Umberto's attention and he recognized Newell, too, and came out to say hello.

"What are you two doing on the night shift?" Newell asked.

"We got tired of those bitches on the day shift. That's all."

"How's Curtis?"

"Oh, honey." Alan's hand on his hip, feeling Newell's eyes slide toward the motion. "Curtis moved to Toronto with Stuart. Thank God. Now we have this nice sane dyke for a boss."

"Luana," Umberto agreed.

"Honey, she weighs two hundred pounds, and she's shaped like a block of ice, I am not lying." Alan raised his brows. "Umberto is supervisor on the night shift. Do you believe it?"

"No," Newell said, and one of Alan's tables beckoned him, and so he tapped Newell on the shoulder and said, "I'll be back in a minute to take your order, sweetie, I have to see what these queens over here want. Yoo-hoo!" and he slashed through the dining room, hips like blades.

Newell said to Umberto, "God, he sure is different. He hated me when I worked here."

"Oh I know, honey. Don't you remember he tried to get me fired, too? I think it's the new medication." Umberto rolled his eyes and they laughed, and Umberto introduced himself to Henry and stood there talking to Henry about how to get a state job like Henry had, more relaxed and assured than Newell remembered him. Alan so different, and Curtis gone for good. Newell asked about the others, learned that Felix was still cooking breakfast every morning, and Frank had gotten sick, stayed in the hospital for a while, and disappeared, nobody knew quite what had happened.

Pleasant to sit there as a customer, even pleasant to pretend with Alan that they had been buddies when

Newell worked here, that everything had been wonder-
ful, when Newell had been terrified most of the time,
wondering if he would make enough money to stay in
New Orleans, never dreaming people who hardly knew
you could hate you so much, and now, tonight, with all
that in the past, to have the face to sit here and pretend
it had all been all right, or maybe that it had all been
Curtis's fault, since he was more the villain and was con-
veniently out of the picture. Newell even found himself
liking Alan by the end of the meal, liking his flair for
bitchy gestures and comments, at least.

Afterward he and Henry went to the Corral, where
they sat in the loud music without talking, shoulder to
shoulder but scanning the room in opposite directions.
Newell thought maybe tonight he wanted to find somebody to go home with. The taste of the margarita cloying,
he licked some of the salt from the rim. He drank it
down, then, around midnight, leaned into Henry's ear
and said, "I'll see you later. I'm going home."

"But it's early."

"I know. I'm tired."

"I bet you're really going to see Mark."

Newell flushed. "I might."

Henry turned away, took his drink in hand, a dramatic
movement like something he had seen in a movie. "I
knew it."

"Give it up, Henry. What difference does it make to
you?" He walked away.

In the street, he headed to Prilla's house, ringing the

bell to get into the gate, Prilla coming out on the porch to see who it was, Prilla in one of those full-length African dresses with a wrap of fabric on her head, probably entertaining this evening, but she smiled at Newell, her voice warm and pleasant as she said how nice it was to see him again and was he looking for Mark? Because she knew Mark was upstairs. Could he go around the back, because she had some sisters in the house for a card reading? Newell answered, conscious of his own lilt and drawl, that she looked awfully nice this evening, so he figured she was having company, and sure, he'd go around back, he didn't mean to disturb her by going through the house anyway, and they chatted for a few moments as easy as if neither had anything else in the world to do, as if it were early in the evening and they both had plenty of time.

The door to Mark's room was open, Mark sitting at the desk with his vein tied off, probing it, a flame burner on the desk, cooking something for his arm. He glanced at Newell, gestured him to come in. "I'll be done in a minute."

"I'll wait out here."

"No. Come and watch."

Something of a dare in the tone, to which Newell had to respond.

"You want some?"

Newell shook his head. "No." It made him afraid, shooting up, though he pretended it made no difference.

Now Mark was filling the syringe with the slightly

cloudy fluid, now touching the needle against one of his veins, now shooting, opening the tourniquet, a cloud of pleasure rising visibly through his body, his lips flushed as if he were kissing, letting the syringe and needle with the drop of blood rest on the desk, Newell watching, the moment too intimate, as if he were watching Mark have sex with someone else. Mark sighed. "What did you want? After you told me off today?"

Newell shrugged. "Just to see you. But I guess I'll come back."

"You can stay if you want."

"I don't think so."

"Did you decide to go the party?" Mark took a deep breath. "Is that why you came."

"No," Newell said. "I came by to see you."

Mark closed his eyes, leaning back in the chair so far it seemed certain he should fall.

Newell wondered why he had come. What had he expected? He walked up the passageway, past Prilla's open front door, through which he could hear gentle laughter. He opened the gate and stepped onto the street, facing the direction of his apartment. Too restless to go home, he landed in the Golden Lantern where he sat for a long time, drinking margaritas. He had not been thinking about anybody, let alone the man he had met months ago, the blow job in the bar; but someone was leaning against him, and Newell gradually noticed the steady pressure, the solid mass of the body, and when he turned, there was Jerry again, the same thick shoulders and neck, the same smooth brown skin. Jerry was breathing on his neck the whole time, leaned close to Newell's ear. "I can't believe it's you."

"Well, I guess it is," Newell said.

"I been looking for you."

"Have you?"

"I went back to the place down the street a million times but you wasn't there."

"I don't go there much."

There was a feeling of quiet between them even in the noisy bar. Nice to have Jerry stand near like this, but why was his heart pounding so? Almost visible beneath his shirt, so that Newell wanted to lay a hand there. "You want to have some more fun?" Jerry pressed himself gently against Newell, but his question rang with urgency. "Not in here, I mean. We could go somewhere."

The noise and confusion pressed close, closer even than Jerry, whose breath ran along the tips of Newell's ears. A shiver passed through him, as he thought of the first time, the way Jerry's body felt, under his hands, beneath the clothes, the smooth brown upper arms, the round hard shoulders. Before, Newell had felt detached, but now he was not so sure of himself. He wanted something, and his own heart was beginning to echo in his chest. "We can go to my room," he whispered, but Jerry was already leading him toward the door.

In the room he fought a rush of panic, because Jerry was there, because his smell would linger long afterward. But Jerry took off his shirt and his body drew Newell to it, and after that he was only thinking about the way it felt to touch this man, the soft gray-black hair cropped close to his skull, the firm corded neck, his mouth, the etched sun-lines of his face relaxing as he drew pleasure out of Newell, and Newell, as he could feel himself giving this pleasure, felt himself inside it, not like the first time, for in here there was no movie, there was only this man pressed close, this man's harsh breath, the noises that came out of his mouth, the look of softness washing over his eyes, the pleasure of it, to be held like this, undressed with such rough hands moving so gently. Without the movie in his head Newell wondered what to do, for a while, till they were on the bed together, and then everything seemed simple, at least at first. Jerry hungry for something, understanding what it was to have Jerry over him, pressing inside him, not at all the way it had looked in the movies, the indignity then the pleasure of it.

But in the aftermath came the sour, beery smell of Jerry's breath, the shit smell from Newell's own ass, and the clammy dampness along their joined skins, a feeling of pleasant heat and unpleasant stickiness. He felt a need to sit on the toilet for a while in case anything might fall out, after all that banging and rattling. The sheets were wet in spots and stained in spots. Jerry sat up on the edge of the bed. He reached for his drawers, then stopped. "You don't want me to stay, do you?"

"No," Newell said, and Jerry put his feet through the drawers, found the rest of his clothes in the dark.

"Did you like it?"

"What? Sure." He knew he ought to say more, so he added, "It was great. I don't remember when I had better."

"You're kidding."

"No."

Jerry grinned then. He was sliding the sleeveless shirt across his shoulders, but he stopped to grin, so big Newell could see it, and he wondered why Jerry would believe such obvious flattery; but the smile made him like Jerry again, anyway, so Newell stood up, naked, and put his arms around Jerry and kissed him on the mouth. For a moment the movie had come back, and Newell could see himself, the languid movement up from the bed, his pale skin, pretty body, shapely arms, tender mouth. Jerry had stopped dressing and waited, so Newell stepped away.

After a moment, cautiously, Jerry said, "I better go, I guess. My wife is probably at home waiting up for me."

"You think she is? You think you're all that special?"

"I'm all she has."

"Then she has a problem." Newell stood, angry now. He walked to the bathroom. "Get dressed and go, please. So she won't have to wait anymore."

"I'm sorry I said anything." Jerry waited a moment, spread across the bed big and square. He was wanting Newell to change his mind, but Newell closed the door and sat on the toilet. In a moment he could hear Jerry moving, and came out.

So satisfying to stand there, to have Jerry's eyes

pore over him like this. Jerry buckled the silver belt buckle. He looked so helpless, standing there. Jerry walked to the door and turned back. "I'll see you sometime, okay."

Newell shrugged. "Sure."

When he was gone, Newell stripped the bed. He lay on the bare mattress under the blanket. For a long time he could only lie there thinking about the way it had felt when Jerry was here, when they were touching each other, the strange cloud that had suffused Newell. He was seeing Jerry's broad back, the warmth of the body, the smells, sweat and pepper and earth. Different from Mark.

Bigger than Mark. It had felt nice, to be under a man so big. A man the size of Jack, he thought, and lay still.

THE NIGHT WOULD LINGER afterward, for many people who would remember it when Newell had vanished, as the last time they saw him; they would remember specifically, because a few days later when he disappeared the rumor circulated that Newell had been murdered. By then he had become, in his small way, notorious, as a cute boy prone to wear leather was apt to become notorious in the French Quarter in 1978. People at the bookstore talked about him, people at the Circle K talked about him, answered a few questions from the police, traded suspicions. He had vanished, taking nothing out of his room. Mac suspected Newell had gotten mixed up in something ugly. Dixie knew something of what really happened, but kept quiet about it for the rest of her life. Louise had her own troubles by then; Henry cleaned Newell's room out, had Newell's phone turned off, drank himself silly afterward, never saying much about what he thought, and soon sickened and died of Kaposi's sarcoma, one of the earliest deaths from that disease in New Orleans.

When Jack came home that night, which is to say, when Jack came to Leigh's apartment, which she had come to think of as his home, she could see something had piqued his interest, but she knew better than to ask. He had been to Mac's, bought the quaaludes she wanted, gave her a couple, and she took them, waiting to feel languid, looking at Jack and thinking she was, maybe, tired of him, now that she had become so accustomed to him. Maybe she was nearly through with him, she was thinking, and he was watching her, hardly seeing her, probably himself already seeing somebody else in his mind, like that friend of Mark's he wanted. Tedious, the presence of anyone, after a certain point, to Leigh. But Jack eventually put his arms around her and his callused hands felt nice on her creamy skin. "Do you ever think you'll get tired of me, Daddy?" she asked.

He laughed. "Of course not."

She laughed, too. But the next morning he was gone and stayed out the whole day and night, the first time in a while he'd been away so long. So later, when she heard about Mark's friend, that he had disappeared the same day, she wondered what had happened, but never asked whether Jack knew. She canceled the Halloween party, to let Jack sweat a little. Pretty soon she decided she really was tired of him, anyway, and told him so, and moved on.

Reason
to Live

I am Jack. I have made Newell an offer and I have waited for an answer. I have been as patient as I could. He has taken some days to come round. I have had to stand in front of him for a long time, show myself for a long time, and even to undress myself a bit and allow him to touch me. His excitement has led him forward, and I have brought him to the very center of the old brewery, near the end that faces the river, all broken glass and corroded iron; I have brought him here because I love him so, tonight. I am glistening when he enters, his face masked and his body still clothed, that slim white body that I ache to hurt, his face sheathed in leather, his hands bound behind him, and the feeling rushes over me, that

I have been doing this for such a long time, that it will always continue, that someone like Newell will appear time after time, fresh and well-prepared by some force already within him.

I take off the mask and the face becomes lost as I watch it, as he runs his hands under my leather vest; but it is he I am watching, cotton underwear against his pale skin, the dark denim bunched around his knees, shirt torn in half, moving as his hands move over the handsome man in front of him, me; sudden roughness when I shove him to the floor, and slam his face into the handsome man's crotch, mine, and I know from these first moments that I am in the presence of something consummate, I slap him hard across the face and he continues to pursue the body with his hands, our body, the scene we have imagined and yet he recreates it so easily, with such simple gestures.

I am greedy to see him struck with the lash, first the one that makes the popping sound, red stripes flushing across his delicate skin. I am greedy to slap his bottom, to see the flesh tremble and the handprints appear, as he lies in the light from this lantern, flickering, in this desolate room, being beaten for me, to make me happy.

He lives in faith, as anyone would in his place, and he accepts my hands, my slapping and pinching, when I hoist him into the sling and fuck him, sweat running under my mask, him lying chained and fetal, his body drinking me into it, his face calling, his soft voice making me shiver, whenever he makes a sound. He lives in faith that his life will all make sense, that he is making sense of things a moment at a time, that each moment when I twist and bite his nipple is a reason to survive to the next.

Here he is sagging forward, exhausted, having given himself, with me tired behind him, harsh breathing and sweat, watching, because it is like a movie to watch him, a silvered image, a surface.

It will seem holy to have my arms lift him so tenderly, to bind his feet in the shackles and raise him up slowly, gently, not too fast so the blood to the head doesn't kill him, to raise him up slowly with the cold sound of the ratchet and tackle and have him shackled that way, spread like a bird in flight, a cloud of terror shining out of him.

I have this boy to remind me that Paradise is coming, and I shall use him for that, until he is all used up, like all the rest, and his burnt-out husk will drift away from me into the air, and I will scent him on the breeze as he dissolves, and I will carry the smoke from his fire inside me, walk down to the river, drift away.

Newell was hardly sure where he was at first, there was only a light, high in a wall of vague shadows. His body hurt, his backside burned like fire, his joints were stiff.

Jack was coming back. He'd said so. Where was this place? Some room in one of the warehouses?

He stood. He found he could. He'd fallen asleep on a pile of rags, filthy.

The cuffs were still on his hands, but when he checked they were open. He took them off.

Now he could see, a bit.

He found his jeans. Not much left of his shirt. One shoe, not his.

Sound, someone coming. He went to the door, found it locked. But there was a window and a table underneath it, and he climbed on the table and opened the window. He knew he was making noise, but as far as he was concerned it didn't matter anymore. He thought Jack would let him go if he asked, but he wasn't going to ask, he was going to leave now, through the window, and when he got it open, sore as he was he climbed out, into a wide gutter between two roofs. He pulled the window closed and ran down the gutter, every footfall making the tin clammer like thunder. A dead man could have heard him running away, but he didn't care about that either. He had seen enough.

It was true he had said yes to everything Jack wanted to do. This was what made it all right, made it possible to think about. But to remember, now that the night was over, terrified him, and he was shivering at the end of the gutter, leaning down to the branch of a baby oak, grabbing it without thinking and swinging toward the trunk, his shoulders with a feeling of tearing, then his bare feet on the solid tree, leaves yellowed.

He climbed to the ground. He was in an alley and headed toward a street. He looked up and saw, now, that he was near the old brewery on the river, maybe that was even where he had been all night, with Jack.

When he stood still, he was shivering, but when he

moved he was all right, so he headed home, down Decatur Street toward the lower Quarter. Stepping gingerly, shivering. Feeling for his apartment key in his pocket, relieved to find it. Early yet, nobody was awake.

When he turned the corner for home, though, there were police cars everywhere, two in the street and two in the carriageway, all with blue lights blazing, and a cop standing at the entrance to the carriageway. Newell could see police in the junk store, in Louise's office, and in the store rooms. Searching through her files and her desk, but Newell only glanced that way, he wasn't entirely certain what he saw, the cops on the street were watching him. "You got any business here, son?"

"I live here. Up there." Newell pointed.

The officer stood aside and said, "You rent from this woman, Louise Kimbro?"

"Yes sir."

He nodded. "Well, you can go on up, I guess. Stay out of the way back there."

"What's going on?"

"Nothing to concern you, son. Now, go on."

He headed along the passage, wondering if something had happened to Louise, but when he reached the loggia he saw her, surrounded by two officers in uniform and two other men in shirts and ties, maybe officers, too; Louise was red-eyed, face impassive, and stared at the ground, refusing to look at Newell at all, though he was sure she could see him.

On the back gallery he lingered a moment, watching,

Louise answering questions in a quiet voice, too quiet to hear.

So Millie had talked to her dad.

It seemed appropriate, to Newell, to be packing while the police searched Louise's house and business, to be packing his own belongings. He had meant to have a bath but suddenly, with the flashing blue lights washing over his room, he was afraid he would turn and find Jack in the doorway. The fear of what it meant to say yes to Jack. So Newell packed some of his clothes, not all of them, because he wanted to take only the bag he had arrived with, and he left all his books since he had read them, and everything else he had bought here, which he would not need when he went back to Pastel, and he got his money out of the four hiding places he had used, counted the three thousand dollars he had saved and divided most of that into two folds, which he put in his shoes. Astonishing how little time it took.

He checked his face in the mirror. No black eyes, no split lip, only a slight puffiness to his cheeks. No one would think anything except maybe he looked hungover.

When the courtyard was empty, he walked down the stairs with the bag, out the passageway and down the street. In a couple of blocks a taxi cruised past and he waved it down, still expecting at any second to see Jack. Or Mark. Or someone.

"To the bus station," he said to the driver, who chewed on his cigarette filter and stomped the accelerator.

He bought a ticket on the next bus to Jackson, figuring

to make the connection there to Pastel, figuring the Jackson buses would leave most frequently. Even so, for an hour and a half he waited for the bus with his bag beside him, nervous as a cat. Seated in a corner of the tiny station, trying to stay out of sight. Not even sure why he thought Jack would be looking for him, not even sure why he had decided to leave, not needing to think it through, sensing the rolls of his money in his shoes and the fact that he was in motion. Nobody in New Orleans could ever find him, he'd never told anybody very much about himself. Only Louise had Flora's address, and she was headed to someplace deeply unpleasant. Nobody would ever go to that much trouble, track him all the way to Pastel, and anyway, it wasn't likely that Newell would stay there long, was it?

He had stopped shivering. The sun poured through a window, and he sat in it, the tropical New Orleans sun, still vivid even on Halloween morning.

Last night, when it had been happening. When he had been in the midst of the beating, the sex that had turned into a beating, the terror that followed, the look on Jack's face, and Newell afraid to ask him to stop, even though Jack had promised he would stop at any point; Newell afraid to ask, in case it wasn't true. When Newell felt himself losing consciousness and wondered if he would ever wake up again. Maybe in the midst of that he had come to some decision.

This has gone too fast, he thought, when the bus pulled up and he realized the time had come and he was getting on it, going home. But I made it fine, for a long time, and I can do it again, somewhere else. As he settled into his seat, watching the other passengers board, the bleak street beyond them, he felt a sudden relief, to be leaving all this without a word, and thought how surprised Flora would be, when he called her from Jackson to tell her he was coming home. Though he'd have to make it clear to her he didn't intend to stay long. There were so many other places to live, now that he had lived in New Orleans.

Miss Sophia, still walking the streets after another bad night, found herself ambling along Canal, the fabulous boulevard making a space large enough to contain her restlessness, when she halted at the intersection of Royal and Canal. A taxi pulled up, and a face swam toward the window, Newell's. He only glanced out the window and reclined out of sight once again, but she saw his face, in the taxi, so that later, when she heard the rumors, she was certain that in fact Newell had escaped. No one had murdered him at all. That morning, standing on the corner, she figured he was gone for good, because he was in a taxi, because he had a duffel bag beside him. She watched the taxi turn on Canal, join other traffic. The news cleared her mind. She decided to head home again, have a strong cup of coffee and a piece of king cake. Another boyfriend gone, she thought, and headed for the bus stop.